THE FIFTH GOSPEL

Visit us at www.boldstrokesbooks.com

By the Author

Getting Lost

Keep Hold

The Fifth Gospel

THE FIFTH GOSPEL

by

Michelle Grubb

2016

ISBN 13: 978-1-62639-447-6

THIS TRADE PAPERBACK ORIGINAL IS PUBLISHED BY
BOLD STROKES BOOKS, INC.
P.O. BOX 249
VALLEY FALLS, NY 12185

FIRST EDITION: JANUARY 2016

CREDITS
EDITOR: CINDY CRESAP
PRODUCTION DESIGN: SUSAN RAMUNDO
COVER DESIGN BY SHERI (GRAPHICARTIST2020@HOTMAIL.COM)

Acknowledgments

It's always tricky writing about topics for which people hold strong beliefs. Religion is no exception.

The intention of this book is not to offend nor disrespect *any* religion. If my book encourages healthy debate and entertains readers, I will have achieved my goal.

A group I refer to in the book called the Order of Purity is fictitious, created by my imagination for the purpose of the story.

Once again, thank you to Bold Strokes Books: Radclyffe, Sandy, Cindy, and the entire team.

My heartfelt thanks to Kerry who helped me form a clear outline for this book and who encouraged me through the planning process.

For the record, I believe in love, kindness, and compassion. That is my religion.

Dedication

For Kerry
For making my world a bigger and better place.

PROLOGUE

Felicity Bastone heard it, but she didn't believe it. Well, not immediately anyway.

"I am telling you," the stylish young Swiss man whispered in frustration, "he is a sodomite."

Felicity glanced up and down the bustling alleyway through grimy windows. Rome was teeming with tourists—it was August after all—and she possessed enough smarts to at least take a deep breath and assess the situation. And this situation required some serious assessment.

Two men, one Italian, the other Swiss, stood staring out the same window of a run-down coffee bar on the crowded narrow thoroughfare called Via Daniele Manin, only two streets behind the Basilica of Santa Maria Maggiore. It seemed odd to be discussing such issues in proximity to a basilica, but then, in Rome, you were never too far from a holy place. Felicity stood a comfortable distance from the men. Her eyes felt heavy from drinking the previous night and she knew she looked less than appealing. To the casual observer, she'd appear sluggish and thoroughly disinterested. She rested her iPod in full view on the bench in front of them before sliding her earphones into place. Nodding her head and tapping her feet, she listened to absolutely nothing but their heated conversation.

In this neighborhood and in a coffee shop barely attractive to locals, let alone tourists, Felicity was convinced the men spoke English, soft and fast, so the locals had little chance of comprehending their conversation. Desperate for coffee, she hadn't bothered to consider the decor; she'd simply followed her nose to the closest scent of caffeine. It seemed that Felicity's olive toned skin and dark features left many Italians believing she was one of their own. With a mixture of Spanish and Australian heritage, she blended in perfectly. Not that her aim was to blend in; she was on holiday after all. Being a tourist had its advantages, but so it seemed did impersonating a local, albeit unintentionally.

The last time Felicity heard a conversation anywhere near the caliber of this one, she had been the instigator. The article she wrote that followed proved to be an award-winning exposé in the small, but highly regarded, *Sunday Experience Magazine*. It had been the one and only time her investigative journalism skills had paid off and the story went global. Of course, she'd had many successful articles, bits and pieces scattered throughout her seven years, but there had only been that one big break so far. At thirty-two, she was doing okay for herself, and freelance work was providing much of her bread and butter. She preferred it that way. Landing a full-time job as a journalist was great in the early days—job stability, food on the table and the ability to regularly pay the rent—but now freelance work provided her with exactly what the name suggested: freedom.

As she systematically considered the impact of what she was hearing, she knew this story, even if remotely true, would, for some, be far more devastating than the corruption, fraud, and downright filthy criminals involved in the international pedophile ring she'd helped uncover. The impact of this current revelation, either partly or completely true, had the potential to devastate the followers of one of the planet's most powerful religious institutions. Over one billion people could potentially wake to find their world had shifted axis.

Felicity sipped her coffee and contemplated what she should do.

CHAPTER ONE

Ten months later

"Felicity, you'd better get down here and quick. I swear to God, everyone is going mental. You really could be on to something with this." Laura Johnson, Felicity's right-hand woman and self-confessed "best friend in the world" left a message on Flic's voice mail. Laura only ever used Flic's full name when she was angry, annoyed, or excited. That was the best thing about Laura; she embraced simplicity. Flic always knew where she stood, and right now, she knew where Laura stood: The Happy Trumpet, one of London's largest pubs. It was next door to Laura's work, and it was precisely where Flic was headed.

Flic walked at a swift pace but paused in the doorway of an electrical retailer. It was packed full of people. Not shoppers, but people watching the televisions that covered the entire back wall. Everyone appeared captivated. The air was abuzz with anticipation. Increasing numbers of people were walking off the street as a news reporter filled the screen and explained that they were waiting on confirmation of a highly controversial Vatican rumor.

Flic's phone beeped, and she read the text message, *Hurry up.* She pulled herself away from the shop front, and increased her previous walking pace to a jog and finally a sprint as she caught sight of The HT only a hundred meters away. Her flip-flops were slowing her down, and the blazer she wore over jeans flapped behind her, but she pushed on, determined not to miss the big announcement. Her pulse raced, not only because of the unexpected and unusual physical exertion, but also through anticipation. If it was the news she was expecting, then her gamble and downright hard work just might have paid off.

"Jesus, we have trains to get around this big city you know." Laura reached through the crowd and pulled Flic, hot and sweaty, unceremoniously through to the front of the bar. Standing a foot taller than Flic, Laura pushed her into prime, front row position.

Flic struggled to catch her breath. "I used the Tube."

"Did you forget to get off again?"

Once, only once did Flic forget to get off the train, and Laura hadn't let her live it down. "I'm so unfit." She sucked in stale pub air. "Has it started yet?"

"They announced they'll be reporting breaking news, but I doubt the Vatican works to the same schedule as the BBC, so we'll just have to wait."

Flic watched as Laura checked her phone for Twitter updates from Rome. "Should be any second now."

Flic shrugged. All this smartphone technology gave her a headache.

"I have a hunch you're right about this." Laura rested a protective arm on Flic's shoulder after an enthusiastic patron roughly bumped into her, a ricochet action from all the pushing and jostling toward the rear of the bar.

Flic glared at the screen. It was midday and a program about antiques had returned to viewing. With no one remotely interested, most people had resumed talking amongst themselves, and she noticed the doors had been closed to prevent overcrowding. At times like these, pubs and cafes were where most people flocked to hear and see the unfolding of big media events, and today was certainly a big event. In recent years, the Vatican had made much noise, albeit controversial, about remaining "strong" and "true" to their beliefs and values on many social issues. With rumors circulating in all levels of media, it was only natural that people would want to bear firsthand witness to possible life-altering revelations.

Although tight, the timing for publication of her manuscript couldn't have been better. Penning the novel had consumed her. The long nights and endless cups of coffee had taken their toll. It was July now, and seven months ago, she'd slept through Christmas and barely registered it was the new year until mid January. If the news unraveled as expected, it could certainly make her, and her publisher, a tidy sum of cash. Maybe enough to upgrade her car and aging computer equipment. Anything beyond that would be a bonus. The small publishing house took a gamble when they signed her, but as things progressed in the Vatican, the gamble might just pay off for them all.

When the volume on the television was increased and a BBC reporter flashed on the screen in a sea of media outside St. Peter's Basilica, over three hundred people in The HT fell deadly silent.

"—while it remains unsubstantiated by the Vatican, close sources suggest that while the rumor surrounding Pope Valentine II's sexuality cannot be confirmed, the undeniable truth is that, at this stage, there is yet to be any formal denial."

"What utter rubbish," Flic whispered to Laura. "Is the church so powerful that even the world's largest broadcasters are too afraid to come right out and say that, according to rumor, the pope is gay?"

Flic had watched with interest in the preceding weeks as attention and talk surrounding leaked e-mails and messages from the pope to his Camerlengo—that could only be perceived as seriously sexy in her mind—were made public and were instantaneously viral. It was about time, too. She had begun to wonder if she'd dreamt up the conversation she'd overheard in Rome. Subsequently, the church—which Flic guessed had more money stashed away than Bill Gates—had released a general statement alluding to the expense of defamation, their only public statement since the rumors began. The statement—a clear warning to anyone publishing supposed and alleged inflammatory content—evidently did the trick, because just about every news broadcaster, commentator, website, and blogger had suddenly introduced the terms "hearsay" and "sources say" and "alleged messages" into their previously lacking vocabulary. In a nutshell, until the pope himself came out and said he was gay, everyone was dancing around the issue, but predictably never straying too far from the dance floor.

Laura rubbed Flic's shoulder excitedly. "This could be big for you."

Flic had been on the phone to the publisher last week. The first run was small, but judging by interest all over the world in the unfolding events, they'd considered a second run almost immediately. In order to facilitate this, the publisher had approached investors. The cash to finance unscheduled and larger print runs just wasn't at their disposal. Flic kept her fingers crossed. She hoped her book would be a success and she hoped View Press found an investor sooner rather than later.

The news coverage crossed back to the reporter in Rome who held aloft an official Vatican document. The crowd in The HT fell silent yet again.

"I have just been handed this official statement. With the world watching and with speculation mounting, we can confirm that the church has canceled, indefinitely, *all* Pope Valentine's official duties and appearances. Sources have also suggested that the Camerlengo, Cardinal Renaldo Caetani, has also had his official duties suspended, although this is yet to be confirmed by the Vatican."

Flic glanced around at the faces in the crowd as the news that the leader of the Catholic Church was most likely in a homosexual relationship with the Camerlengo, sunk in. Jesus, news that the pope was in any sort of relationship was enough to shake the world, let alone a homosexual relationship. Until reporters began descending on Rome by the hundreds, most people simply assumed the rumor about the pope was a joke, or at most, a trumped up rumor about an ambiguous and inflamed incident that might or might not have happened. To the billion plus Catholics of the world, it was all in bad taste. Nevertheless, the lack of denial from the church left many wondering if there was any truth in the rumor, and with an official Vatican announcement looming, albeit a lame one regarding the cancellation of official duties, public interest was the highest Flic could ever remember witnessing.

The chatter in the pub continued long after the television channel changed. The irony that the leader of the Catholic faith, a faith that condemned homosexuality, was most likely gay was not lost on the patrons. Reassuringly, however, not one conversation she overheard focused on Pope Valentine's sexuality as being abhorrent. On the contrary, most people, probably few of them actually Catholic, were shocked by the news, but certainly not repulsed by it. The consensus was that the Vatican should let him get on with his job. It seemed that the only people concerned that the pope was gay were homophobic people who hated all gays—leader of the Roman Catholic Church or not.

The crowd, including Flic and Laura, poured from the pub to be greeted by a crisp yet bright summer day. The air wasn't as fresh and as clean as it could be, after all they were in central London, but it was better than the stifling heat in the pub. Flic pulled her phone from her pocket. One missed call and one voice mail message. She continued her discussion with Laura concerning the pope as she distractedly listened to the message.

Flic froze. She pushed her free hand against her exposed ear to block the city noise and gave her full attention to the message.

Laura quickly pulled her into a doorway. "You'll get trampled to death if you pay any less attention."

Flic replayed the message and held the phone to Laura's ear. "This is Dee Macintosh. We need to talk. Are you watching the news? Call me."

CHAPTER TWO

Flic couldn't remember the last time Laura found herself speechless. Slightly amused, she watched as Laura mumbled and muttered before finally managing to speak.

"She rang you while watching the news. Dee Macintosh is the best of the best, and she just called you." Laura pushed her stylish short blond hair from her eyes.

"Yes, seems like it."

"What do you suppose she wants?"

"How the hell should I know?"

Laura stopped fidgeting. "You don't know who she is, do you?"

Flic shook her head. "Nope. Not a clue."

"Griffin's. She's the publisher."

Flic had certainly heard of Griffin's Publishing House, but she had no idea who owned it. "Why is she calling me?"

"Did you submit to Griffin's?"

"I submitted to everyone, so I guess so."

Laura began pacing, an awkward sight in a narrow doorway for someone nearly six feet tall. She became serious. "We have to think about this, Flic."

Felicity nodded. Her mind was racing. She already had a publisher.

"No, I mean *really* think about it."

"No, seriously? I wasn't aware there were varying degrees of thinking. I thought you just meant the half-assed kind of thinking."

She smiled and linked arms with Laura, dragging her back onto the bustling street. "Coffee?"

"And that's just for starters. You need to know exactly what to say when you return her call."

"What to say? I need to know what she wants first."

Laura worked for a management group that specialized in elite sports people. She represented some of Britain's top athletes. Her current favorites were aspiring Olympians and female footballers trying to crack the prestigious US leagues. Her least favorite were the male footballers. Flic loved her dry sense of humor. Laura's latest line to her whining boys was apparently, "The moment you play like Beckham, I'll make sure you're paid like Beckham."

Flic's palms began to sweat. "Maybe *you* should make the call?" She was suddenly nervous at the thought of talking to Dee Macintosh. "I mean, you talk people into paying you more commission for a living, and then they thank you for it! I think you should see what she wants."

Laura grabbed Flic by the shoulders. "Man up, woman. It's just a phone call. Do not, and I repeat, *do not* discuss figures over the phone."

"Figures about what?"

Laura ignored her. "And don't sound desperate."

"What? When do I sound desperate?"

"Every time you want something from me."

Flic smiled. "And do I get it?"

"Shut up, that's not the point. Just try to sound calm and cool." Laura maneuvered Flic by the shoulders to face her reflection in a shop window. She sighed. "Okay, cool will be a stretch, but at least you're wearing pinstripes."

Flic shrugged Laura away and straightened her pinstripe jacket. "Let's just find out what she wants. First."

They eventually pulled up stools in a café and ordered coffee. As an afterthought, Flic ordered a slice of thickly iced carrot cake.

"They must know to sign you now would be too late." Laura was thinking aloud. "Maybe they're trying to cut View Press's lunch." She stole the last of the carrot cake from Flic's plate. "Underhand tactics if it's true."

Flic loved Laura's enthusiasm and the frequency with which she used a phrase out of context or a word that was nearly the right one, but not quite. Flic often wondered how she wooed her clients at all. Perhaps her genuine nature was what set her apart. "I think you only cut someone's lunch when you steal their girlfriend or boyfriend."

"Not client?" Laura frowned.

"No, not client." Flic drank the last of her coffee, even the dregs at the bottom. "Right, no time like the present."

She listened to the message one last time and pressed the appropriate number to return the call. "Hello, my name is Felicity Bastone, and I'm returning Dee Macintosh's call." She indicated to Laura that she was on hold.

Laura nodded but was playing with her phone, and Flic was relieved that Laura's attention wasn't fully on her.

"Miss Bastone." A Queen-like accent greeted her. "This is Dee Macintosh. Thank you for returning my call."

Flic attempted to speak, but the muffled sound of a choking ant was all she produced. Laura gave her a gentle nudge. Flic shook her head and finally managed, "Hi, thank you for calling."

Dee, probably used to twits like Flic stammering their way nervously through conversations, continued. "I'm sitting here with a rather interesting manuscript on my desk. You're an investigative journalist, Miss Bastone, not an author, as far as I can see. Should I be concerned about the contents of this document?"

"Not unless you're Pope Valentine." Flic joked before her brain filtered the thought.

Dee Macintosh offered an indifferent tut.

Flic inhaled deeply. "I was in Rome last year and an idea came to me. It's as simple as that."

"I doubt if this particular novel was conceived in that manner, Miss Bastone, but regardless, I am interested in speaking with you about it."

"I'm sorry Miss Macintosh, but I've already signed a publishing contract for that manuscript with View Press."

"Ah, yes. Well, you have, but you also haven't. I just made an offer to the publisher of View to purchase the business."

Flic eyed Laura to gain her full attention. "I'm sorry, did you just say you're going to buy the entire View Press publishing house?"

Laura's eyes bulged wide.

"I want to market and sell your book. It's as simple as that."

"So you bought the publishing house?"

"Well, in theory I have. You know how it is, lawyers, contracts, finer details, all those tedious shenanigans. Please rest assured it was a generous offer."

This time Flic was speechless.

"So, the crux is this: I'm in the process of buying the publishing house, so therefore, I'm now in the process of publishing your book."

"Wow. I honestly don't know what to say."

Dee Macintosh laughed. "First things first. Come into the office. I'd like to meet you. Say half an hour."

The phone beeped in Flic's ear. Silence.

Laura held her phone aloft, showing Flic Dee Macintosh's most recent Twitter post. Time stamped *Just Now* it read: *Holy Father, Holy Secret. How much is a secret worth?*

Laura raised her eyebrows and shut down her phone.

Flic was gobsmacked. It was all happening so fast. *Holy Father, Holy Secret* was the title of her novel. Dee Macintosh had just posted the title of her novel for the entire world to see. She looked at her watch. "What are you doing in the next hour or so?"

Laura shrugged. "Why?"

"We have a meeting with Dee Macintosh in thirty minutes."

Laura's feet, massive as they were, became entangled in the legs of the stool. She steadied herself. "Now? We have a meeting with her now?"

Flic stood nervously tapping her hand on the coffee bar. "Can you Google the address, please?"

Laura focused, and with the amazing technology now expected by all smartphone users, she was able to calculate the distance and time of arrival at their destination. "Guess how long it takes to get there?"

Flic already knew the answer as they rushed out onto the street.

"Cheeky cow," said Laura.

"Not a spare bloody minute to do anything but rush to get there."

After racing to the Underground, down escalators, and through tunnels to reach the correct train, Flic and Laura finally sat puffing on the Piccadilly line to Finsbury Park. Although Flic had no reception, she saw eleven missed calls on her phone. "She's something else, isn't she?" She was referring to Dee Macintosh. "That bloody Twitter post or twat or twit or whatever it's called, that's why I've got all these phone calls. Christ knows who follows her on that thing."

"Tweet," offered Laura.

"What?"

"A post on Twitter is a tweet. I can't believe you don't know that."

"Whatever."

"It's ingenious really."

"Well, I don't think someone needed a degree to think up the word tweet."

Laura frowned. "No, I don't mean that, you idiot, I mean Dee Macintosh's schedule."

There was too much adrenaline surging through Flic's veins to flush with embarrassment, but she was hardly convinced about Dee Macintosh. "I feel like we're being played. She gives us no time at all and then she practically boasts about it on social media."

Laura shut her eyes.

"What are you doing?"

"I'm putting myself in her shoes."

Flic eyed Laura's larger than average feet. "I doubt you'd fit into many strangers' shoes, let alone Dee Macintosh's."

Laura's eyes snapped open. "That's why she's the best. It's not boasting rights; it's Dee Macintosh displaying just how good she is. She's read the manuscript and she wants to publish the book. Buying View Press in order to publish it is an amazing marketing tool. I estimate she spent less on the deal to buy View than what she will to market your book. The very fact alone that she actually bought out a publishing house in order to publish a book is massive news. That tweet just shows that she's snared her rabbit. You're all hers now."

"*Hers?* I'm not a prize."

"Oh, yes you are. She's outsmarted everyone. The book's ready to go. All they have to do is sell it. I have to say, Flic, I like her style."

"Well, I have to say that I don't. I'm a respected journalist. I don't like being treated like an idiot."

"What's a post on Twitter called?"

Flic sighed. The conversation had occurred only seconds ago. "I don't remember."

"See, you actually are an idiot. Don't blame her for treating you like one."

"Fuck off." Flic sulked for a moment. "If she wanted to print it so much, why didn't she just offer a deal when I first sent her the manuscript?"

"I can only imagine that the person who made the decision to disregard your manuscript no longer has a job."

Flic was about to question how Dee knew about the story if that was the case, but then she remembered View Press was on the hunt for investors to increase the print run. Now it all made sense.

Laura gave Flic a wink and dragged her to a standing position. "Come on. This is us."

Upon returning to ground level, Laura consulted the map on her phone and set off in the right direction, Flic in tow.

Set on the top floor of an old building, recently redeveloped for exclusive office space, Griffin Publishing House looked more like a set from *Downton Abbey* than a workplace. Conflicting with the age of the building were the state-of-the-art computers, security gadgets, and the smell of expensive coffee emanating from the elaborate machine near reception that Flic was convinced could be larger than a small car.

Although hot and sticky, Flic was thankful she'd at least worn a blazer that day. She was choosing to believe her flip-flops were simply trendy and not just the first thing she bothered to find rushing from the door that morning. Indeed, all Flic seemed to have done that day was rush.

A smartly dressed young man said he had been expecting them, and his almost imperceptible glance at the clock, followed by a faint smirk, suggested he knew how tight their schedule had been.

Although she knew her book was safe, that it was the sole reason Griffin's bought out View, impressing Dee Macintosh was suddenly of utmost importance. Griffin Publishing House was Britain's largest and most respected publisher. She had to get her shit together. Ms. Macintosh was obviously a tough cookie, and she couldn't afford to become tongue-tied. At least she had Laura. Two against one were good odds, and they were in her favor.

The receptionist ushered them along the thickly carpeted hall and politely knocked on a heavy timber door. The brass nameplate read Publisher. Flic took a deep breath and held it as the weighty door swung open easily. The breath she wanted, indeed needed, to release became trapped in her throat. The vast room, which she guessed she couldn't even kick a football the length of, housed a massive mahogany table with five people sitting toward the far end. In the center sat Dee Macintosh. To the left of the table, projected onto a large expanse of white wall, was an image of a book cover. It was glamorous, it was Rome, and although View Press had designed a great cover, the one she was looking at, wrapped around an image of a hardcover book, was absolutely stunning. *Holy Father, Holy Secret* by Felicity Bastone beamed back at her in all its glory.

Flic finally exhaled and promptly passed out.

CHAPTER THREE

"Y ou sure showed them."

Flic registered the voice but was too frightened to open her eyes. She felt something soft touch her cheek.

"Come on, Flic. I think you've adequately demonstrated how swiftly you can transform from an upright position to flat on your back. Open your eyes for me." Laura sounded amused.

Flic wanted to open her eyes, she hoped to God it was a bad dream, but when she cracked her left eye open even a fraction, she saw the massive book cover on the screen and the nausea engulfed her all over again.

"It's okay. They all dashed from the room when you hit the deck." Laura poked her in the ribs until she squirmed.

"They're going to print me in hardback?" Publishers only printed best sellers in hardback. A paperback and an eBook format always followed, but it was the ultimate to have written a hardcover novel.

Flic finally opened her eyes to be greeted with a cup of tea and a biscuit sitting beside her. She could smell the strong tea, immediately knew it would be well sugared, and couldn't resist any longer. Laura helped her into a sitting position.

"Everyone was super concerned, wanted to call an ambulance, but when you started moaning and groaning, I said you would be fine. I explained that we had missed lunch—what with the announcement and all—and I guessed you would have skipped breakfast—although Dee did do a little *tut tut* at that."

"You told her I miss breakfast?"

"Well, you do."

"Not every day. I was in a rush today."

"I don't think she cares, Flic, and anyway, I was under a little duress when I had that conversation."

"But she *tut tutted*. I can't believe you told her I don't eat breakfast."

"Get a grip before I whack you over the head with a blunt object and knock you out again." Laura shoved the biscuit toward Flic. "Here. Eat."

Flic took a deep breath after finishing the tea and biscuit. "They could have given me more than one measly biscuit."

"They did." Laura hauled Flic up to sit in a chair. "I ate the others waiting for you to open your eyes."

There was a purposeful knock at the door before Dee Macintosh and her entourage re-entered.

No longer distracted by a stunning book cover with her name on it, Flic gave Dee her full attention. "Sorry, Ms. Macintosh. I don't know what came over me."

Dee Macintosh was average in every single way, except that she was *the* Dee Macintosh. Average height, average weight—a little on the heavy side—and besides the fact that she was wearing an expensive dress, she was rather average looking. Her expensive, highlighted, middle-aged haircut was perfect, not a strand out of place, both sides swept back and tucked behind her ears. Her face was well made-up but subtle without seeming to try too hard.

She intimidated the life out of Flic. Nausea threatened her again until the young man from reception delivered a tray of pastries, sandwiches, and unknown chocolate delicacies. Flic ignored protocol and selected chocolate immediately.

Dee smiled warmly. "Not at all. But you should see a doctor if it happens again." She held out her hand. "As far as a formal introduction goes, yours was a little flamboyant for me." Flic took her hand. "I'm Dee Macintosh."

"Felicity Bastone. It's a pleasure to meet you." Flic laughed nervously. "And I'm upright." She glanced to Laura for help.

"You must be a busy lady. I imagine it was difficult to slot this meeting into your schedule?" As expected, Dee's eyes followed Laura's as they drifted toward the projected front cover image.

Dee nodded in understanding. "Let's just say this meeting was something I was willing to clear my afternoon for."

Flic relaxed. Laura was experienced at levelling the playing field.

Dee relaxed, too. "Please, ladies, sit. We have much to discuss. And, Felicity, do eat something more than chocolate. We don't want you passing out on us again."

The atmosphere in the room altered, and Flic was suddenly famished.

"Firstly," said Dee, "I'd like to welcome you aboard and assure you we're the best publishers to handle your book. Let me introduce you to my team."

Oddly, Flic had forgotten anyone else was in the room. She took in the man and woman flanking Dee.

"This is Cameron Humphries, one of our most experienced editors."

Cameron wore smart tight jeans and a figure-hugging navy blue knitted top. His pink-and-white striped shirt, of which she could only see the cuffs and collar, indicated he was no fashion slouch.

"And this is Anna Lawrence, our marketing guru." Anna was attractive. Flic was hopeless at ages but guessed Anna to be mid to late thirties. She wore a simple black suit, not cheap, but not Armani either. Her face was sweet looking, round and cheerful, and her wavy auburn hair sat just below her shoulders.

Flic shook hands with them both, wondering how such a young pair could be so experienced, let alone "gurus." Regardless, her eyes lingered on Anna longer than she had intended. There was something about her that she couldn't put her finger on; perhaps it was that she maintained the air of aloofness even Dee Macintosh had abandoned.

"We'd like to offer you a new contract."

What?

Dee mistook Flic's dumbfounded silence for an indication she should continue.

"The advance is £50,000, paid however you like, and we commence marketing immediately. Publishing your book is a time game at this stage."

Flic began choking on an egg sandwich.

Laura rolled her eyes and handed her a glass of water.

Dee smiled, but continued. "We can't afford to be complacent with time or quality. The news about the pope is big, and it will only get bigger. At some point, the Vatican will have to deny or confirm the rumors and with no denial forthcoming, I think it is safe to assume that the pope is gay." She shrugged. "Although why that's a problem, let alone big news in this day and age, I'll never know." Anna flinched and Flic wondered why. "Either way, we're producing a work of fiction. If we get our story out before the pope has a chance to tell his, we're printing nothing but a story full of coincidence." She paused for effect. "Do you understand me?"

Flic understood; of course she understood. All she'd thought about for the last ten months was the pope. When her mind hadn't been consumed with writing the manuscript, she'd either been sleeping or wondering how she would explain a book that so closely resembled the truth if it were ever to become known. Thinking about the latest Vatican revelations, there was no way the pope's sexuality was going to remain a secret. She needed to explain. Her book was far from fiction.

As if reading Flic's mind, Dee held up her hand. "How you came about the *idea* for your story is irrelevant to me and the rest of the world, Felicity. What is important is that it gets out there before the truth, regardless of how similar our story and the truth may prove to be."

CHAPTER FOUR

I t's absolutely ridiculous!" Anna said.

Seb lifted the pan and flicked something laced with garlic back and forth like a professional chef. "It looks like it's true, Anna. You might have to rethink your view on this."

"So what? Maybe it is true. Why do we have to sensationalize it? Some idiot writes a book that now happens to be coming to fruition—"

"Wow, big word, tiger. I thought you marketing mob liked to keep it simple."

"It shits me, that's all. This chick is going to get mega rich from this—"

"Um, excuse me, but isn't that your job? You really need to get over this, Anna. She'll make Griffin's a bucket load of cash. Everyone benefits, not just her. Your Christmas bonus, just like everyone else's, will be a big one this year."

Anna mumbled as the Pilates DVD rolled the credits, and she drank from her water bottle. Seb hated Pilates.

Dee Macintosh had made some questionable decisions about publishing in the past, she was only human after all, and Anna was far from perfect herself, but buying into the misery that her beloved church was currently enduring was beyond her understanding. Dee had admitted herself just that morning that things were becoming prickly in Rome. *Holy Father, Holy Secret* was a gamble on many levels, especially when she had to buy an entire damn company to get it, so why not let one of the other publishers take that risk. Why Griffin's?

"Is it that she's gay?" Seb had read the bio Anna had brought home of the author who wrote the soon-to-be-published fictional exposé. "You know, your religion can be completely fucked sometimes."

"Hey, that's not fair, and no, it has nothing to do with her sexuality." Anna said the words, but she wasn't entirely convinced they were true. "It just seems a little unfair that a lesbian without faith is writing about a gay pope. There must be some agenda. She must have some sort of grudge." Anna nodded her head. "It's her grudge that offends me, not her sexuality."

"I don't see any evidence that she bears a grudge against the church. It's your church that openly condemns her sexuality."

"I've not witnessed one person suffer discrimination at the hands of any parish I've attended."

"Oh, come on, Anna, that's utter rubbish. The priest is hardly going to stand up during Mass and send out the faggot, is he? Your church condemns and discriminates on a global scale. It doesn't have to pick and choose individuals."

"It feels so inclusive to me," she said.

"And I'm not disputing that, but your experience was different. You believe because you choose to, because you were lucky enough to encounter great priests who nurtured your faith and your morals. You have to accept that not everyone has that experience."

"Well *I* don't condemn homosexuality. I know loads of gay people."

Seb rolled his eyes. "You know two."

"Well, that's *people*."

"And they're my friends."

Anna picked at the mushrooms and onion in the pan before Seb smacked her hand away. "But you can't argue that I do *actually* know them."

"And perhaps you ought not try to argue that you might *actually* be a little bit homophobic."

"That's rubbish!"

"I get that the axis has shifted on everything you love and trust, but this is the twenty-first century, my friend. Love is love."

Seb had been Anna's flat mate for nearly two years and they often shared heated discussions. He made valid points, she knew that, but on this occasion, it was just too big for her to swallow without serious consideration.

The pope wasn't supposed to love *anybody*, let alone another man. The scandal rocking the Catholic Church was the biggest challenge to her faith that she could imagine. There was a structure to Catholicism that had stood the test of time. It kept the flock safe. The pope kept everyone safe, so what was going to happen now? The pope was a man, yes, but he was God's highest representative on earth. He was the one man who stood above all men, he was the holiest of men, and this scandal would see him crash to earth unceremoniously.

Anna found it impossible to comprehend that the pope was just human, just a man. So human in fact, he was probably in love. He preached love, he encouraged love for all human beings, but he had no right to find love for himself. Anna fought the overwhelming feeling of disappointment, but it was too strong and she was hastily developing disgust for those so callously keen to tear her church down.

Dee didn't have to ask how Felicity Bastone had written a novel that was fast becoming true. Gossip was rife in the office about how she came across the facts. Of course, you could tell she was sensationalizing the tale for maximum sales effect, but the rest bore an alarming similarity to real life. An informant in the Vatican wasn't unheard of, but for her to then selfishly pen a novel exposing the truth, Anna could only surmise that she must have betrayed her informant's trust. Felicity Bastone was on unsteady, dangerous ground. How dare she assume the right to tell the world private Vatican affairs?

Flic's one-bedroom flat was in an outer London borough, well beyond her means until cashing in from the story she wrote breaking the pedophile ring. She and Laura sipped wine in the lounge, carefully reading the thirty-page document that set out the new terms of her contract.

She'd already signed it of course. Dee Macintosh was hardly going to let her leave the office without the deal secure. Not that she had much choice. If she wanted her book published, and she did, signing on the dotted line was a foregone conclusion.

The contract was the same as her previous one with View Press with the exception of a lengthy promotional clause and the all important advance and royalties section. Laura bothered to read the additional clauses while Flic stalled on the section that clearly stated, upon arrival of the manuscript—already delivered—a cool £50,000 would be deposited into her bank account. Forty-five thousand more than View Press could offer. She took in her modest surroundings; if she made more from royalties, the one-bedroom flat would nearly be all hers.

"Besides the section about publicity and marketing, I think it's pretty standard." Laura sipped the expensive wine, purchased as a well-earned celebration. For her own peace of mind, she'd used Flic's computer to forward the contract to her firm's lawyers who'd confirmed there were no hidden traps.

In fact, Dee had been frank about the inclusion of the publicity and marketing clauses.

"We need to feed the press something more to focus on," she'd said. "I want that focus to be you."

Flic wasn't convinced.

Dee had been adamant. "If we give you and your book to the press, they can say exactly what they want to say, what they're dying to say but don't have the balls to put out there. They can do it all from bloody Rome for all I care, but the pope remains in the news and they need that. Suddenly, they have a brand new avenue to report exactly what's in your book and that's everything they're desperate to report now."

Laura had nodded when Flic looked to her for guidance. "She's completely correct. They'll latch on to you like a leach. They're struggling for legitimate ways to report it now. They're out of credible experts, out of historians, and if we deliver them an author with a novel that has practically predicted the future, well, that's gold to them and to us."

It had never occurred to Flic that her involvement in the book would be so intense and extensive. Sitting in the vast room listening to people talk at her, she hid her naivety well. Nothing could prepare her for what was to come. In her mind, she'd already put in the hours and done all the hard work. The book was written, edited, and ready. She imagined a rigorous social media campaign, maybe a few radio interviews, but that was nothing in comparison to the scale of involvement Dee was suggesting.

"So, how are you feeling?" Laura stretched on the sofa and eyed Flic.

"It all feels so surreal." She rolled her eyes. "I know that term is overused and usually completely out of context, but I can't think of a better way to describe what is suddenly happening in my life. I don't suppose you can swing a week or so off to help me get through Dee's publicity stuff?"

Laura thought for a moment. "Dee will probably do London bookshops first, then perhaps Manchester, Liverpool, and then head to Scotland or maybe Ireland. I have a feeling she'll squeeze in a few smaller venues along the way. It'll be busy." She accessed the calendar on her phone. "I reckon I can reschedule some appointments or Skype the clients. The initial push should only take a week or so. Yep, I'm in."

CHAPTER FIVE

E urope?" Flic asked.
　　"What were you thinking, my dear, Charing Cross Road
and then out for high tea?" Dee replied.

High tea sounded just perfect.

Dee couldn't help but smile. "My gut tells me you've written a
best seller. Regardless of what comes out about the pope, it's a good
yarn. My business decisions reflect my direction with your book.
We need to make it big and I believe I can do just that."

Flic and Dee were back in the boardroom discussing vague
details of the publicity tour while waiting for Anna Lawrence—the
apparent marketing genius—to present them with a solid schedule.

Flic felt alone. Laura wouldn't be able to take enough time
off to gallivant around Europe, especially when she wouldn't be
paid and especially when she had clients to manage of her own. Flic
had fallen asleep last night safe in the knowledge that the publicity
tour would take a week or so of intense appearances in the United
Kingdom with Laura by her side. Discovering now that she was
kidding herself and that half of bloody Europe was being scheduled,
sent her spiraling into a panic she couldn't suppress.

Before anyone could allay her fears, Anna strode in the room,
greeted them with a brief nod, and wirelessly projected a map
onto the same wall where a day earlier her book cover had been.
She handed them all a thick document entitled *Holy Father, Holy
Secret—Publicity Itinerary—Felicity Bastone*.

The map listed destination after destination. Flic gulped her tea and forced down a biscuit, determined at least not to faint again. She rarely underestimated many things, her line of work ensured she remained open-minded and she'd long ceased being surprised or shocked by the world around her, but she was kicking herself now, and she was only just beginning to understand the anticipated scale of interest in her book.

"As we all know, today is going to be a long day. And probably a long night," Dee said. "Since five this morning, we've had our marketing and graphics team working on your book. The sleeve on a hardcover is important. It's imperative we get it right."

Dee kept a close eye on Flic. She knew it was to gauge her reactions, and since holding a poker face wasn't her greatest skill, she guessed Dee knew exactly what was racing through her mind.

Dee turned to Anna who clicked a button on her tablet and a run sheet appeared on the screen.

Flic's eyes popped out of her head. "Two weeks? Is that even possible?"

"The book's ready to go, Felicity. I've called in some favors and we have multiple print runs scheduled here, continental Europe, and the States. By the time we leave here this evening, the graphics will be finalized and Griffin Publishers will begin marketing your book, complete with stunning cover, all over the world, first thing tomorrow."

Anna was nodding. "We're making the news already. By simply leaking that we bought View Press, we're already creating interest and intrigue. By the time we ramp this up, everyone in the developed world will know who Felicity Bastone is."

"Surely you understand we need to move on this quickly, Felicity."

Dee paced the room. "Ideally, we want your book out before the Vatican or the pope confirms or denies anything. We can't control what they do, but we can make damn sure we do everything in our power to make the best of the slight advantage we have. The Vatican isn't renowned for being predictable in these circumstances. Hell, we haven't seen a crisis of this scale in the modern world. But this is big and I don't think the church will make any rash decisions. Time, in that sense, is on our side. In contrast, to have a hardcover book hot off the press in two weeks is a race against the clock, and certainly not a feat I've ever undertaken. Griffin's don't, and won't, produce a substandard product. It has to look like the masterpiece we're going to market it as."

Anna stared directly at Flic before adding, "The timeframe is tight, because when you attack an institution like the Catholic Church, you need to move quickly while you have momentum and before you get shot down in flames."

"Anna." Dee's tone was unquestionably a warning. "I don't bring my private life to work, and neither should you."

Anna flushed from below her shirt. The red rash spread to her cheeks. "I asked you to assign this to someone else."

"And I'm asking you to do your best. I respect your beliefs, but I don't pay you for them."

Flic coughed, reminding everyone she was in the room. The exchange had caught her off guard. Why was Anna hostile? She was confused. "I don't know you, Anna, or your religious persuasion, but can I ask why you interpret this as an attack on the Catholic Church?"

Anna leapt at the chance to elaborate. "The church, my church, provides the framework to hold over a billion people on this planet together. It provides them with a sense of hope and a moral grounding. Our church will welcome everyone. Support everyone. It should be left alone." She couldn't disguise her trembling hands.

Flic nodded, inwardly rolling her eyes. She had traveled the world, visited many holy sites, and witnessed the good and bad of countless religions, but by the end of all that, she believed in God no more than she believed in Santa Claus. To argue with Anna was fruitless, and she understood her opinion was no more valid than Anna's when it came down to it. Faith was simply that, faith, and Anna was a means to an end she would endure until the book promotion was over. Unable to let it go without one final comment though, she said, "That didn't answer my question, but I accept you have strong faith. I would question, however, the validity of your claims that the church supports everyone. I, for one, am condemned by your faith, and the children that suffered at the hands of the abusers in your church would certainly not share your opinion. But it *is* your opinion and I respect that. Perhaps you can respect mine?"

"You're out to destroy our church!"

Flic remained calm. "Only those people who form part of a homophobic institution would view the pope being gay as destructive."

"Homophobia has nothing to do with this. The pope has allegedly been conducting a forbidden relationship with a cardinal. The pope is married to the church."

"Well, he sure as hell isn't married to the Camerlengo, nor can he be under Catholic rules."

"I know all that," said Anna. "It wasn't the point I was trying to make."

"So, you're trying to tell me that if the pope were to be in a similar situation but with a woman, the response from Catholics all over the world would be exactly the same?"

"Yes. Precisely."

"Rubbish."

Anna turned her back. "You don't understand. This will destroy us."

Flic sighed. She didn't want to leave things on a sour note. "For what it's worth, I think it's fabulous news that the pope is in love with a man. Your perspective is not mine. I'm not out to destroy anything, let alone the Catholic faith."

"I think that's enough, ladies." Dee stood as Anna turned with an icy stare. "Time for a break I think."

Anna marched from the room.

"I'm sorry if I'm offending her." Flic poured tea and then turned to Dee. She had been blindsided by Anna's standpoint. It hadn't occurred to her that someone in the publishing house wouldn't be supportive. It was good practice, she convinced herself. When the entire world had access to her book, she would probably face far worse than Anna Lawrence.

"Anna has a unique perspective on many things. When it comes to her job, it serves her exceedingly well, and she can usually separate her personal opinion from that of a professional one. This is, however, proving to be a personal challenge."

Flic nodded. She found it difficult to dislike Anna, which was strange because usually someone with such narrow-minded views would certainly have bored her by now. The knowledge of marketing and the competent manner in which she conducted herself was keeping Flic engaged for the time being.

Dee smiled. "I suspect Anna could serve just as capably as a nun as she can our head of marketing."

A nun? Flic wasn't sure what to make of that. "She's prudish?"

Dee laughed outright. "If I gave Anna a brief to come up with the sexiest, dirtiest condom campaign Britain has ever seen, it would be outstanding."

Flic frowned.

"You don't have to have tasted the cherry to know it's sweet," said Dee.

"She's a virgin?" The question spilled out before she could stop herself, let alone remember the manners her mother taught her. "Sorry, that's out of line." She wondered about the possibility of someone in their mid to late thirties actually being a virgin. It was possible but unlikely.

Dee waved off the apology. "Cut her some slack, though. I don't think she's had much experience, but she's a smart woman. Her faith and her job are the two most important things in her life."

Flic nodded, wondering if there wasn't an important "someone" in Anna's life. When Dee's attention returned to the schedule in front of her, the conversation was over.

Before Flic finished her tea, Anna returned and quickly reverted to full professional mode. On the screen, she displayed a detailed publicity schedule. "Ireland is first, predominantly Catholic in the south but, as we know, less so in the north. We need this book to be talked about, so from a marketing perspective, this is the best chance we have to manufacture momentum in these early stages of promotion."

Flic understood the Catholic south versus Protestant north divide in Ireland. Obviously, things had improved significantly since "The Troubles," but a religious angle would certainly generate interest from the press. It was a clever tactic.

"France is next," Anna continued. "The French like to protest, and it will be our job to provide them with something they can form a clear opinion on. On the back of Ireland, this is our challenge, but it can certainly be accomplished."

Anna detailed the locations she intended to lock in as sales took hold. After France, the tour would take Flic around most of Western Europe before returning to England. It was a grueling timetable, and without even factoring in the lucrative US market, the tour was already a month long.

Felicity began to comprehend just how life changing the book might prove to be. She watched in awe as Anna outlined the strategies they would employ. Even as they spoke, the social media department at Griffin's was frantically building a website, a Twitter account, a Facebook page, Instagram account, and a huge array of digital downloads associated with the book and Felicity herself. In between all the marketing and decision-making tasks associated with the actual book, appointments had been squeezed into her personal itinerary—a makeover, photo shoot, and sessions with experts to deliver her a crash course in breathing and interview techniques to name but a few.

Beyond their obvious difference of opinion, she couldn't help but be impressed by Anna's professionalism. After faltering that morning, Anna appeared to have gathered herself and seemed incredibly committed to the task, indeed, committed to Dee. The fact that she didn't personally believe they should be pursuing publication of the book strangely impressed Flic.

The graphic team submitted a set of possible covers, including the one she'd seen yesterday, by mid afternoon. Although she loved them all, she was forced to choose her favorite. The image she selected conveyed strong religious undertones, and predictably, it was Anna's least favorite.

"Will you always dislike what I like?" Flic grinned.

"I can't help it if you have appalling taste." Anna was gathering her documents from the table but didn't hide her amusement.

"I don't believe for one moment you didn't have the last say on the final cover proofs."

"Then you overestimate my authority. Dee always has the last word."

Flic briefly doubted that but knew better. "I imagine you went to Dee with the final proofs and she agreed with your selection. Tell me I'm not wrong?"

"I'll tell you nothing of the sort. Besides, you selected the least appealing cover of the final proofs." Documents secure in her stylish bag, Anna held the door open for Flic with her free hand. "I reiterate—appalling taste."

Flic stalled on the threshold, dangerously close to Anna. "In some situations, I have outstanding taste."

"And dare I ask those situations?"

She wasn't expecting Anna to entertain the conversation any longer than necessary. Flic liked her cheeky response. "Maybe I'll show you one day."

Anna finally blushed. "You should get some fresh air now before the real hard work begins."

"You're changing the subject."

"No. I think you might be doing that."

"And is this topic so bad?"

They had been walking toward Anna's office. She paused before entering. "I'm not entirely sure what the subject is, but I think I'm holding my own."

Flic laughed as she continued toward reception and the futuristic coffee machine. "Yep, you're doing that all right."

CHAPTER SIX

The only break came at seven that evening when Dee ordered food and sent those in for the long haul home with orders to shower, freshen up, and return by nine to continue into the night.

Anna stretched back in her luxurious office chair. She enjoyed the challenge of a big project, but it invariably took its toll. This time next week, she knew she'd be dead on her feet.

She was impressed with Felicity's attitude and dedication. She had been the last to leave and the first to return for the evening stint. On any other project, Anna thought she might like her more. It was a pity she held such radical views. Flic was charming, even she could tell that, and genuine too, with her sense of humor and warm attitude toward everyone. She just wished Felicity hadn't been the author of *Holy Father, Holy Secret*. In fact, it was beginning to annoy her that she couldn't write Felicity off as an unsavory lost cause. The annoyance was, in turn, causing her a great distraction. Felicity's niceness was distracting, but what a stupid notion.

Anna stopped swiveling on her chair. She was becoming dizzy. A distraction indeed.

Her task that evening was to build a framework for the logistics of the tour schedule. On this occasion, marketing and location went hand in hand; the order of appearances would influence her marketing approach. The priority for her team in the morning was to confirm flights, hotels, transfers, and schedule appearances. She was pleased with her team. They had produced an abundance of ideas on how to market the story to maximize interest, and while she was personally struggling with the concept of the pope being gay, something Felicity had said that morning seemed to motivate the others, and the team had run with it.

The angle they had developed was acceptance, not scandal, and it was brilliant. The only problem was that she didn't buy it, not for a second. Anna knew the outing of their leader would crush the church, but would the rest of the world take something from their angle? She had to concede it was a unique selling point, and the innovations her team had brainstormed already were inspired. The only problem was, no one on her team was Catholic, and few of them comprehended the magnitude of these revelations. Even fewer cared. In essence, their marketing strategy was to idolize and revere the man they were outing and the man many Catholics would despise. It was a tough sell, but on the balance of probabilities, it could work. She hated and loved the idea simultaneously.

❖

Flic sat surrounded by piles of paperwork to either read or complete. She had no idea there would be so much information to absorb. She clouted her knee on the desk when a knock at the door startled her. Without waiting for a response, Anna poked her head in.

"Can I interrupt you for a moment?"

Flic nodded, rubbing her knee, but relieved by the welcome disruption. Her eyes were tired from reading, and the thought of being distracted by Anna lifted her spirits.

"I didn't know you wore glasses." It was more of an observation than a question.

Flic smiled. "They just relieve some of the strain. I tend to over focus."

"Well, they suit you." Anna blushed as if she'd spoken a thought out loud.

"Thank you. I certainly need them tonight."

"I have a couple of things to run by you if you have a moment?" Anna replaced her friendly persona with slick professionalism. Flic admired the seamless transition and nodded for her to go on.

"This is the press release we're running with in the initial stages. Depending on what's happening in the media, we have other directions preplanned, but on the whole, this is the direction we'll be taking."

Flic glanced at the press release. "Whoa, it outs me as a lesbian in the first sentence. Don't you think that's a little personal?"

Anna nodded. "In normal circumstances, yes." She then handed Flic the publicity and marketing proposal. "But as you can see, we're not trying to create a scandal. On the contrary, we're trying to distance ourselves from the negative press that is surrounding this whole situation. We can control that to a certain extent, then eventually, the media will do what they like, but at no stage will we actually suggest that the pope is doing anything wrong. Our line is to suggest that the entire thing has been completely blown out of all proportion."

Flic was amazed.

"What you said to me this morning made sense on some level, and if *you* don't think the pope being gay is outrageous, then perhaps the public won't either. From a marketing perspective, it could be a winner."

"Could be?" Flic was pleased her little talk had sunk in.

"Yes, could be. It certainly won't be what the press and the public are expecting. It will work in our favor."

Flic couldn't help be a little disappointed. "So, it only made sense for the purposes of marketing?"

Anna straightened. "I'm not suggesting you're ignorant. I think you believe what you're doing is morally sound. But I don't think you have any understanding of the impact of what you've written and the subsequent publishing of your book."

"Anna, the pope is gay whether I've written it or not."

"Perhaps, but for the sake of over a billion people, the Vatican can manage this situation, repair the damage, and in time move on. That can't happen when there is a novel out there sensationalizing this, fuelling the fires of anti-Catholic demonstrators, and putting into question everything that the Catholic faith holds dear."

"Don't you mean that *you* hold dear?"

"Yes, me and over a billion people."

"And you think *I'm* ignorant?" Flic was astounded by Anna's attitude. "You can't possibly try to tell me that over a billion Catholics abstain from sex before marriage, refuse to use birth control, or haven't participated in adultery?" How was someone so highly intelligent and educated so uninformed? "There are loads of gay Catholics in the world. Poor Pope Valentine isn't the first, you know?"

Anna turned for the door, flustered and close to tears. "When I was a child, the Catholic Church was all I had. Forgive me for not wanting that to change. And forgive me for not wanting to be a participant in its destruction."

Flic had more to say, but Anna was gone. She had more to say to prove her point, but also floating around her brain were the words she might have used to placate or even console Anna regarding the future of her beloved church. Destruction certainly wasn't what Flic had in mind. She hoped to God Anna's marketing strategy would work, otherwise the hatred of the world's Catholic believers might be aimed solely in her direction.

At one a.m., Dee called everyone to the boardroom. Still looking alarmingly refreshed and alert, she stood relaxed at the head of the table and requested updates from every team.

Anna reported that her publicist team would work through the proposed schedule when they arrived later that morning at seven o'clock. She produced the first draft of the marketing proposal and markups, including images from the social media team. It all looked stunning and amazingly professional.

Flic was exhausted. She wondered how these people could remain so focused and effective at that hour of the morning. Dee was the rock and driving force.

❖

Although they remained guarded, Anna and Flic established a favorable middle ground and continued to work efficiently together as the days passed.

As it stood, the Vatican remained silent and gave no indication that an official statement would be forthcoming. This was good news for the exhausted team at Griffin's, but the public were becoming increasingly twitchy. It was possible, due to the tight time frames, that her book might be delayed, but it was imperative that it was released prior to any Vatican confirmation of a gay pope. Of course, if they denied the pope's relationship with the Camerlengo, her sales would likely soar.

Silence or a denial was Griffin's preference, and a confirmation would cause a major rethink. The whole thing was incredibly stressful.

Anna had come to Flic's office to discuss her preferences on hotels, and not for the first time, had taken five minutes to catch a power nap on Flic's sofa away from her own office and Dee Macintosh.

Flic was usually so far behind schedule that she barely noticed Anna, but tonight she was struggling to keep her eyes open. Without really noticing, she began to watch Anna sleep between tasks, then more frequently until she quit working altogether and simply just watched her sleep.

She couldn't remember ever seeing anyone sleep so peacefully. Anna's eyes finally twitched open, and Flic didn't bother trying to hide her stare. "Can I get you anything?" she asked. "Tea or a coffee?" Flic's voice was soft and gentle. She hadn't meant it to be; it just came out that way.

"I'd love a cup of tea."

Flic smiled.

"And a doughnut, please? Maybe a jam one if there's any left."

Flic returned with hot drinks and a selection of snacks.

"Do you always watch people sleep?" asked Anna.

"I'm not always around sleeping people, so I'm not sure. I'll make a mental note next time to see where my eyes wander though."

"So there's no one waiting for you at home then?"

Flic laughed. Something told her Anna didn't want to be interested in Flic, but curiosity had evidently won out. "If there was, I reckon they'd have pushed off by now or they'd have forgotten what I look like."

"Everyone will know what you look like soon."

"Yes. I suppose they will."

"Does it bother you?"

"I'm too tired to be bothered by anything other than lack of sleep, but I guess it will sell books."

"If this works, you'll be famous. Have you thought this through?"

"Nice try." Flic offered the last pastry, and when Anna declined, she ate it herself. "And a new tack and all."

Anna smiled. "I didn't mean you should pull out. You're many things. I doubt a quitter is one of them. It's just that you seem very private. I simply wondered if you fully understood the impact your book is probably going to have."

"If your marketing strategy works, my book should have a massive impact."

Anna rubbed her eyes. "Yes. Perhaps I'm my own worst enemy."

"What's your strike rate?"

"Pardon?"

"What are the chances of your strategy working? Do all your strategies sell books?" Flic clarified.

"Put it this way, I'd be surprised if you didn't hit the *New York Times* number one spot sooner rather than later. You'd better develop a tough skin."

"I think I can handle it."

Anna's face softened. It was the first time Flic thought she might be seeing a real person, not just a professional searching for the best-selling angle on a book. "I'm serious and I'm not trying to frighten you, but when your book is released, everyone in the world will have access to it. Everyone will be an instant expert, a critic, and there will be some people who will try to do everything to drag you down. They will write horrible things about you and about your book, and they won't care that you're a real person too, with feelings." Anna smiled knowingly. "I'd hate for you to go into this blind, that's all."

Flic had only thought about fame briefly, and then it was only the good bits like a new car, a bigger house, and a *long* holiday. The fact that Anna had bothered to counsel her about it gave her cause to set her perceptive comments aside and afford them due consideration later. Anna didn't have to look out for her in this way, and the notion was touching.

Not wanting to miss an opportunity, Flic steered the conversation back to personal ground. She wanted to know more. "But an eye for an eye, Miss Lawrence. Tell me about the special someone waiting for you at home?"

"I wish. Waiting at home is my flatmate, Seb. We've been friends for years. I don't seem to have much luck in the romance department."

The response was far more candid than Flic had expected. She returned the favor.

"Me neither."

"What? Surely you have a girlfriend?" Anna blushed. "I mean, you're a nice person. I wouldn't have thought you'd be single."

"Yes, I am a nice person. Glad you noticed." She winked, but her humor was brief. "I think that might be the reason I'm single." Flic's last relationship, and most significant by far, had failed miserably, but she refused to harbor the classic brooding routine. She just cracked on with things.

"So, we're two single chicks just hanging out in the office until...well, until I go gallivanting off to Europe, I suppose." Flic finished her tea.

"Do you believe in God?" Anna pulled her knees under her chin. "I mean you seem to be someone who I'd imagine has faith of some description."

Flic hated this question at the best of times, and religion certainly wasn't something she felt comfortable talking to Anna about. Unless she lied, there was no chance of any common ground between them.

She hated liars. "If I'm being completely honest, I don't believe in God."

"At all?"

"I think he's a myth, just like the tooth fairy and just like Santa."

"So why write about it?"

It was a fair question. Flic considered her response. "Just because I don't believe in it, doesn't mean I'm not interested. With absolutely no evidence of validation, I find it fascinating that so many people's lives are ruled by, or in some way affected by, religion. But don't get me wrong, I don't judge people for their beliefs. I simply find it all quite intriguing. If there were a machine to measure judgment on beliefs, I'd wager yours to be a higher reading than mine."

"Oh, that's utter rubbish." Anna was wide-awake now. "You've written a book you know full well will damage the church."

Flic had been enjoying their conversation until now. It was the first time she'd felt at ease with Anna and she liked it. She thought that perhaps Anna had too. It was too late to remove herself from the conversation without looking like a rude bitch, so she calmly explained. "On the contrary, I hope it enhances the church, but that's not the issue here, and from the tack you've taken on the marketing, I presume we're agreeing to disagree on that. Besides the obvious, there's a marked difference between an atheist and a religious person and that is that an atheist can understand why people *are* religious. We see the world and all its intricacies through many different levels. A religious person, on the other hand, can't for the life of them fathom why an atheist has no faith. They seem incapable of understanding that some people don't need what they need. The fact that you work in marketing is somewhat odd in that respect, so there might be hope for you yet."

"That's a little generalized, isn't it?"

"Is it?"

Flic wasn't expecting an answer. If she was right, Anna was admitting her own ignorance.

"I'd better get back to it." Anna stood abruptly and was out the door in a matter of moments.

Flic didn't want her to leave this way. "Thank you," she shouted.

"For what?" Anna returned to the doorway.

"For your advice. I know it's not your job to help me with all that stuff. I appreciate it."

Anna's shoulders dropped a fraction. "You're welcome." She left.

❖

The church had brought Anna so much joy as a child, there was a huge part of her that didn't understand why other people, especially those with troubles or those who had lost their way, didn't seek solace within its loving arms. Inside the church, she had found contentment and inner peace, and it had been so simple. Even now, she felt a sense of warmth and belonging just thinking about it. It was true that she had wondered why so many others didn't follow that path. Nevertheless, thinking about Flic's stance on religion contributed only a fraction of the current reflection she was engaging in after their conversation. The thought of being watched while sleeping was unnerving, but it hadn't bothered her in the slightest with Flic. In fact, it had felt pleasant not to wake up alone, and the advice she had given Flic was well intentioned. It suddenly occurred to her—God watched over her, but without faith, who watched over Flic? It certainly wasn't her job, but it felt good to provide a little assistance.

There was a gentle tap on her door.

"Anna, it's me, Flic, can I come in?"

"Of course."

"I'm sorry if I offended you. I wasn't trying to. Are you okay?"

"I'm not offended. You gave me something to think about." Anna smiled and leaned back in her chair, pleased Felicity had returned. "Your nickname is Flic?"

"Yes. All my friends call me that. You can call me that, too, if you like."

Anna simply nodded and Flic turned to leave.

"Do you like sushi?" asked Anna.

Flic nodded.

So did Anna. "Of course you do. Do you like jam and peanut butter sandwiches like they eat in the States?"

Flic shook her head. "I've tried it, but I prefer them on their own. You?"

"I love them. They're my weakness."

"Good for you. It's nice to have your own little indulgence sometimes."

"I guess we can't all like the same things, can we?"

Flic seemed to understand. "No. We can't. But I reckon that's okay."

Anna tidied her desk and switched off her computer. Flic took that as her cue to leave.

"See you bright and early, Flic," Anna called down the hall after her.

Chapter Seven

Although the team working on Flic's marketing and print run schedules was exhausted and bleary eyed—sipping strong coffee and chatting excitedly—anticipation gripped the entire office. It was seven a.m. on Thursday morning, and nearly one hour ago, Griffin's listed *Holy Father, Holy Secret* as a forthcoming new release on their retail webpage front and center. Word from Griffin's IT department only minutes past six indicated their computer server was struggling with demand for prerelease orders of her book. While demand was a nightmare for IT, it was fabulous news for Flic and Griffin's.

Dee's mobile rang, and the room fell silent. Everyone's eyes fixed on the vibrating rectangle placed squarely in front of her. She answered while everyone held their breath.

"Yes. Thank you." She hung up.

Flic stood, no longer able to remain still. "Well?"

"Thirty-five thousand preorders in the first hour."

The room erupted.

Flic grabbed the person closest to her for a hug. That person was Anna. She was struck by the intense unisex perfume that gave Anna a confident air, the solid embrace that held her from the waist and shoulders firmly to Anna's body, and the faint sigh that escaped Anna's lips as she gently squeezed Flic.

The phone rang again, but no one except Dee bothered to take any notice of it this time. She answered, nodded, and then hushed the group. "Anna, the server's crashed. Get an announcement on social media ASAP. You know what to do."

Flic froze, remaining in Anna's arms. Momentum was important at this time surely. This was a disaster. "This isn't good, right?"

Anna gently touched her cheek. "It's fine, honestly. I'll work some magic, I promise." Anna gathered her tablet off the table.

Dee smiled. "On the contrary, my dear. This is extremely good. Demand for our product is so high it creates more interest and generates more sales. People will want to know what the fuss is about. The best way to find out is to buy the book. Please don't panic."

"But the book isn't even out yet. And we can't guarantee when it will be. Won't this just create problems if there's a delay?"

"Hardcover book buyers are a resilient lot. It'll do more good for sales than harm, trust me."

Flic relaxed. Anna gently squeezed her shoulder. "The server will be back soon, and in the meantime our customers will wait, chat about it on social media, or even shop at another retailer. Either way, it's good for us. We use system crashes like this all the time in marketing to our advantage. This is no different."

Flic felt a pang of cold reality. Soon everyone would have access to her work, to the thoughts in her mind. Anna had been right. The thought of people having an opinion on her work was daunting.

Flic called her parents and then Laura with the good news. Laura was disappointed she was missing all the fun, but she'd remained in constant contact, offering moral support and an ear or a shoulder for when the times got tough.

Flic poured another coffee and stared at the projector screen. The finished product was simply stunning. The cover encapsulated Rome, the Vatican, and other religious imagery. Her book was a modest 270 pages, but it was well paced, well polished, and extremely professional.

The marketing campaign was being executed to perfection. Anna had worked tirelessly with unwavering dedication. After the announcement of an impending novel emulating current events surrounding the pope's sexuality, the media, both TV and print, ran with it beyond even Griffin's expectations. They had skillfully created an air of mystery surrounding Flic, electing not to expose publicly her tour dates until the day after the book release. That way, Anna hoped to exploit sales on day one, create speculation about the author, and then produce Flic in the ensuing days. Obviously, with information available at the click of button on the Net, people would be able to research Flic as the author, but Anna relied on the media wanting to get hold of the real deal, and for that, they'd have to wait. It was a gamble, news only ever lasted a short time on the front page, or any page for that matter, but given the subject, she was willing to bet Flic would remain a hot commodity on day two.

After a week of determined effort to the point of near exhaustion, Flic found it odd to be sitting around watching and waiting for updates. She had nothing else to do, no more publicity tour decisions to make, and for the remainder of the morning, her only job was to sit and relax and let Griffin's marketing machine work its magic.

Anna's team had released some preliminary sales numbers to media outlets, and by mid morning, when sales reached fifty thousand, radio, TV, and Internet broadcasters had published or broadcast the news of an exciting New Vatican exposé, poignant in the current climate.

The speed at which consumers were reserving *and* paying for her book was overwhelming, and in the end, Flic was pleased to leave the boardroom for some last-minute media training and publicity photos in preparation for the following days.

After the training, the photos, and nearly an entire week indoors, pure relief struck her. She understood that the journey had only really just begun, but to have the book finalized and on sale in a prerelease was indescribable. Not quite ready to face the confines of the boardroom, she caught sight of the small park diagonally across the road. The opportunity for precious moments to herself was too tempting.

Big mistake.

She made it no more than five steps into the crisp sunlight before a reporter recognized her and pounced, a camera operator close behind him. In no time, that reporter and camera operator grew to about ten, surrounding Flic.

"Miss Bastone, what do you make of the presale figures for your book?"

"Miss Bastone, are you religious? Do you discount the Catholic faith as an ancient cult?"

"Is your book fact or fiction?"

"Miss Bastone, are you yourself gay?"

"Miss Bastone, you can't expect us to believe the release of your book is purely coincidental?"

Flic had nowhere to go. The words and questions surrounded her, bombarded her, and until she felt the solid arm of Dee Macintosh expertly usher her to the rear of the group, she was convinced she would faint again. Anna took Flic by the hand and led her inside, leaving Dee to fend off the reporters.

Flic watched behind mirrored glass as Dee capably addressed the gathered press. Realizing she was still holding Anna's hand, she left it in her grasp, content to wait until Anna was ready to relinquish their connection. She hadn't felt such soft skin for a long time. Of course, Laura hugged and kissed her every time they met, but it wasn't the same. She savored the sensation.

"After your media trainer left, she called to tell me reporters were gathering. I was already on my way down to see just how many when she called back to say you'd inadvertently walked right into them." Anna briefly glanced at their entwined hands and quickly severed the contact.

"Sorry." Flic felt terrible. "Have I stuffed things up?"

Anna smiled, flexing her fingers and staring at her hand before gathering herself. "In this game, you'll soon learn that unless you get arrested for murder, most press is good press. There are so many variables in publicity and marketing, that over the years we've created ways to turn just about any situation to our advantage."

Flic shook her head and smiled back.

"In actual fact, a murder charge could work for us at this stage, but I'm not advocating such extreme measures."

"No. Murder is a sin."

Anna raised her eyebrows.

"And I'd go to jail for it."

Anna raised her eyebrows even further.

"And it's morally wrong, and to be honest, I just don't have it in me and it would make me a very bad person."

"That's better." Anna smiled.

"Thought so."

The early evening news broadcast played in the boardroom when Flic, Dee, and Anna returned. Dee was a master at convincing people they wanted what they couldn't have. The media were running the story on the book, but they wanted Flic. Predictably, they behaved like a petulant child; the more they were told they couldn't have her, the more they wanted her. The only mystery that surrounded Felicity Bastone was the one Anna created, and it was working brilliantly.

Dee switched off the footage. "We'll be printing this in all corners of the world." She eyed Flic who must have looked clueless because she explained. "Why print and ship when we can print right where we need to distribute."

It made perfect sense and Griffin's was a big publisher. It wasn't surprising to learn their strategy was global.

Dee's phone rang. She nodded, smiled, said thank you, and hung up.

Dee then dialed her PA. "Bring it in now, please."

Ethan wheeled in a trolley filled with champagne and fancy platters of food. Everyone was summoned to the boardroom.

"Preliminary reports from sales and marketing are just to hand." She waited until everyone had a full glass. "Worldwide presales have exceeded two hundred and fifty thousand."

A huge cheer erupted as everyone raised their glass.

Flic was astounded. A quarter of a million people had bought her book before it was officially released. Occasionally, she was overcome with the sensation of floating outside her body and peering in. This was one of those moments. She could hardly believe the impact her book was having and how much time and resources Griffin's were pouring into it, not only in the UK, but globally. She felt elated, receiving congratulatory hugs and kisses from colleagues, some she'd never even met. As the group toasted their newest sensation, all she could do was smile. Her achievement was outstanding, but it all felt so mind-numbing.

Flic invited Laura to the office to share in the celebrations, and late that evening when everyone except Dee, Anna, Flic, and Laura had gone home, they sat quietly drinking in Dee's office lounging on the sofas periodically receiving global updates on book sales. It was anticipated that the first twenty-four hours could yield sales of up to a million copies worldwide.

At midnight, Dee canceled all Flic's media engagements for the following day, creating even more hype. She announced to the media that the first glimpse of Felicity Bastone speaking about her book in public would be in Dublin, Ireland, the following Tuesday evening. While sales figures soared, pressure mounted on the printers and distributors. A dedicated team was established simply to manage companies all over the world to meet the deadline.

On Monday, as long as everything went smoothly, Flic and the team at Griffin would celebrate the release of her book. The throngs of people who purchased it during the presale would finally see what all the fuss was about. Flic hoped it lived up to expectation. She felt nervous and exposed. Her work was about to be revealed to the world. The thought terrified her.

She felt relieved not to have to face the media the following day, but it did place more pressure on the bookshop appearance Tuesday.

Exhausted and barely able to keep her eyes open, Flic allowed Laura to call a cab and take her home.

The journey was mostly silent with Flic resting her head on the seat behind her. Laura's shrill voice startled her.

"Stop!" yelled Laura.

Flic's eyes snapped open. She recognized her surroundings. "What is it?"

"When have you ever seen so many vans in your street?" She directed the next comment at the driver. "Change of plan, I'm sorry. We need to go back."

The driver seemed to understand the urgency and swiftly turned the vehicle.

Flic rubbed her eyes and scanned her street. She counted at least seven vans, and as the cab exited the street, at least a dozen people streamed onto the footpath, all eyes trained on the car they knew contained Felicity Bastone.

Flic phoned Dee immediately. All she wanted, tonight of all nights, was a decent sleep in a comfortable bed. Her bed.

Dee was clearly annoyed with herself. "I'm sorry, Flic. I thought of everything except the probability that reporters would have discovered where you lived and would be lying in wait."

Flic couldn't tell, but she guessed Dee was already in bed.

"My mind has been so focused on printing and marketing your book, as has everyone else's, that something so downright obvious was overlooked. I'm truly sorry."

"It's not your fault. I can stay with Laura tonight." It wasn't ideal; Laura lived in a small one-bedroom apartment.

"Nonsense. I'll make a call and get right back to you." She hung up and within a minute had called back. She was sending her to the Safire, one of London's most exclusive and contemporary hotels. Dee would arrange a car to take her to the house in the morning, collect what she needed, and return her to the office where they were scheduled to meet at eleven.

Upon arrival at the hotel, Flic sent Laura home; she was wooing a new client first thing and needed all the energy she could muster to deal with him.

Flic felt alone. It was an odd feeling compared to the constant interaction she'd had with Griffin's staff this last week.

Nearing the end of the most exciting and hectic two weeks of her life, Flic was asleep as soon as her head nestled into the expensive feather and down pillows. Her last thought was the hope that the media weren't causing her neighbors too much grief. When they realized she wasn't coming home, she hoped they would bugger off and find something better to do. But then, that wasn't really what her publicity campaign needed. She needed those reporters, every single one of them. Dee and Anna had made it clear that the media were an ally and the enemy all rolled into one. Nevertheless, like everything else, she was assured they could be manipulated; that's what marketing geniuses like Anna were for. Why then, thought Flic, did she feel like the one being manipulated?

CHAPTER EIGHT

I didn't think of it. I can't think of everything." Dee sat reclined at her desk while Anna stood explaining herself. She hadn't yet been invited to sit, and that alone annoyed her. The fact that no one had thought of reporters at Flic's house was an oversight, but the blame lay squarely with both of them, not her alone.

"That's your excuse?"

"I know it's not good enough, but it's been a fortnight like no other. Either my brief is to babysit her, or sell her books. I'll need a lot more manpower if I'm going to run her life, too." She danced precariously close to the edge of Dee's patience and she knew it.

Dee's eyes flashed anger before they softened. She nodded toward the chair, and Anna sat. "I need you to clear your calendar for the next three weeks."

Anna didn't like the sound of this. "Why?"

"This thing with Felicity is big. I know we've sold some brilliant, top-selling books in the past, but this is on another level altogether."

Anna nodded. Being part of the team that published *Holy Father, Holy Secret* was a privilege and a thrill, and yet because of its content, it was the work she was least proud of.

"I want you to accompany Felicity on the publicity tour—"

Anna shot to her feet. "Not a bloody chance in hell!"

Dee remained composed. "That's rich coming from you, Anna. But I've made up my mind."

"Well, unmake it."

"I beg your pardon?"

"You heard me, unmake it!"

"Anna, you're treading on some very thin ice here, my dear."

"I don't care if I'm wading in iced bloody water. I'm not going on tour with this book!"

"Sit down!" Dee's voice reverberated through the entire office. Anna disobeyed her. "I gave you exactly what you wanted. Absolutely *everything* has progressed as planned. The campaign, if I do say so myself, is outstanding, and this book *and* Felicity are being marketed and sold to the world with such precision, even I'm in awe. But all I've done is my job, exactly what I'm paid for. I don't *like* the book. It's utter rubbish. I certainly wish it wasn't Griffin publishing it, but most of all, I *certainly* do not want to babysit Felicity Bastone around Europe while her book and her inevitable supporters, all with very little understanding of the Catholic Church, indiscriminately tear it down."

Anna knew what she was saying was hardly fair to Flic, but there was something dangerous about traveling and spending time with her. Not dangerous in the physical sense, but just dangerous. She couldn't put her finger on it. She just knew she shouldn't go with her.

❖

Ethan had sent Flic through to Dee's office, and she was poised to knock when Anna's tirade roared through the door. Bitter disappointment filled her. She thought they'd been getting along so well, but now she realized it was all part of Anna's professional act.

Flic wanted to run, get out of Griffin's bloody offices, just for one day, and do something normal for a change, something less stressful and something less complicated, but then she remembered the reporters out the front and it all became too difficult to even contemplate.

Half expecting an equally venomous retort from Dee, Flic listened intently, but she heard nothing. She retreated to the foyer and informed Ethan that she'd heard voices and that Dee must already be with someone. Ethan phoned through and confirmed Anna was with Dee and that Flic was to join them. At least walking back and forth to Dee's office was wasting time and delaying the inevitable.

She was beginning to feel like Griffin's was a prison. Spending the best part of two weeks practically living in the office was not the adventure she had tricked herself into believing it could have been. Escaping to Europe was looking like a better option every minute. There was no way Anna would be going with her after that outburst, and maybe that was for the better.

She tentatively knocked on Dee's door. Entering, she felt the air heavy with hostility. Anna was bright red, her eyes bloodshot, and Dee, although smiling encouragingly toward Flic, appeared as if she needed a cigarette and a stiff drink.

"About last night—" Dee began.

Flic held up her hand. "The Safire is lovely. I'm just as responsible for not thinking about it as anyone here at Griffin's."

"Nevertheless," continued Dee. "I've spoken to the manager. He understands that discretion is paramount, and until you leave for Ireland, you're to stay there."

Flic nodded. She'd guessed as much.

"And I've got some good news for you." Dee brightened and moved to the coffee machine, selecting three cups and pressing numerous buttons to produce hot, smooth lattes. "Anna will be accompanying you on tour."

Flic stared at them both. Anna refused to meet her gaze.

"Is that necessary?"

Dee sipped her coffee. "We need to milk this for all it's worth. The window of opportunity is not indefinite. The Vatican will make an announcement sooner rather than later. We have to assume it will be sooner."

"Announcement or not, what impact will Anna have on that?" Flic pushed her luck. "I can't see the relationship between the two issues."

"I want Anna to go with you. It's as simple as that." Dee smiled, but her voice remained firm.

"But you've delayed my press conferences today. What's to suggest the church won't make an announcement over the weekend?" We may have blown it altogether."

Dee nodded and glanced momentarily at Anna. "Yes, we may have, and that was my call. But we've created as much hype as we were ever going to at this stage of the process. From Tuesday evening, we will be full steam ahead. Do you agree, Anna?"

Anna nodded and sighed. "The gamble will be worth it if there's no Vatican announcement this weekend. If there is, we've lost a bit of ground, but then *no* story will be as big as the pope being gay. If there's a denial from the Vatican, we have a strategy in place to make that work for us. Dee's call to cancel the press conferences was a good one. I believe it will work in our favor."

"I get the feeling you're sending Anna to babysit me." Flic used Anna's words, and it triggered a reaction.

Anna found something interesting to stare at on the floor.

"I need someone on the ground, someone I can rely on and someone with enough experience to ensure this runs smoothly."

Flic raised her eyebrows.

"Our preparation has been so fast, we're bound to have forgotten things. Last night is a prime example. I refuse to send you out with an inexperienced team and risk fucking this up."

It was the first time Flic had heard Dee swear, and it denoted the seriousness of the situation.

There was little point in continuing to argue. The truth was Flic felt a sense of relief knowing that Anna was going to be there. She just wished Anna would afford her some credit for her opinion on a gay pope. They had had many conversations, albeit in a guarded manner, where they had both shared and listened to the other's opinion. Well, Flic had reflected on Anna's opinions; obviously, Anna had not afforded her the same courtesy. So while it was fabulous to have someone with the necessary knowledge and experience Anna clearly possessed, she would have preferred someone a little less judgmental.

Flic eyed Anna squarely. "I realize this isn't your favorite project, and I don't really care what you think of me, my book, or my motive for writing it, but I respect your position and expect the same in return. If we both do what we're getting paid to do while we're away, I imagine it will work out just fine."

Dee attempted to interrupt.

"If that's all"—she eyed Dee—"I presume I'll hear from you as required." Turning to Anna, she added, "I'll see you at the airport on Tuesday."

❖

Flic scanned the minibar, cursed at the exorbitant prices, and then proceeded to open the most expensive bottle of wine. "Drink?" she asked Laura who was in awe of her impressive hotel room.

"Yes, please." Laura's eyes lit up. "This is a great hotel, Flic. Must be costing them an arm and a leg." She found the light control panel and proceeded to switch on all the lights before making the entire space turn purple. "But then, even after only twenty-four hours, I should think you'd have earned them an arm and a leg too."

Flic agreed, and the expensive wine rapidly tasted better. "Griffin's have done an outstanding job. Books take time to market. They gain momentum, word spreads, and then after an indefinite period, you have a best seller. I take my hat off to them marketing this so well before it was even available and in such a short timeframe."

"You've got a little soft spot for Miss Anna Lawrence, haven't you?" Laura teased her.

Flic wasn't entirely sure what was going on with Anna, but the small pang in her lower abdomen at even the suggestion she might have a soft spot for her was unnerving. "Well, apparently Dee thinks we're a good team. She's coming on tour with me."

Laura laughed. "So Dee sends her prize possession to keep an eye on you, eh? Doesn't she trust you or something?"

"Something like that."

"Pardon?"

Flic had gone over Anna's words a million times that day. She had honestly thought they'd reached an understanding regarding the contents of her book. She explained what she'd overheard to Laura.

"That's pretty full-on."

"Tell me about it." Flic shook her head. "I feel like she lied to me, or used me in some way just to keep me sweet and sell the product."

"That's just business, Flic. She was just doing her job."

"Yes, but I was genuine with her. I could have agreed with her, smiled sweetly, and then bitched about her behind her back, but I didn't. I thought we were becoming friends."

"You want to be friends with Mother Bloody Teresa?"

"Yes, well, no. I guess for the sake of the book I wanted it all to run smoothly."

Laura suppressed a grin. "It has run smoothly, Flic. One could argue her way of handling you was correct. For the sake of the book and all your media engagements, she's achieved her goal."

"But that's not the point. I was straight with her and she played me."

Laura stood and gestured for Flic to finish her wine before fetching a top up. "The point, my darling Felicity, is that you like her and you're hurt and worried she might not feel the same about you."

Flic flounced to the bathroom. "That is complete rubbish. Don't be so bloody ridiculous."

❖

"Don't be so ridiculous!" Anna stormed to the kitchen to fetch something, but she couldn't remember what. Her brain had been mush since Ethan mentioned Felicity Bastone had probably heard her argument with Dee.

"If you meant what you said, why do you even care if she heard?" asked Seb.

Anna returned with soy sauce.

"What is that?"

"Soy sauce. What does it look like?"

"You're putting that on spaghetti carbonara?"

She scooped the sauce from the table and stormed back into the kitchen, this time returning empty-handed. "You're enjoying this aren't you? Can't you see I'm in turmoil?"

"It is okay to admit that liking someone scares you."

"I don't *like* her like that!"

"There was no implication to how you like her at all. I'm simply saying it's okay to like someone, or be friends with someone," he added quickly before she could protest again, "and not share the exact same views as them."

"Yes, but this isn't just any view. It's my entire life perspective."

"I'm not religious and we're friends."

"Yes, but you haven't written a book on the subject. You won't be tearing down the Catholic Church with a book that will probably go down in history as one of the most famous of all time."

"Anna!" Seb rarely raised his voice.

This moment obviously warranted her full attention.

He continued. "The story is already written. The pope is probably actually gay. He just hasn't come out and said it yet. Felicity Bastone didn't make him gay, nor did she force him to act on his feelings, no more than she could force him to deny them. It's not her book that will bring the church down; it's the fact that the people won't just accept it and move on. Homophobic people are the only ones making a big deal out of this, and you're dangerously close to fitting squarely into that category."

"Don't you dare call me that."

"Then stop behaving like it."

"I am not, Seb. I don't have to like everything you like."

Seb lowered his voice to a whisper. "Then accept that the pope is gay."

"It's not just that he's gay. He's not supposed to fall in love with anyone."

"So you're seriously trying to tell me this is all about the pope having feelings for just someone? Woman or man?"

Anna hesitated.

"I thought so. The pope in a relationship with anyone is bad, I get that. But a gay pope is the ultimate hypocrisy, right?"

Anna was close to tears. She rubbed her eyes. This reaction was so unlike her. "If his sexuality wouldn't change my church, I'd accept it if he were gay."

"And Felicity?"

"What about her?"

"She's gay, she's written about the pope being gay, and it's okay to like her, you know."

Anna fought to suppress the memory of when she'd pulled Flic through the reporters outside Griffin's offices and held her hand watching as Dee managed the press. Frightening things were happening to her body and her brain every time she remembered the softness of Flic's hand and her reluctance to withdraw immediately. She looked at Seb who in turn was looking at her knowingly. "This is confusing for me right now."

"You're not asexual, Anna."

She gasped, not at the notion, but at hearing the word and her name in the same sentence. It had once occurred to her that she might be asexual. She'd researched the subject and on why others defined themselves that way, but she wasn't convinced she really fit into the broad definition. She was embarrassed.

Seb went to her and pulled her close, his stubble scratching near her temple. "I'm not trying to say things to hurt you, but I think there's a reason why you're single. You're confused because your mind is constantly in conflict with your beliefs."

Anna slipped from Seb's embrace and ran from the room. She couldn't have this discussion. Now was not the time to even contemplate those demons, let alone try to deal with them. She needed time and space, and most probably from Flic more than anyone else, but spending at least the next three weeks with her was exactly the thing that was keeping her going. She just wished she hadn't written that damn book.

Seb could say all the stuff he liked, but there was no such thing as a true atheist. In her experience, an atheist wasn't simply a non-believer; they also thought others shouldn't believe, just like them. In addition, while it was true Anna struggled to understand why others didn't seek fulfillment from the church like she did, she had never preached that her way was the only way. That kind of talk always came from those without faith. It seemed ironic to her. She had convinced herself it was only a matter of time before Flic attempted to persuade her that faith was a sham and that she was a fool. She'd experienced that enough as a child; there was no way she was putting herself through that again.

CHAPTER NINE

The weekend had been long, the Vatican had remained silent, and the *Holy Father, Holy Secret* campaign had lost little, if any, momentum.

Flic celebrated her book release with Laura over a long lunch.

"I guess you'll be spending enough time with Anna in the coming weeks to not really miss her now?"

"Why would I miss her now?"

"Well, everyone's so busy at Griffin's you've just got me for lunch."

Celebrating with Laura was exactly what Flic needed. She'd been so consumed with the book in the past two weeks, her life had become distorted and insular. Before she embarked on her book tour, a long, expensive lunch courtesy of Griffin's was exactly what she needed.

"It's out there now." Flic shrugged. "It feels so weird I can't even begin to describe it. But lunch without my newly appointed shadow or my boss is perfect because I'm sharing this occasion with you."

Laura held her glass aloft. "To my amazing and talented friend."

Flic mirrored Laura's image and raised her glass. "To friendship and a successful book tour."

"And to yet another 'straight girl' conquest."

"Do you want to wear that expensive champagne?" Flic had bed one straight girl in her time and subsequently fell in love with her. She had been seventeen, young, and stupid, and Laura still found the whole episode highly amusing. From that day forward, Flic had stayed away from straight girls.

"Actually, do you really think Anna's straight?"

"I'm not bedding Anna or any other straight girl for that matter," said Flic.

"But you want to."

"In case you haven't listened to a word I've said lately, I think she might actually hate my guts."

"That's just your guts; you have many other redeeming features to woo her with."

Flic ignored Laura and beckoned the waiter to fetch another bottle of champagne. The truth was Flic felt conflicted. She wanted Anna on tour with her, but she also didn't want her there because she'd protested so fervently.

The maître d' approached the table looking sheepish. "I can't help but notice that your lunch is courtesy of Griffin Publishers."

Flic nodded. Dee had said she'd arranged it all and they were to treat themselves.

"If you don't mind me asking, are you Felicity Bastone, the author of that new book?"

Flic nodded.

The maître d' produced a shabby piece of paper. "Can I have your autograph, please?"

Laura whistled and Flic knew the grin on her face must have looked ridiculous. "Of course." She paused briefly, wishing she'd thought about her signature and tag line before now. She scribbled, "Don't stop believing. Felicity."

"Oh, hang on," said the maître d'. "I'm not Catholic or anything."

Flic smiled. "Me neither, but there's so many things to believe in. Just believe in yourself if that's what you'd like to interpret it as meaning."

The maître d' nodded and placed the piece of paper securely in her back pocket.

Laura reached across the table and took Flic's face in her hands before kissing her sloppily on the cheek. "You're made for this shit, Felicity Bastone."

Flic was riding with Anna and Dee in a black limousine to the airport. She was now well and truly on show and the circus had only just begun.

Ethan had prepared a memo with some news headlines from around the world. The impact of the book was astounding.

Dee read aloud some of the headlines as the limo sped toward Heathrow airport. "Holy Father, Holy Prophecy. Gay Pope, But Is He Happy. Twisted Exploitation from a Wannabe Novelist."

Flic cringed at the last one.

"Some of these are actually quite amusing," Dee said. "Oh, this has got to be my favorite—Holy Father, Holy Violation."

Flic glanced at Anna. Riding in a limousine with Dee reading headlines that clearly disturbed her was probably not endearing her to becoming happier with the current arrangements.

"Some of them are far from favorable." Flic was concerned it was all going sour.

"It's just an angle." Anna snapped out of it. "Imagine if the press wrote something like: English Woman Writes Book about Pope's Sexuality. Not exactly catchy is it?"

Flic shook her head and she understood, but as a journalist, she didn't write sensationalist pieces, and thank God, none of her pieces attracted such pathetic attempts at word play headlines. She wondered what idiots thought up such tripe.

"Try not to take it personally. You know the business. But remember, any press is good press at the moment."

Anna had appeared nervous when she delicately positioned herself away from Flic in the vast backseat of the limo. Dee and Flic easily filled any silences, and it seemed that speaking about work, a subject on which she always spoke with confidence, eased Anna's obvious tension.

It was ironic, being less than an hour flight away, but Flic had only ever been to Ireland once, and she barely remembered a thing.

If she entered a few bars it might all come back to her, but on the way to Grafton Street, she didn't recognize one single landmark.

The famous Dublin Book Emporium was a labyrinth of shelves and reading nooks with a large café on the mezzanine floor. Anna had briefed Flic regarding the layout of the store, and from photos, it looked like the kind of bookshop she could become lost in for days. Tonight's appearance involved a direct address to the audience, a small reading, and then questions from the floor. With the exception of question time, everything appeared straightforward, but there was no way of filtering the difficult questions. She would just have to do her best and answer them as honestly as she could. Dee and Anna had discussed this with her and had decided that Flic should remain resolute on her reasons for writing the book and subsequently her opinion that a gay pope made little, if any, difference in his ability to lead the Catholic Church. What she was adamant to mention though, was that perhaps the church, in light of the revelation looking more and more likely to be true, should reconsider its stance on many subjects, not simply that of homosexuality.

Not only were Griffin's selling the book, they were also selling a brand. Felicity Bastone was that brand. Her style, her attitude, her clothing, her hair, her transport, the hotels she stayed in, they were all designed around an avant-garde, yet wholesome look. In this respect, Flic's attitude would remain sincere, but her clothing and outward appearance was not her own. It was dictated by Anna and her stylist advisors.

Flic would appear in public wearing expensive trousers, chinos, jeans, shirts, tops, and jackets. Anna had designed a smart, feminine look within the guidelines Flic had specified—no dresses, no skirts, and no heels unless they were small and worn with her black suit.

Her transportation was in smart black SUVs, nothing too flashy, certainly not a limousine, but not a beat-up old taxi either.

With the windows tinted, Flic touched up her modest makeup, applied faint colored lip gloss, and jiggled her leg nervously as Anna ran through the evening one last time while the vehicle negotiated peak hour traffic. They were on schedule for the six o'clock start, but Flic could only concentrate on suppressing the urge to pee.

"Do you need more color on your cheeks?"

Flic applied additional bronzer without question.

"And you're comfortable in your outfit?"

Flic nodded. She wore designer label jeans, brown boat shoes, a tweed jacket, and a low-cut white top. She felt stylish and professional even if she looked a little pretentious.

"And your glasses are in your jacket breast pocket, okay?"

Flic nodded again, patting the pocket.

Anna cleared her throat. "If they're brave enough, they'll probably ask you about your sexuality. You have to be ready for that question, and try not to look shocked when they ask."

There was so much to remember. Panic began to cause Flic's heart to beat faster.

"Be there in five," the driver said.

Flic took a double intake of breath.

The Dublin Book Emporium was at the St. Stephen's Green end of Grafton Street, and the black SUV slowly made its way down a cobbled side street as close as it could be without encroaching on designated pedestrian zones. The owner, Mark Duggan, was there to greet them.

"Miss Bastone, Miss Lawrence, lovely to meet you."

They all shook hands.

"Is everything ready, Mr. Duggan?" Flic knew Anna would delay the appearance for five or ten minutes if it meant having everything run smoothly and according to plan.

"Yes, yes." The slightly chubby Mr. Duggan, probably in his late forties, beamed a smile. "Probably a few more here than I expected, to be honest, but we'll shut the doors if we reach capacity."

Anna seemed relieved and she saw Flic eyeing her. "A few more is a whole lot better than a few less," she explained.

"So, it's show time, I guess?" Flic stood clenching and flexing her hands.

Anna pulled her aside, and again the touch of her hand caused a chemical reaction. "You're prepared. We've been through this and you know exactly what to do. You have your cue cards in case you lose your train of thought?" Flic nodded, pushing them securely into her back pocket. "And your book will be on the rostrum with the correct page marked." Flic inhaled deeply; just the thought of her work in hardcover print made her dizzy. "Just be yourself. You'll be fine." Anna awkwardly shifted weight as if she wanted to hug Flic, but instead uneasily touched her elbow.

Mr. Duggan held out his arms in an ushering gesture and led them along the side street toward the front of the shop.

There was no turning back now. Somehow, Flic managed to turn her nerves into excited adrenaline. She reminded herself of her journey from Rome many months ago to a European book tour and an international best seller. She turned to see where Anna was.

"I'm right behind you. You'll be fine."

The words were the antidote for any residual nerves, but they inexplicably stung. They carried such warmth. Flic wished anyone other than Anna Lawrence had said them. She wanted to be able to feel something mutual with the person who melted her heart that way.

Grafton Street was bustling with workers dashing for transport on their way home, but the entire front of the bookshop was no less than twenty people deep. Flic was anxious; by the time they let that lot in, it would be well past six o'clock, and she really wanted to be through this first appearance sooner rather than later. The crowds were contained behind a barrier, and when Mr. Duggan led her to the front of the queue, she realized many were being denied entry.

She turned to Anna. "What's going on?"

Anna pointed to the inside of the shop. There were people everywhere, and by the look of things, an extra sound system was being erected for patrons to hear her speak from downstairs. The mezzanine looked full to capacity.

Upon recognizing Flic, some of the crowd became vocal. "Leave the pope alone," yelled one.

"Fuck off back to ye girlfriend," yelled another.

"Catholic homos."

"Free the Church."

"Burn in hell."

Soon, all the words became a chorus of insults until Anna's firm hand in the small of Flic's back ushered her into the shop.

"Nothing we hadn't expected." Anna eyed Flic.

Flic held it together. How could she convince these people that a gay pope was not the tragedy they perceived and that writing about it was neither blasphemous nor a denigration of their faith? But then, her own colleague, the one guiding her through the insults, thought little more of her than the protestors. She wasn't sure who was on her side anymore.

Burdened by nervous anticipation and wishing Laura were with her, Flic enacted her positive self-talk regime. It began with the phrase: what would Ellen do? Flic felt better. Knowing that Ellen would bluff her way through this ordeal and have the audience in stitches, gave her strength.

Mr. Duggan's introduction was brief. Flic made her way to the rostrum imagining every member of the audience was dressed like a leprechaun. It didn't help.

After the modest applause died down, she took a deep breath and began. "Does anyone know how many popes have been before our current pope, Pope Valentine II?" It was her opening line, and although her voice wavered in the beginning, she gained clarity toward the end of the question. Members of the audience yelled various numbers until she heard "two hundred and sixty-six."

The Internet was handy for those wishing to look like a smart arse.

"That's correct, two hundred and sixty-six. Conservative estimates now suggest that around two to six percent of the population is gay and probably always has been." She paused for effect and to allow the mathematicians in the room time to calculate the statistic she was about to reveal. "Taking that into consideration, at least five, and up to sixteen, popes in history have been homosexual." Again, she paused, allowing the information to be absorbed.

"Why then, is the world shocked to think that our current pope might be gay? He is, after all, a man like the rest of men, born from a mother like other mothers, and I honestly can't see why he requires no more or less love than the rest of us. Affection, companionship, passion, lust, friendship, desire, and ultimately love are what makes the world go round, surely?"

The audience mumbled, clearly not convinced.

Flic continued, undeterred. "If those things weren't so important, why would one in ten people in the United States have used a dating website? Why do we spend so much time searching for 'the one'? Think back to your teenage years. Think back to your early twenties. Think about your life now, the important people in it, perhaps the person you're here with tonight. Is that important person not your significant other?" Flic took a breath, shocked by how passionate her delivery was. "We live to be loved. I simply can't fathom why the pope, ultimately just a man, can't love and be loved, too, and why"—she raised her voice over the groans of disagreement—"can't that person be a gay man?"

Half the audience applauded; the other half shook their heads in dismay.

Flic stole a glance toward Anna who was standing directly to her left. She wasn't smiling; in fact, she sported a face any poker champion would be proud of, but she nodded her encouragement and Flic proceeded to read an excerpt from her book. She had deliberately chosen an innocuously lighthearted passage, and she even managed a few laughs.

At the end, questions came thick and fast.

"What you've written seems to be coming true. You're an investigative journalist. Have you disguised a journalistic piece as a novel?"

And there it was, straight up. The question everyone wanted to know. Flic had an answer prepared. "It's true, I am a journalist. When I conceived the idea for this book, I was in Rome on holiday. I have not investigated the pope or the Vatican." It was the truth. She attempted a joke. "Even I'm not brave enough for that." It scored a giggle, even with the skeptics.

"But, Felicity"—she turned her gaze to a middle-aged woman toward the rear of the mezzanine floor—"surely you agree that the similarities are startling?"

Dee had warned her that readers would walk a fine line between discussing her book and discussing current events. Her answer came quickly and naturally. "Of course, without question, but I read *Angels and Demons*, like most other people, and I watch the conclave when a new pope is elected. My book is a novel, and the people in it are characters. I had to choose one of them to have a relationship with the pope. Naturally, I chose the Camerlengo." She smiled, maintaining a casual air. "Plus, from an author's perspective, it's a fabulous word. It sparks a pang of recognition in readers, and it gives the impression you actually know what you're talking about." That earned her a laugh. "It's purely coincidence. The Camerlengo was chosen in my book for his great title and his standing in the church." Flic twitched at her first lie.

"I believe you're a lesbian, Miss Bastone. Is this book an attempt to have the church return the tired equal rights argument to its agenda?"

Flic ignored the answer that sprang to mind. Her media coach had said an emotional response was ill-advised on occasions like this. Instead, she counted to three, nodded as if contemplating such an outstanding question, and then looked the audience member in the eye as she answered. "In my opinion, sir, the equal rights debate, regardless of the forum in which it's conducted, will never be tired. But no, that's not what my novel attempts to do. My novel attempts to entertain, provide alternative perspectives, and hopefully encourage people to think and discuss, in any forum, the contents of the book. I imagine that is what most authors would like their work to achieve."

"Are you Catholic, Felicity?" The question came from a young girl Flic estimated to be in her twenties.

"No, I'm not."

"Do you believe in God?"

Lie number two coming up. "No, not in any God you will find revered in institutionalized religion. I believe there's *something*"— she used rabbit ears to make her point—"but not a single God as such." In truth, she believed in nothing at all.

A man bouncing a baby on his lap asked, "What difference does it make to you personally then, if the pope is gay or not?"

Flic considered responding with the scripted answer, but chose a different tack instead. She refused to make eye contact with Anna, fearing her reaction at this diversion. "Is there anyone here, besides me of course, willing to disclose that they're gay or lesbian?" To her surprise, at least a dozen people raised their hands, some tentatively, others boldly.

She turned her attention to a young man wearing a suit, probably having just come from work. "Perhaps I can turn the tables and ask you a few questions?"

He nodded, and she was both amazed and relieved to see she held everyone's undivided attention.

"Do you have a job, sir?" Flic was briefly distracted by a movement in the corner of her vision and chanced a fleeting glance toward Anna. She was frowning with her arms folded across her chest.

He nodded. "Yes, I'm a schoolteacher. I teach geography."

Flic was so relieved by his occupation she could have kissed him. If he'd have said porn star, she was stuffed.

"Does your sexuality in any way impede your ability to teach geography and deliver what your employer expects of you?"

He shook his head. "I'm head of my year, so not at all."

"Are your students aware of your sexuality?"

He thought for a moment. "Yes, the majority of them know, but it only occurs to them to mention it when they're on detention."

The audience laughed.

Flic turned to the man who asked the question. "I'm not trying to make you look silly, sir, but I do want to make the point to everyone here in context when I answer your question. You essentially asked if the pope's sexuality makes any difference to me or not, and the answer is no. Not because I simply don't care, but because last month, when no one knew anything about his alleged relationship with the Camerlengo, everyone thought he was a good pope. I believe he's the same man, gay or not, and equally capable of performing the duties he more than adequately performed before the speculation on his sexuality became leading news."

The man acknowledged with a tilt of his head that she'd made a fair point.

Others disagreed and the audience grew louder in discussion.

Flic interrupted them. "Just like sexuality has no bearing on my work or the work of that gentleman"—she gestured to the teacher—

"I firmly believe the pope's sexuality has no bearing on his ability to be pope."

Just as comments flew at her, thick and fast, Mr. Duggan stepped toward the podium and Anna gently drew Flic back.

"Well done." Anna smiled. "You had me a bit worried there."

"But it was okay, right?"

"Yes, you pulled it off this time."

Flic detected a "but" although she didn't push the issue.

Mr. Duggan was making a thank you speech in the background when Flic glanced at her watch, adrenaline tearing through her. "I think we could have squeezed in a few more questions." The audience was engaged and some remained unconvinced. She thought leaving so soon was a mistake.

Mr. Duggan turned to them and Anna nudged Flic who instinctively smiled and waved to the audience in thanks.

Anna explained. "These people aren't here to change their opinion based on what you say." Flic was confused. "They're either here because they're genuinely interested or they might simply want to listen, but the rest, the vocal crowd, they're here to voice *their* opinion, not be convinced by yours."

Flic nodded. Realistically, she could debate the pros and cons with certain members of the audience all night trying to convince them, but she didn't want that. She knew she had to accept that she could no more convince them as they could her.

Clearly impressed by the turnout, Mr. Duggan approached with an outstretched hand. "That was simply wonderful. This is a big store and I've never seen it so full for an author appearance."

Anna was pleased. "Thank you. Perhaps we can sneak the star of the show out a back or a side entrance?" She glanced toward the crowd that was slow in dispersing, either from the sheer number of people, or the fact that many people appeared engrossed in discussion.

"Of course. This way."

Flic hung back. "Hold on a minute." They glared at her. "Isn't that suggesting I'm a bit of a coward? I come and say what I have to say and then sneak out the back door? I'd like to go out the front. Say thank you to my supporters."

"And say what exactly to your critics?" Anna's charm had deserted her.

Flic wasn't entirely sure what she would say to her critics. It just wasn't in her nature to sneak out the back. "Look, I get the distinct impression people are leaving here holding on to their own opinions, yes, but also valuing the opinions of others. I think I should go out the way I came in."

Anna looked at Mr. Duggan who merely shrugged. Flic knew he could no more predict the outcome from that course of action than she could.

"We need to start this as we mean to go on," said Flic.

Anna raised her hand, buying time to think. "Okay. I agree with you. It's a work of fiction. It's only a book. We shouldn't appear intimidated by anyone who disagrees."

Anna was trying to convince herself more than anyone else, but Flic was getting her way, so she just went with it. "Good. Then let's go."

With Anna behind and Mr. Duggan leading a path through the crowd, they made their way to the shop front. Some people smiled their good-byes to her, others nodded, and she knew that those who turned their backs simply didn't want a damn thing to do with her.

As they reached the front door, one of the shop assistants pushed through the crowd toward Mr. Duggan. He was clearly distressed. "Um, sir, you might not want to go out there."

They all stared through the window. There were a handful of protestors, but nothing Flic didn't think she couldn't handle. She pushed past Mr. Duggan and out onto the street, not willing to wait around for yet another discussion on a subject that had already been agreed upon.

It was an avoidable miscalculation.

CHAPTER TEN

Flic had seen only a small section of protestors. To the left of the shop, about fifty people deep, was an incensed mob, and within seconds of her stepping onto Grafton Street, they surrounded her.

She had foolishly and arrogantly marched into the middle of a thuggish rent-a-crowd.

Every single placard bore an anti-religion or anti-gay message, some intertwining the two with the most horrific of them claiming homosexuality was akin to pedophilia. Anger stirred inside her.

The mob closed in. They yelled obscenities and spat at her feet. Mostly men and all Caucasian, they screamed that the pope was a filthy faggot, that he sodomized young boys, and that she should be burned on a cross or fuck a man like all women should. The noise was deafening, and her personal space decreased with every passing second.

She struggled to remain on her feet as the crowd constantly surged and retreated. Flic's anger disappeared as pure fear constricted her chest and esophagus. She fought to breathe as freely as she could just moments ago, and she began gasping for air, short and shallow. She had made an amateur mistake. She should have waited for the others, at least discussed a plan, or reassessed the best departure point under the circumstances. It was irrelevant that these hooded men hadn't even bothered to set foot inside the bookshop and listen to a single word she had to say. They had probably received the call on some social media site and flooded Grafton Street to play the heavies. They weren't interested in healthy debate or sharing opinions or ideas, they were redneck thugs taking pleasure in yelling abuse and making trouble for any cause where their dominant white male supremacist egos could shine in all their glory.

The men groped her, pushed her, and one handsome young man snarled at her that she should have her clit cut off if she didn't know how to fuck properly.

Terrified, Flic struggled to fight her way back to the shop, back to Anna, but that was a foolish strategy. The more she grappled through the men, the more they touched her, yelled at her, and propelled her deeper into the fray.

"Anna!" Flic roared so hard her throat hurt. She had wanted her scream to bellow above the din of the mob, but it provided little contest and was barely audible to even herself.

Her clothes were being pulled in all directions when suddenly, just as her panic was about to reach suffocation point, her arms were pinned powerfully to her sides. Preparing one final act of defiance before she was sure she would pass out, she glanced down to try to locate her captor's feet, thinking she would aim what she hoped would be a bone-crushing blow to the bridge of his foot. Her eyes, however, didn't search past the arms that encircled her, and she felt a wave of relief. From elbow to wrist, she was enveloped in fluorescent-clad arms. It was the police. Her debilitating panic began to subside.

The crowd quickly dispersed. *Cowards, the lot of them.* They certainly didn't believe in this cause passionately enough to be arrested for it.

Flic was rapidly ushered to a waiting police car, driven no more than three streets away from the shop, and transferred to an ambulance. There had been little chance to talk to the police. They were busy negotiating traffic and talking on the loud CB radio. Before she could utter a word through her shallow breathing, the ambulance doors banged closed and the van began to move.

"Wait," she panted. "Where's Anna?"

A paramedic wearing a name badge that said "Andrew," smiled warmly and placed an oxygen mask over her face.

"The others will meet us at the hospital," he assured her. "For now though, I'd like you to look at me and breathe slowly." He sat directly in front of Flic, holding her hands gently in her lap and breathing animatedly for her to follow. "You're hyperventilating a little, but we'll have it under control soon. My name's Andrew."

She involuntarily eyed his name badge.

"I guess you already knew that." His smile soothed her.

Flic felt like her brain was running at a thousand thoughts a second. She felt dirty, and even through the antiseptic aroma of the ambulance, she could still smell the alcohol and cigarette smoke from many of the men.

Lightning fast, Andrew produced a bag and smartly whipped the oxygen mask from Flic's face. She vomited bile and what looked like watery vegetables into the bag.

"How did you know I—" She vomited again.

"Your hands have gone clammy and your face went as white as my shirt."

Flic felt embarrassed. "I'm usually tougher than this."

"Really? When was the last time a bunch of idiots accosted you in the street?"

Flic shrugged.

He handed her a paper towel to wipe her face before replacing the oxygen mask. "Just until we reach the hospital."

"I'm okay," she mumbled through the plastic.

"Good. But I want you to sit back and relax and enjoy the ride in my shiny van."

As if her body had been waiting for permission, she relaxed back into the seat and let her head rest on the slightly cushioned panel behind her.

Andrew checked her over, asking if she'd suffered any head trauma or any other trauma to the rest of her body, mainly her vital organs, but to each question she shook her head. Her body ached, but it sounded ludicrous when she mumbled she'd simply been pushed, groped, and manhandled. Maybe bruises would show tomorrow, but when Andrew removed her jacket and checked over her stomach and back, she had barely a scrape on her.

Anna rushed through the emergency department with such gusto, Flic became embarrassed; she wasn't that injured. Upon seeing Flic staring at her, Anna's cheeks colored and she slowed down, sucked in a deep breath, and looked awkward attempting an air of nonchalance.

"I'm okay, Anna. Nothing broken and hardly a mark on me."

Anna held her emotions in check. "I can see that."

Flic nervously adjusted herself on the bed. "Good." She was annoyed that she'd allowed herself to think Anna cared. "If you'll excuse me, I need to go to the bathroom. Now you've seen me, I assume you'll let Dee know I'm in one piece and fit to continue with the tour."

Masking slight shock at her early dismissal, Anna simply nodded and retreated.

The emergency nurse returned with a clipboard and a pen. "Did I hear you say you needed the bathroom? It's past the nurses' station, second on the right."

"Thanks, but I'm fine." Flic shrugged because she couldn't think of a decent lie. "Crowd control."

"I see. Is she your boss?"

"No." Flic laughed. "She's gone to call my boss. She's… difficult." Flic wasn't sure if she was describing Anna's personality or her own inability to understand her. Either way, the clipboard housed a discharge form, and Flic eagerly signed it.

Sitting next to Anna in the waiting room was a police officer. She figured he knew about as much as she did and wondered why he was there.

"I'm Officer Bourke. I'd like to take a quick statement from you and drive you home."

Anna nodded when Flic looked to her. "It's just precautionary, but we've changed hotels and we thought a lift there might be appropriate."

"There were protestors at the hotel?"

"No." Anna was quick to reassure her.

"We just don't want anyone getting any ideas," Officer Bourke explained.

Flic sat in the rear of the unmarked police car while Anna sat beside her making phone calls to arrange an increase in security. Not that Anna shared the details with her, but as far as Flic could ascertain, someone would meet them at the hotel in the morning to take on the role of personal security. Flic felt vulnerable and alone watching Anna arrange things. She at least had a purpose, something to take her mind off things, while in contrast, Flic felt useless and violated with no one to talk to and no one to share her emotions with. She shifted her body toward the window as tears slid onto the lapels of her filthy jacket.

The new hotel was just as lavish as the previous one, but it failed to impress. Upon entering her room, Flic stripped, leaving a trail of clothes toward the bathroom where she spent considerable time allowing a powerful stream of water to bounce off her head, neck, and shoulders. She was tired. It had been a long day.

At ten o'clock, barely thirty seconds into the news, there was a faint knock at the door.

"Flic, it's just me, Anna."

Flic rose from the bed slowly, staring for a long moment through the tiny peephole in the door. Anna was still dressed in her suit, although her makeup had all but disappeared. It annoyed Flic to notice how attractive she was with or without makeup. She unlatched the door and swung it open, barely greeting Anna before returning to the bed.

"We should watch the news." Anna ignored Flic's indifference.

Flic gestured to the TV just as the newsreader returned to the screen. A photograph of Flic's head and a fade-in of her book cover filled the top right hand corner. The headline read "Anti-gay Clashes."

Flic sat up.

"No arrests were made at St. Stephen's Green this evening immediately following hostile scenes at the conclusion of the book launch of Felicity Bastone's controversial novel, *Holy Father, Holy Secret*. Police say an angry mob of approximately fifty protestors moved from Grafton Street after Miss Bastone was taken to hospital and proceeded to clash with members of a Catholic Church group peacefully supporting Pope Valentine II. The crowd dispersed as the guards arrived."

The newsreader then crossed to a reporter at St. Stephen's Green who described the events of the evening before interviewing a woman in her mid forties.

"Catholicism is not exclusively for heterosexuals," she said. "We support a gay pope and the right to share your love with a man or a woman."

There was more, but Flic was too astounded by the courage of this woman. The report had finished by the time she refocused her attention.

She stared at Anna. This news report had been the only thing able to put a smile on her face all evening. "Well, there you go."

Anna remained impassive. "Breakfast in my room tomorrow morning at eight. We have a teleconference with Dee and some security issues to discuss."

Flic nodded.

Anna reached the door. "I just wanted to say..." She stalled. "I'm glad you're okay."

The door closed softly behind her as she left Flic to her own thoughts.

After a nightcap and about an hour tossing and turning, Flic drifted into a restless sleep, confused about Anna, but deeply thrilled to have seen the woman on the TV. She wasn't the only one willing to speak out that a gay pope would not cause the apocalypse.

The fact remained, Pope Valentine II had been gay all this time, and the world had not ended.

CHAPTER ELEVEN

Anna sipped wine and paced her room. She couldn't sit still and weaved between bed, desk, and sofa while she finished her drink. Day one and it had all gone belly up. She couldn't believe it had gone wrong so soon. The phone call to Dee transpired as expected, although she was annoyed by Dee's inference that it would make great headlines and sell more books. Who was she kidding? If Dee hadn't made the connection, she would have brought it to her attention. That was the job of a marketing expert after all.

The main thing was that Flic was okay. Their schedule would suffer a slight disruption. Dee was spot-on; book sales and interest in Flic would only benefit from the incident.

She took a large swig of her drink and sighed. Again, who the hell was she kidding? The fact that this clash with protestors was great for publicity wasn't at the forefront of her mind. What was disturbing her was her genuine concern for Flic. Cold, heartless, and sales-driven she could deal with, but this caring and concerned side to her polished personality scared her half to death. She poured more wine and wondered if she paced for long enough would she wear another pattern into the already hideously patterned carpet.

Anna felt like an idiot, running through the hospital to see Flic. No doubt she looked like one too, but as it turned out, Flic couldn't have cared less if she were there or not. Perhaps Flic associated her with the mob clash that evening, but surely even Flic understood that she would never condone violence and intimidation whether it supported her cause or not.

Obviously, there was no reason for Anna to want to be close to Flic, but she'd been willing to offer support and comfort. Regardless of their differing opinions, she cared for Flic on a professional level, and she endeavored to do better in the future.

She stared at the bed. It was late. A new security detail was arriving tomorrow, and she had to coordinate Flic's press in the morning. She needed sleep, but she knew it wouldn't come soon.

❖

Flic's body ached, and it weighed her down, heavy and tender. When she looked beneath the covers at her naked form, she was surprisingly pleased to see faint bruises forming all over. They acted as a reminder that nothing in life came easy but standing up for what you believed in was worthwhile. It was six in the morning, and she just knew she looked like shit. An old shoulder injury from her days of volleyball had resurfaced, and sleeping on her left side had caused the pain that had woken her.

Without a second thought, she took the ibuprofen the nurse had sent her home with and settled back down, drawing her knees up to her chest, this time on her right side.

She checked her phone—a message from Laura who'd obviously just seen the news, and a message from Anna informing her that the scheduled morning and afternoon radio show appearances had been postponed until further notice or until solid arrangements could be made to improve her security. She imagined she would conduct them via the telephone if need be in the ensuing days.

She felt the tablets begin to work as she messaged Laura to tell her she was still in one piece, and she simply wrote the word "okay" to Anna.

Within fifteen minutes, there was a light tap at her door. Her heart faltered when she recognized the knock as Anna's. She recognized the knock. When had she committed the gentle tap and rhythm of Anna's knock to memory? Her stiff body protested as she pulled on the hotel robe. Anna didn't wait for an invitation when she opened the door. She was dressed in a pair of jeans and a shirt, and the aroma of coffee wafted with her. She looked tired and lovely all at once.

"I thought you'd like a real coffee this morning." Anna held the cardboard carton out. "They're both for you."

"How did you know I was awake?"

"You just messaged me." Anna stepped around Flic and into the room.

"Did you go and get these after I messaged you?" Anna was certainly sending Flic's head spinning.

"Well, I'm not telepathic. I was already up." She fidgeted uncomfortably, her relaxed persona fading.

Anna stood swapping her weight from leg to leg. She appeared to have something to add, so Flic sipped the coffee and waited. "I know I was all business last night." Anna made the briefest eye contact before separating the tall curtains a slight crack and staring out over a waking Dublin. A heavy fog had settled overnight. "I had things to arrange, and Dee would expect some progress before we spoke this morning. You said you were okay."

Flic was struggling to see Anna as a whole person. She'd never encountered anyone like that before. Their personal—albeit strained—relationship seemed to run parallel to their professional one, rarely ever in synchronization and certainly never uniting. It was problematic for her that she could never predict Anna's behavior regardless of the situation.

Last night she had wanted some personal understanding, not professional.

"I think I would have just liked a hug." Flic could have sworn those words were only audible in her head, but the saddened expression on Anna's face suggested otherwise.

"I'm sorry. I—"

"It's okay. I know you're not the hugging type, and I'm perfectly fine this morning," she added as Anna stepped awkwardly toward her and then retreated in the same uncoordinated movement.

Flic stared at the black plastic lid of her coffee. "I was scared, I guess. When I encounter bad guys, either they're on the end of a computer or they're contained within a piece I've written days before and long forgotten about. Physical confrontation isn't my thing."

"If it's any consolation, you handled yourself well." Anna stepped closer.

Flic smiled. "Other than pure fear, I really don't remember much."

As if overcome by a burst of confidence, Anna roughly grabbed Flic into a brief embrace, culminating with a manly pat on the back before she released her. Obviously not convinced her actions were adequately demonstrating the platonic nature of their relationship, Anna proceeded to whack Flic on the shoulder before saying, "Righto, champ. See you at eight." She practically ran out the door.

Champ?

Flic flexed her aching shoulder.

Flic knocked on Anna's door, only three doors down from her own. She wasn't sure what she was expecting, but it wasn't what greeted her. Spread on the dining table was a lavish breakfast, and Anna looked small curled up in the corner of her sofa, typing on her laptop. Considering the events of last evening, the picture was too serene, too contrived.

"What's going on?"

Anna smiled and handed Flic a piece of paper. It was a press statement.

"Seems we have a couple of days off." Anna gestured to the table and Flic sat.

"What?" Just when she'd psyched herself up for the grueling tour, it was stalled. All this stop-start business was driving her mad.

"Belfast is up in the air for tomorrow."

Flic continued to read the press statement. "But I'm not seeking counseling for emotional distress, nor am I seeking the second opinion of a doctor today. Am I?"

"Five o'clock."

"But I don't need a doctor. All I have is a few bruises. Do you want to see them?"

Anna flinched as if she'd been asked to remove her own teeth with pliers. "We can't ignore this opportunity, Flic."

"Opportunity?" Anna remained silent. "What happened last night wasn't an opportunity. It was a contrived assault. Should we really be milking it like this?"

Anna poured fruit juice for them both and helped herself to a croissant, offering the plate to Flic. "Do you know what my job is, Flic?" Her tone was light.

"Besides making my life miserable, yes. You're here to make sure this all runs smoothly."

Anna shrugged, ignoring the jibe. "Sort of. That role is a byproduct of my actual job."

It was too early for Flic's brain to function effectively.

"My job is to facilitate the sale of as many books as possible and make as much money as I can for Griffin's."

"I see."

"Do you?"

Flic shrugged. Maybe she didn't.

"I have to make the most of these events, unfortunate or otherwise, when they occur."

"So we're going for the sympathy vote? Nerdy author ambushed by thugs, needs time off?"

"Something like that. Nevertheless, we do need to increase your security. We have Max arriving any time now to take on the job."

Flic couldn't shake the notion that Anna's calmness unnerved her. "You didn't arrange that little scene last night, did you?"

Anna laughed briefly but was clearly insulted. "I don't engineer what happens, certainly not when you could be put in danger, that would rarely end well, but what I do know is how to turn just about any situation—"

"To your advantage. Yes, I know. I've heard it before."

Anna looked perplexed. "What's wrong?"

"I look pathetic. I've had one day on the job and now I've got two days off. Who's calling these shots, you or Dee?"

"As I was saying, my job is to run with the line you're giving about the pope and his sexuality, and I try to work everything to our advantage in the process, attempting to maximize our exposure and capitalize on our investment."

Flic understood the concept, but yet again couldn't reconcile the professional Anna with the personal one. "So, essentially, you disagree with my ideas, believe that Griffin's shouldn't have published my book, but by the same token, you're doing your best to make sure it's a best seller."

"It's my job."

"It's hypocritical."

"I really think you need to get over this, Flic."

"Me?"

There was a knock at the door. Anna was poised for a counter argument, but inhaled deeply and obviously reconsidered. She answered the door instead. A heavy silence filled the room until it was broken by a burly man lumbering in.

Again, Flic wasn't sure what she was expecting. Perhaps she had visions of Kevin Costner from *The Bodyguard*, but Max looked more like Hagrid from *Harry Potter*, and he practically filled the room. His beard was unruly and his hair could have had something nesting in it for all anyone knew.

"Hello, love. I hear you're being bullied a bit out there." His accent was Northern, Yorkshire somewhere.

Flic liked Max immediately.

Anna explained that Max had flown in from Greece that morning—their urgent need for security meant he'd been recalled from his holiday.

"Excuse my lazy holiday look. Better things to do than shave." Then he added in a softer voice, "Until now, anyway."

Flic soon realized that Max's physique wasn't all it appeared. Underneath his substantial layer of holiday cheer, lay some impressive muscles.

He declined breakfast but drank three coffees as they discussed their requirements. With his vast experience in the armed forces, he provided some excellent solutions to already encountered and perceived problems and suggested exit and entry strategies for buildings and vehicles. Max requested he be informed of their daily movements and that, in public, Flic should follow his lead and follow his direction.

"You do realize the easiest way to avoid the problem you encountered last night was to not get yourself amongst the crowd in the first place?"

Flic lowered her head. Yes, she had realized this.

"Working smart doesn't mean I protect you in a crowd. It means we avoid the crowds. It's simple risk assessment and control."

It made perfect sense. She just wished she'd given it more thought the previous evening.

"Right, ladies, I'll leave you to it." Max shook Flic's hand. "Lovely to meet you, and trust me, we won't have a repeat performance of last night. You'll be fine from here on in."

Anna handed him a USB drive. "It has our schedule and the details of every hotel, car hire company, et cetera, for the remainder of the tour. If you need anything else, just let me know."

They arranged to meet again the following morning, but other than that, Flic expected Max would be off catching up on sleep and reading about her schedule for the next few hours.

The call to Dee was, Flic expected, for her benefit only. It was evident from the conversation that Dee and Anna had already spoken, probably numerous times, but Dee's reassurance was welcomed, and by ten o'clock, Anna and Flic had just about exhausted all conversation.

"There's a pool here." Flic didn't want to leave the hotel, but she wasn't keen on spending time alone in her room either. She looked at Anna expectantly.

"I've got loads of work to do, sorry."

"Oh, come on. Surely you have a measly hour of free time?" Flic produced her tried and tested impersonation of a dog at the pound waiting for adoption.

Anna smiled but didn't fall for it. "Give me an hour. If I'm finished I might come down."

❖

Flic floated in the pool and lazed in the steam room and sauna, but after two and a half hours, Anna still hadn't surfaced. It bugged her that every time the door swung open she snapped up her head expectantly, but was disappointed when strangers entered.

Every time she thought of them in the changing room, dressing to return to their rooms after chatting easily and swimming in the pool, butterflies danced in her stomach. Flic wasn't entirely sure where the attraction originated. It wasn't as if Anna showed her any interest; she just hoped her thoughts were purely serving to distract her from last night's mob attack.

Bored out of her brain and wrinkly from the pool, she eventually returned to her room for a nap before plucking up the courage to visit Anna. Bottle of wine in hand, she knocked purposefully on the door.

"Flic. Sorry I didn't make the pool." Anna glanced at the wine, but didn't move from the doorway.

"That's okay. Figured you must have been busy. But all work and no play makes Anna boring." Flic waved the bottle around and internally cursed herself for saying something so ridiculous.

Anna stepped aside. "Have you been drinking already?"

Flic flopped on the sofa and groaned. "No." She was beginning to wish she had. "It's just so boring."

Anna laughed.

"I can't begin to think of the times I've dreamt of being stuck in a hotel with nothing to do. I've wished for those days—minibar, room service, pool, and little else to do but relax and enjoy—but I'm so Goddamn bored."

"You *can* leave the hotel you know. Just take Max with you."

It had crossed Flic's mind, but after last night, she felt a little intimidated by the unpredictability of the outside world. Until last night, she embraced unpredictability and opportunity, but not today, maybe tomorrow.

"I've got some e-mails to reply to. Why don't you turn on the TV and pick a movie for us to watch? I'll only be about fifteen minutes." Anna had softened.

Flic dismissed the notion that she was probably imposing on Anna and grabbed the remote.

"Wine?"

About to say no but obviously thinking better of it, Anna agreed.

Flic poured two glasses and selected a movie scheduled to begin in twenty minutes. She turned the volume down low and watched Anna work.

She was impressed by how easily Anna typed, how she regularly paused to read what she'd written, and how she could tell by the furrow on her brow or the slight haste with which she typed that she'd said something important or possibly creative.

Flic finished her first glass in minutes and wondered why she hadn't had a little tipple the previous night to settle her nerves.

"Can I ask you a personal question?"

Anna cocked her head. "I guess. Can't guarantee I'll answer though."

"Have you ever been in a long-term relationship?"

Anna's eyes remained on her computer, but she shook her head. "No. You?"

"I was in a civil partnership once."

"Really? I didn't know."

"Why would you?"

"We make it our business to know about your life when we sign you to a tour like this," Anna explained. "We knew you were gay and single. Things happened so quickly it must have been an oversight not to look more deeply."

"Does it really matter? I mean, I'm an author, not running for PM."

"If someone from our office digs around and finds out stuff about you that you haven't told us, others can do that too. If we know it might rear its ugly head, we can be prepared for it."

"Civil partnership, six years. Amicable separation and subsequent divorce. We're friends now."

Anna raised her eyebrows.

"Well, she lives in Newcastle, and we don't see each other anymore, but we don't hate each other either."

"At least it wasn't messy."

No, it wasn't messy. Compared to some of the dramas her friends encountered, her separation had been upsetting, but necessary. It had been the wisest option for two people who realized they were no longer lovers, but best friends.

Flic pounced on the opening. "So now you know the inside scoop on my significant relationship. Tell me about yours?"

Anna blushed. "I haven't had one. Not a significant one."

Flic wasn't surprised. "So what's your longest?"

Anna picked at the seam of her jeans. "A couple of months, I guess."

"Closer to one month or two?"

"Five weeks."

"A boy or girl?"

"What?" Anna leapt from the sofa.

The wine bottle was nearly empty, and even Flic was surprised she'd asked such a confronting question, but it was out there now. "I don't mean to offend, but sometimes when people are a little homophobic—"

"*Homophobic?*"

"Well, only a little."

"Just because I'm Catholic, doesn't automatically mean I'm homophobic. I know I'm older than you, but it's hardly an entire generation. What a ludicrous notion." Anna was all over the room, evidently unsure what to do with herself.

"I don't like to assume—"

"You don't *assume* someone's homophobic or not, Felicity."

"No, I know. It's just that when some people are a little uptight—"

Anna stared wide-eyed.

Flic wondered where it all went wrong and why was she still putting her foot in it?

"Anna, I'm sorry." She recovered with a firm tone.

Anna released her clenched fists.

"I guess I'd wondered if your religious beliefs might be clouding your judgment on your sexuality. Or not so much clouding it, but perhaps making things difficult in your mind."

"Why is it that all lesbians think single women are gay or in the closet?"

"Wishful thinking, I suppose," muttered Flic.

"Pardon?"

"Nothing." Flic regrouped again. "I'm sorry I offended you." In a show of friendship, Flic drew Anna into a hug and was surprised when Anna didn't pull away. "You know it's okay to be gay and Catholic, don't you?" The words came out softer than she'd intended, and this time Anna did pull away.

"I'm not gay! You know there are factions of the Catholic Church that claim homosexuals try to recruit others? Well, you're not doing anything to dispel that notion right now."

"Recruit you? I was just saying, that's all."

Flic poured the remainder of the wine for Anna who took the glass reluctantly. "I believe in the Catholic Church's view that homosexuality is unnatural. I don't begrudge you the lifestyle you lead, nor do I think you are in any way a lesser person than me. I just don't believe that being with someone of the same-sex is what God intended for us."

"Do you agree with same-sex marriage?"

"I believe beyond the four walls and sanctity of the church, same-sex marriage is a personal choice."

"But Catholics shouldn't be gay?"

"No. Not if they have true faith."

"And that includes the pope?"

"Especially the pope."

Flic couldn't argue with a belief. Faith was personal and Anna wasn't suggesting she be lynched or anything archaic like that. She had to delve further. "Do you accept that people are born gay?"

Anna hesitated "I believe those with true faith would choose not to be gay."

"Have you ever met a practicing Catholic homosexual?"

Anna ignored her. Eventually, she reached for the remote. "Come on. Are we watching this movie or not?" The conversation was shut down.

Flic reined in her questioning, resigned to the fact that the conversation was too uncomfortable for Anna. Had she gone too far? Before Anna switched on the movie, they both stared at a familiar sight on the screen—the cover of *Holy Father, Holy Secret.*

The early edition local news was on, and the story centered on a stubborn few protestors who refused to leave the foyer of the hotel Flic had previously been staying in. She suddenly felt detached. What had been going on? Flic logged on to her social media sites on Anna's computer only to be inundated with both support and heavy criticism. Her website alone had over five hundred thousand hits in the last twenty-four hours, and her inbox was full of messages, some of them positive and uplifting, others downright disturbing.

Anna peered over her shoulder. "Oh my goodness."

Post after post, comment after comment, filled her news feed. Groups were forming and gathering momentum. Those with opposing views sent comments back and forth, and even those with similar views began infighting.

"I need to say something." Flic was in shock. She couldn't believe the speed of the escalating social media.

Anna quickly closed the computer. "I'll gather my team together to deal with this."

"I need to be the one who deals with it."

"And it will look like you're dealing with it. But this has happened so fast. We need to consider our response first."

"We can't just let these people write whatever they like. Some of that is pure evil and inciting violence!"

Anna rested a firm hand on Flic's. "We can't stop people writing a damn thing. That's the downside of social media, but what we can do is formulate a measured response."

Flic nodded and stared at their touching hands.

"If you could say anything, what would it be?" asked Anna.

Flic's heart raced. "Love is love. The pope loves another human being. He happens to be a man. It's as simple as that."

Anna paced the room. "Let's keep it simple. Remove the pope from our discussion, and go with your uncomplicated message—love is love."

"But the pope *is* a part of this. How can you ignore that? It's the premise of my book."

Anna knelt before her, their eyes locked. "It's not the premise for most of these idiots, though, Flic."

Flic knew she was right but rolled her eyes regardless; hearing this from a pope-loving Catholic was not helping.

"It's not me talking now, Flic. It's Anna the marketing and publicist specialist. Promote the message, we stay away from all the other crap, and the book will promote itself."

A heat rose between them, and Flic realized Anna was practically kneeling between her legs. Not convinced she could make a sound, she whispered, "I thought I was only ever talking to the professional Anna."

"What?"

"Do I ever see the real you?"

Anna went to move away, but Flic caught her hands and pulled her back to her knees.

"You hate me because of my sexuality and my book."

Anna's eyes popped wide open. "I don't hate you. Not at all."

"You're so guarded around me."

"I'm trying to be professional."

"And I'm trying to be your friend."

"Our relationship *is* professional, Flic."

"I like you." It was out before Flic had a chance to engage her filter.

This time Anna moved to the opposite side of the room. "To hear that is beyond confusing."

"Confusing?" It wasn't the response Flic had expected. She imagined Anna might have used the words repulsive, ridiculous, or downright offensive, but *confusing*?

"I know you like me." Anna was barely audible.

"And that's confusing for you?" Flic's hand covered her mouth. Realization dawned. "What are you trying to say?"

"Nothing. I just think for the sake and ease of this tour, we should remain professional, colleagues, you know, keep everything aboveboard."

"Is there a chance it can go below board?"

"What? No, of course not."

Flic stood tall. "I challenge everything you believe in, don't I?"

Anna was calming down. "Perhaps you do."

She turned to leave the room. "Good."

CHAPTER TWELVE

The press release Anna drafted firmly sold the message that love is love and that Felicity, together with Griffin's, in no way condoned the violence that was being threatened on social media. She sought advice from the police and lawyers in relation to some of the wording, but their angle remained clear and concise. Some extremists attempted to argue the view that if love was love, was it okay for man to lie with a beast or a child if they truly loved them. There was no requirement for Anna to make a statement regarding this. Supporters on social media shut down those conversations quickly and efficiently. After the troublemakers had their fun and the conversation became too intellectually difficult for them, what remained were two distinct camps: pro choice supporters—Catholic or otherwise—citing that a pope's sexuality held no bearing on his ability to perform his duties, and the other side that felt the church should be protected at all costs. The latter appeared to be a combination of pro-Catholic supporters and antigay supporters, Catholic or otherwise.

It hurt Anna to see the sadness in Flic's eyes when she realized her book had been the catalyst for the social media frenzy.

In a way, she envied Flic and her simplistic view of the world. Love is love, sex is sex, black is black, and white is white. Although when she thought deeply about it, in reality, Flic's views weren't simplistic and they weren't black-and-white. Felicity Bastone embraced gray. She likened her to someone floating down a long river where every adjacent river was a possibility, an opportunity awaiting exploration. Anna wondered what her river might look like. More like a canal in England, she concluded, interrupted by low-lying bridges and loch after loch, hindering her progress and posing the question: Was it worth it to go through the loch, or should she simply tie to the shore and be content with never moving forward?

Not only was Anna questioning where she was going, she was now questioning exactly who she was.

❖

It took a double take before Flic recognized Max entering the dining room the following morning at breakfast. He was cleanly shaven, and his mop-like hair was now only a few centimeters long and styled with product. He wore a smart white shirt and dark denim jeans.

Flic whistled. "Hello, sailor."

"Morning, love. Thought I'd better smarten up for work." He selected a massive bowl of yogurt and fruit with two mugs of coffee. "So, we're Belfast bound today?"

Flic nodded. "Should be interesting."

"You worried?" Anna spoke as she took up a seat at the table.

Flic regarded her closely. "Morning." She smiled awkwardly.

"Morning." Anna did the same, and Max glanced between them several times.

"I'm taking a wander through town this morning if you fancy coming along?" said Max.

Max didn't look like the shopping type, and when he shot a reassuring nod in Anna's direction, Flic knew there was a conspiracy at play.

She really wanted to call their bluff though, tell them she didn't need anyone facilitating a bogus shopping trip to get her out of the hotel, but the fact was she couldn't say that because it wasn't true. Since the incident in Grafton Street, she'd balked at any talk of exploring the city or playing tourist. Anna had assured her with a hat and dark sunglasses, no one would know who she was, but it simply felt easier to stay in seclusion. It wasn't like Flic to be so intimidated, and she found the whole thing unnerving.

Anna pushed her egg back and forth before finally addressing Flic. "Our Belfast gig is going ahead as scheduled. Today."

"What? I thought things were postponed for a couple of days?"

"Dee wants to get back into it while the press is still keen."

Dee changed her mind like the wind. Flic couldn't keep up with what Dee bloody well wanted. What about what *she* wanted?

"What about those idiots out there? What if *they're* still keen?" Flic began to sweat under her arms. She could feel the uncomfortable heat radiate from her chest to the crown of her head.

Without hesitation, Max reassuringly touched Flic's shoulder. "This afternoon will be different. We've learnt from the Grafton Street experience so there's no need to worry. You can trust me, okay?"

Flic was far from convinced. "I trust you, Max. It's those other thugs out there with complete disrespect for my personal space that I don't trust. Some of these people are fanatical, too, you know, not just rent-a-crowd twats with nothing better to do before their mummies put dinner on the table."

"Max is liaising with the police, who've assured us they'll have a presence at the bookstore, but you have to understand, Flic, this is about book sales and exposure. We need to maximize this for the next week or so. The Vatican can't sit on this much longer. We need you back in the saddle." Anna certainly appeared convincing, but she didn't sound it.

Flic struggled to keep her nerves in check. "Fine. Then let's go. The sooner we get to Belfast the better." She left breakfast hastily, just as her appetite had left her only a minute before.

The drive from Dublin to Belfast on the M1 motorway took only two hours, mostly spent in silence, and by the time they arrived, Flic felt ill from the pungent deodorizer the car hire company had obviously felt the need to spray in copious volumes.

They arrived by lunchtime and Flic disappeared to her room. The schedule swapping back and forth unnerved her, and she needed time to psyche herself up for another reading, more questions, and possibly another confrontation. With the slight chance her hotel could be targeted again, Anna had arranged an alternative, and while it was old, it was certainly comfortable enough. Dark timber and effective lighting somehow made it homey.

At three o'clock, dressed in dark olive green chinos, a white T-shirt, and black blazer, Flic answered the knock at her door. Max, dressed in all black, and Anna, wearing a black pantsuit and a pink shirt, greeted her. Black clothing seemed the order of the day. Flic liked to hide behind it. It was the only color that seemed to ease her sense of vulnerability.

"Ready to roll?" Anna's eyes focused on the small empty bottle of vodka on the coffee table. "Are you okay?"

The vodka had worked its magic when, five minutes earlier, Flic drank it in one gulp. "I've never taken Valium, but surely vodka's the next best thing."

Anna regarded her for a long moment then pulled a small packet of mints from her bag, opened the left hand side of Flic's blazer, and slipped them inside. "Here, keep these in your pocket and suck on them regularly."

Flic laughed. So did Max. Anna shook her head and led them all to the stinky car.

The bookstore was only ten minutes' drive, and Flic sat in the back with Anna, her leg jiggling and her palms sweating. She'd never been anxious like this before. Nervousness was one thing, a good thing if she thought about it, but this was something else altogether.

It was a chilly day in Ireland, and every man she saw wearing a jumper with the hood over his head sent a sharp twinge of panic through her midsection. She should really have eaten something before drinking the vodka.

Anna produced a makeup case. "How many drinks did you have? You're as white as a sheet."

Flic glanced at her face in the tiny mirror on the inside of the case. She was certainly pale, but the sheen of sweat on her forehead glistened even in the dull sunlight. "I don't feel so good. I think we should go back."

"What?"

Turning back was not an option she knew Anna would be willing to explore.

Max eyed her warily in the rearview mirror.

"I don't want to do this today." The words tumbled from Flic as if her life depended on it.

"After Tuesday, today is crucial," Anna replied quickly.

"After Tuesday, today is just absurd. Anything could happen. I could be stabbed. Jesus, I could end up in the morgue."

Max swiftly pulled the car to the curb. Calm as you like, he unbuckled his seat belt and turned to face them. "Ladies, this is not helpful. I mean no disrespect, Felicity, but those idiots you encountered before were most likely there because it was a bit of fun to them." Flic rolled her eyes. "I'll grant you, not harmless fun, but they weren't protestors passionate about the cause. You know that as well as I do. Rent-a-crowds at book launches don't usually hurt people."

"Yet still, I ended up in hospital!"

Anna placed her hand on Flic's. "And you were okay."

Flic felt her breathing slow, and she knew the reason was Anna's soft touch. The notion irritated and comforted her simultaneously.

"And today we have Max," continued Anna.

Max nodded. "We have a greater police presence, you have me, and it will all be fine." He lowered his voice. "If I get even a sniff of something going down, I'll have you out of there and away from it all so quick you'll wonder what happened."

Flic nodded and linked her fingers through Anna's.

Max continued. "We don't endure and survive episodes like Grafton Street. We actively avoid them. Please don't worry. I have your back."

Flic closed her eyes, attempting to relax. "Just give me a minute." Her tense shoulders lowered, and she felt tiny droplets of sweat slide down her lower back. Until she heard Anna's voice, she could have sworn the world stood still.

"Felicity? Flic?" Anna squeezed her hand, prompting her back to the present.

Flic cracked her eyes open the smallest of margins. She didn't want to face the world, and she didn't want Anna to release the firm grip on her hand. Reluctantly, she conceded, "I think I'm okay now."

"Tuesday night was confronting, wasn't it?"

That was an understatement.

"You have to remember though, you handled yourself amazingly well."

"I wasn't just scared. I was terrified."

"That's why you didn't leave the hotel yesterday," added Max.

Anna raised her eyebrow. "I knew you were shaken, but I'm not a mind reader. You need to talk to me when you feel this way. Max and I are worried about you."

The words hurt Flic more than she had imagined possible. Unless it was to talk about marketing or publicity, Anna was possibly the least approachable person she'd ever met. "You don't see that incident as anything other than a publicity opportunity, do you?" She removed her hand from Anna's. "You could have asked you know? Would that have been too much for you, just to ask if I was okay?"

"I did ask." Anna paused and frowned for a long moment. "Didn't I?"

Flic shook her head. "Not really. Not until yesterday morning."

"Well, I'm sorry. But you *were* fine."

Physically I was fine, but mentally, I needed someone. Flic didn't say the words aloud. They sounded pathetic and weak, and she couldn't bear Anna knowing she wasn't the tough investigative journalist everyone obviously thought she was.

Flic tapped Max on the shoulder. "Let's just go. I'm ready now."

"I'm sorry, Flic."

"You're here to do a job, not be my friend. I understand how this works."

"But I am your friend, or at least I should have been a better person for you. Honestly, Flic, I'm really sorry."

Flic wanted to defend herself, be strong and tell Anna she was fine without her help, but the words wouldn't form in her mouth. It seemed that what she wanted and what her brain and body were telling her she needed, were polar opposites. She chose silence instead, forcing Anna to go on.

"You can do this today. We can do this. You, me, and Max."

From beneath her lowered gaze, Flic saw Max nod his encouragement to Anna. He'd ignored her request to drive on.

"I wasn't going to use it—mostly because I didn't know if it would be useful—but Max gave me an earpiece and microphone yesterday. For everyone's peace of mind, I think it will be valuable today. Max will be our eyes and ears, and I'll make sure you can see me at all times."

This perked Flic's interest and encouraged Anna to continue. "I'm your focal point today, okay? I promise to be where you can see me at all times, and if Max wants to pull the plug, I'll give you the signal." She drew her finger across her throat in the universal sign for "kill it."

Max intervened. "Um, let's not get too dramatic, ladies." He grinned, easing the tension. "How about we use a thumbs-up for all good and a thumbs-down to wrap it up."

Flic clocked a flash of disappointment on Anna's face, and it was amusing to think Anna was upset that her thumb would now dictate her foray into the world of personal protection. She wondered if Anna had ever used a thumbs-up signal in her life. For whatever reason, it worked. Flic relaxed, content with the plan. "Okay. And you'll have communication with Max the entire time?"

"Yep. Focus on me. I'll be there for you."

Max turned on the engine and edged back into traffic.

The crowds were bigger than Dublin, but the police were in visible attendance, and Max assured her there were probably some undercover officers mingling in the crowds. Although initially concerned about the sheer volume of people, Flic studied them more closely. The demographic had altered. There were far fewer young men sporting angry scowls and chips on their shoulders. These seemed to be replaced with middle-aged people, men and women, some smiling and joking amongst themselves while others stood rigid in the early evening chill, their hands pushed deep in their pockets.

The messages on placards had altered, too. *This is not a gay rights issue. This is a church issue. Leave us alone.* Then there was a group of people with no placards at all. They simply wore a prominent rainbow accessory like a scarf or hat. Of course there was the standard *Homosexuals are against the word of God* placards, but tonight, instead of a young thug holding it aloft, a frail old man stood silently with it by his side. Flic wondered what the chances were of convincing a man entrenched in seventy-plus years of bigotry, to change his view.

She pointed him out to Anna. "I can't hate that man. He's of an era where it was okay to keep slaves, okay to openly suppress women. I'd like to think that if he were my age, he'd be bothered to protest for *my* rights, for the freedom to love. He's just defending what he thinks is right."

Anna pointed to a young woman holding a sign not dissimilar in ideals to the old man. *What next? Legalizing pedophilia?* "And what about her?"

Flic shook her head and turned away as their vehicle came to a halt. "She chooses to be ignorant. A bigot. She hasn't had years of brainwashing in a time when people honestly didn't know better." Flic shrugged. "And the likelihood is that she has homosexual tendencies but was probably raised in a conservative family. Go figure."

"Not everyone who's raised conservatively and who doesn't believe in homosexuality is in the closet you know."

"Believe? Homosexuality isn't like the Easter Bunny. You don't believe or disbelieve it. It just is."

"She has a right to protest."

"Yes. And making a complete twat of herself is also her right. One she accomplishes with alarming success. But why care? Why does she care what someone else does in the comfort of their own home? Why so publicly voice an opinion on something you are clearly ignorant of? Why? Because you're scared and in the closet, that's why."

Anna smiled. "I think you're ready for today."

Flic shook her head but smiled. "You infuriate me sometimes."

"It's part of my conservative charm."

"What would your placard say?"

Max had exited the vehicle and was deep in conversation with what appeared to be a senior police officer.

"Me with a placard? You've got to be joking."

Flic conceded it would be out of character. "Okay, no placard. In one sentence, what would your argument be?"

Anna gave it some thought. "God, Jesus, and the Catholic Church—God's representatives on earth—don't believe homosexuality is in the name of God. I believe in the church and therefore believe the pope shouldn't be gay."

"That's two sentences."

Anna grinned.

"And you're just regurgitating stuff the church says umpteen times in umpteen variations. What about what *you* think? Surely that conflicts with your own beliefs or personal experiences even just a little?"

Anna became distracted with a burly policeman opening her door, but she quickly addressed Flic. "Perhaps it's beginning to."

The car door swung open and the noise of the crowd entered the sanctuary of the vehicle. Flic's calm state scurried into the recesses of her mind, making way for fear and anxiety to return. Between Anna, Max, and Sergeant Blakemore, she regained control and pushed through the most debilitating nerves she had encountered in her life.

CHAPTER THIRTEEN

Although Flic stumbled on her words in more than a few places, her reading went well and she received laughs on cue. Anna was never too far from her, and she remained in Flic's line of vision at all times. Intermittently, Flic's eyes lingered on her, waiting for a reassuring thumbs-up, which always came. She relaxed a little as Anna smiled and nodded encouragingly, and although she was asked many difficult questions, her answers remained clear and always within the overarching message that love is love and that homosexuality in no way diminished your abilities in life.

"Unless of course you're a gay man and can obviously dance with more rhythm and coordination than other men." The crowd laughed, and she glanced up to see Anna giving her the thumbs-down signal. The gesture briefly panicked her. Her entire body flushed with heat as anxiety triggered the initial stages of a natural fight or flight response. It lasted only moments before Anna's warm smile and sparkling eyes indicated it was merely time to finish up. Tonight's appearance was only half the duration of Dublin, and warm, fuzzy relief overtook her fear.

It was over.

Anna was by her side in moments. "That was fantastic. Really well done."

Flic wasn't convinced.

"I know you were more nervous, but I honestly think it was better than Tuesday."

"It was shorter." Flic allowed herself to be guided to the rear of the store by Anna.

"It was, but I think that's how we need to proceed from now on. What do you think?"

Barely lasting thirty minutes, her appearance seemed an appalling waste of time, but Flic nodded her agreement. "No, I think it's good timing."

"We've been invited to dinner with Martha Devlin, the store owner, and her family. Do you feel up to a little celebration this evening?"

Day three and the promotional tour had become exhausting. Where was her stamina? No, Flic didn't feel up to it. For the past few weeks, she had lived, breathed, and dreamed about her book, the pope, sales figures, marketing, and the media. It hadn't occurred to her that defending her book and her ideals would be so draining.

"Can we not? Not tonight."

Disappointment briefly flared Anna's nostrils.

"I will get better at this stuff, I promise, but just not tonight." Flic dared to speak her mind. "I was hoping you and I could have dinner. Just the two of us. Do you like Italian?"

"I don't know…"

Distracted by Max's approach, Flic didn't catch Anna's reply. They were standing at the rear door of the premises, bidding farewell to Martha, when Flic froze, aware that this was the junction upon which everything had unraveled Tuesday evening.

With impeccable manners, Flic let her mouth switch to autopilot and deliver the appropriate gratitude to Martha and her staff, but all the while, her eyes scanned the dingy alleyway where Max stood, one arm outstretched ushering her to the black SUV. Her ears began to ring.

Every logical cell of her brain told her that there was no need to believe that her previous experience would be repeated. There was nothing stirring to suggest she was in any danger. In fact with Max reassuringly standing directly in front of her, statistically, she was in considerably less danger than Dublin, and the crowd had been confined to the front of the store with all access blocked by the police. Her sense of irrational fear had another name—anxiety.

Anna wrapped up the pleasantries with Martha, a little disappointed Flic wasn't keen on socializing, but she understood why. Max appeared to be giving her the eye. She turned toward Flic who was frozen on the spot. She went to her, taking Flic by the shoulder and with Max's arm firmly holding her waist, they worked as a team to usher her into the backseat of the vehicle.

Relief spread across Flic's face, and Anna guessed she had probably been on the verge of another panic attack. Flic closed her eyes, and Anna could tell by the lowering of her shoulders that her fear was subsiding. It was awful to watch. She moved closer to Flic on the backseat, the only gesture she felt comfortable making. It occurred to her that a hug might also be soothing, but that felt like a giant leap she couldn't make at that time. They remained silent while Max negotiated the traffic. Anna took out her tablet and read an e-mail from Dee.

Minutes passed before Flic opened her eyes. They were now well away from the store and en route to the hotel.

Anna was busy typing.

"E-mail from Dee?" asked Flic.

Anna nodded. "She's worried about you."

"But you've told her today went okay, right?"

"Of course." Anna eyed her curiously and paused for a long moment. It was difficult to know how much to tell Flic and how real to make it all sound. She had no idea where Flic's breaking point was, and if she reached it, to what lengths would she be willing to go to bring her back. "It's getting big, Flic. We're continually making news headlines. Sales are through the roof. You're breaking sales records in just about every country we've released in."

"And Dee's worried because on day three I bottled it?"

"No, she's pleased you pulled through."

"But you told her it was a close call, you know, getting me there." Flic blushed.

Anna cleared her throat. "The vodka worries her."

"You told her about the vodka?"

"To be honest, Flic, the vodka worries *me*."

"I can't believe you told her!"

"Calm down. She pays me, remember? Not you." The moment the words came from her mouth, she regretted them.

"And I'll be funding your generous Christmas bonus this year, so perhaps afford me a little leeway here."

Anna lowered her eyes. "And perhaps afford me a little leeway, too. I don't hide things from Dee, and I'm not hiding anything from you."

Anna counted all the way to thirty-seven before Flic spoke again. "I'm sorry. I know you had to tell her."

"I know you might not always see it, but often doing the right thing by Dee actually means I'm doing the right thing by you, too. I am on your side, you know."

"I understand that. I'm learning to trust you, I promise."

Anna shifted uncomfortably in her seat as Flic's words stung. *She doesn't trust me.* Of course Flic didn't trust her. Why would she trust the person who so openly dislikes her book, her lifestyle, and who's accused her of trying to destroy the Catholic Church? Anna liaised with Dee, with Max, and with absolutely everyone else who was involved in publicizing the book. It finally occurred to her that Flic was probably feeling isolated and out of her depth.

"Would you like to be more involved in the decisions we make about you?"

"What do you mean?"

Anna shifted in the seat to face Flic. "Your anxiety might ease if you feel like you have more control over the things that happen to you."

"You should be a politician."

"What? Why?"

"What you really just said was that we'll still do what we like with you, but we'll tell you about it sooner and then you might feel better because you're under the impression you have some say in it, some control."

Before Anna really felt like the lowlife Flic was implying she was, Flic smiled. Anna did too. "Yes. That's exactly what I was saying."

"I thought so."

"So would you like to be involved more?"

"Involved but actually have no real say in my own life?"

"Exactly."

Flic grinned. "Yes, please."

Anna winked. "Good. Then I'll keep you informed."

"So what do you say to dinner?"

Anna hesitated.

"How about we agree now to not mention the book, religion, vodka, or anything to do with our work if we go out?"

"What would we talk about?"

Flic pounced on the opening. "Anything. Just not those things. Come on. If nothing else, it'll be a good exercise in human behavior."

"You want to experiment and use us as guinea pigs?"

"Yep. Food, wine, and not one mention of *Holy Father, Holy Secret*. Actually, every time we slip up we take a shot of Pernod, and the person who shoots the most foots the bill."

"Dee always foots the bill."

"You're avoiding the subject."

"Half a shot, not a full one."

After due consideration, Flic nodded. "You're on."

It might have been the fact that Dee would ultimately foot the bill that encouraged Flic to persuade Anna to buy a bottle of Pernod and have the waitress leave it on the table with two small glasses. Dessert was being served, and the bottle was half empty.

"It's not as easy as it sounds to avoid talking about work, is it?" Anna spooned sticky toffee pudding and cream into her mouth. She'd recently been to the bathroom and had reapplied a pale plumb lipstick, her moist lips causing Flic to shudder slightly. The fact that Anna had bothered made her all the more curious.

"Um, correct me if I'm wrong, but did you just mention work?"

"Steady on. I mentioned it in the context of this experiment, not *actual* work."

"I've had a great night." Flic smiled.

"Me too." Anna sounded surprised. "Your work—your real job—sounds very interesting."

"As does yours. I can see why you've succeeded so early in your career."

"You're only hot when you're hot," said Anna. "It just takes a couple of rubbish decisions and you can come crashing down. I've been lucky."

"I guess there's no loyalty in marketing."

"No. You're an expensive liability if you lose your mojo, and there's always someone younger with fresh ideas ready to take your job."

"Well, now you can add babysitting authors to your CV if you ever find yourself out of a job."

Anna smiled. "So what exactly is the expected outcome of our little experiment?"

"Excuse me?"

Anna rolled her eyes. "An experiment is usually conducted to find something out, test a theory, you know? What's your theory?"

Flic hadn't the faintest clue. She only came up with the hook line to entice Anna to dinner. Something sprang to mind. "Very few people can spend little time one-on-one without talking about their job. I was interested to see if we could spend considerable time and do the same." It sounded plausible, even intelligent. "Have you ever seen people out to dinner or in cafes staring out the window and generally looking anywhere other than at the person they're with, let alone actually conversing with them?"

Anna laughed. "I see it all the time. I love to people watch."

"Well, under altered conditions, we managed not to have a single pause in the conversation. Pretty good considering our work is what ties us to each other."

It was true. They'd maintained conversation, interesting conversation, without one awkward silent moment.

"So, Professor Smarty-Pants, you're avoiding the question. What's the outcome of your little experiment?"

"Sound relationships are based on the foundation of good communication and respect for the opinion of others."

"Are we in a relationship now?" Anna's tone suggested she was teasing, but her eyes conveyed panic.

"No, I meant friendship."

"So we're friends?"

Flic wanted to remove her smarty-pants; they no longer worked. She took a gamble. "Yes, I think we are, and we have the foundation to be very good friends. I don't know if I could sit and talk to some of my oldest friends for as long as we have tonight."

Anna nodded, staring at her napkin as she placed it on the table. "You're right. It's been remarkably easy."

"So, friends it is then?" Flic prodded, seeking clarification. "No more of this professional courtesy stuff? Actual friends?"

Anna smiled. She beamed and it caused the muscles in Flic's pelvis to contract. "Yes, you're on my Christmas card list."

The waitress had placed the bottle of Pernod into a gift bag, and they shrugged on their jackets to leave. "What about birthdays? I'll get a present, right?"

"Don't push your luck."

As if their agreement on friendship had provided a newly found sense of relief, they chatted incessantly on the journey back to the hotel. Perhaps realizing it was fruitless to even try to fit a word in, Max remained quiet and concentrated on driving.

"One more?" Flic held the Pernod aloft in the hotel hallway.

"We have a big day tomorrow." Anna hovered on the threshold of her room. "Paris will be big; you know how the French like to protest."

Flic didn't want their fun to end. "Just one?"

Standing her ground, Anna smiled but shook her head. "I have work to do before I turn in. And you could use a restful sleep. I doubt you've had enough the last couple of nights."

It was no use. Anna had made up her mind. "Okay, you win." Flic advanced with outstretched arms.

Suddenly, it all began to go wrong.

Anna advanced in the same manner, but their arms became entangled and Flic accidentally brushed Anna's breast.

"Sorry." Flic worried it might be the shortest friendship ever.

Finally, with arms securely embracing each other in the appropriate places, Flic gave a gentle squeeze. It was her usual routine. Laura once told her she was the best hugger this side of her lovers, but on this occasion, the squeeze prompted Anna to emulate the move, bringing them closer. Anna released an audible, contented sigh.

In that split second, Flic somehow transitioned into a completely alternative reality. In her arms, Anna was soft and fragile, yet strong and reassuring. Her right arm encompassed Anna, her hand resting on her side, directly on her ribs, and because her frame was slight, her hand held this area firmly, as if ownership was her right. Flic's lower abdomen tingled for a long moment.

Anna continued the embrace.

Flic felt the juices flow in her most sensitive place. The Pernod left her feeling deliciously pickled and happy.

Anna's hand moved to gently stroke the hair that sat above Flic's collar. Just once, but it felt divine, and it certainly wasn't anything Laura had ever done during their extensive friendship hugs.

Instinct took over, and Flic pulled away, just far enough for her eyes to lock on Anna's lips. She edged closer. The touch was electrifying. It was clichéd, but beyond the first kiss she'd had with a girl in year nine, Flic had never felt that earth-moving feeling again. Until now.

Anna pushed her away. "No."

Flic's transition back to real time was far less rewarding than her digression. Realizing exactly what she had done, she watched helplessly as Anna backed out of reach. "I'm sorry."

"Go to bed, Felicity." Anna swiped her room door and pushed it open.

Hearing Anna use her full name stung. "I didn't mean it."

Anna glared at her.

"No, that's wrong. I meant it, I just didn't plan it. I didn't know I was going to do that. You held me and sighed—"

"Now it's my fault?"

"No, of course not, but—"

Anna grasped a handful of Flic's top and dragged her through the door. "Get in here. You'll wake the entire hotel."

The touch, as rough as it was, turned Flic on even more.

She gathered herself. "I don't know how to explain this to you. Look, I know it was wrong, but it felt right—"

"Is that what a pedophile says in defense of raping a child?"

Whoa. Flic raised her arms in surrender. "Okay, that's enough. I'm not a pervert and your implication that I'm somehow on the same level as a child rapist is just fucking insulting." Flic paced the room, riled and distressed. "I happen to like you. A lot. And trust me; it's as much of a surprise to me as it is to you. It was an innocent display of affection, and while we're laying our cards on the table, I'll admit there was a hint of passion in the mix, but I'm not a perverted freak." Flic fought her emotions. Anger and guilt didn't mix well in the bowl. "How the hell did I even fathom hoping for a friendship with someone who barely thinks I'm one step up from a pedophile?"

"You kissed me. You were out of line."

"Yes, and I'm sorry. God, you freak out because a lesbian kisses you, but I bet if I were a man you'd be flattered. A greater percentage of men rape and fiddle with kids than women—gay or straight—and you've got the gall to suggest I'm as wretched as a filthy fucking pedophile. Fuck you and fuck your twisted, suppressive religion."

"I knew it would come to this."

"Yeah, well here *this* is." Flic shook her head, advancing toward the door. "I apologize. I displayed affection you hadn't asked for. I apologize because I read the situation wrong."

Flic marched from the room, but before the door slammed behind her, she was able to shout, "But what I really feel sorry for is pathetic little you."

CHAPTER FOURTEEN

Picture perfect, Paris looked glamorous and cultured, exactly like it looked in every *National Geographic* Flic had ever read. She wasn't fooled, though. She'd seen Paris plenty of times in winter, and it was bloody freezing. On this occasion, however, the sun was hot and high in the sky. Even her olive skin was burning as she lounged, dozing on the balcony of the hotel on Rue Benjamin Franklin. Just above the building opposite, she could see the Eiffel Tower barely five minutes' walk through a park and over the River Seine.

The flight from Belfast had been fine. She had sat next to Anna, but they barely spoke, and she was grateful her iPod held enough charge to last the journey. There were no unpleasant exchanges, just a cold silence so vast it could fill the Grand Canyon.

A knock startled Flic from a nap, and she was pleased to wake before she caught too much sun. "Hang on."

Max greeted her with a cheesy grin. "Hiya, Flic. Can I come in?"

Flic was pleased Max was tactful. He would have had to be blind and deaf not to realize there was tension between her and Anna.

"I've picked up some tension. What's going on?"

Max had apparently lost his tact.

"Have you spoken to her?"

Max cringed. "By *her* I assume you mean Anna."

"Yes, sorry. Have you spoken to Anna?"

Max poured them both a glass of iced water. "No, not yet. I wanted to know how you were feeling after yesterday."

Flic paused. *Yesterday?* Were they on the same page? Surely Anna hadn't mentioned their little altercation to Max?

He clarified. "Your nerves. You feeling okay about the signing and appearance this afternoon?"

Since the altercation with Anna, nothing else had entered her mind. She was, in fact, calm about the impending public appearance and naturally concluded that because yesterday had run smoothly, and to plan, her fear had subsided. She felt safe with Max on board and smiled. "I'm good. It's all good. I think just over half an hour is long enough in the public eye for the time being."

Max nodded.

"Can we stick to the same routine as yesterday?"

"Of course, but if you two can't even look at each other, the system we had yesterday now has an obvious flaw."

So Max did know something else was going on. This snag hadn't occurred to her. "So, you'll talk to her then?"

"Not on your life. That's your deal, but cut her some slack. She's looking after you on a professional level and trying to be your friend. It's a high pressure job, and I think she's doing her best."

Flic contemplated Max's advice after he left. He rarely spoke great monologues, but when he said something, it was usually worth listening to. Flic threw a T-shirt over her bikini top and left her room in search of Anna. She found her staring at her laptop in the luxurious and expansive hotel foyer, sipping coffee.

"Hello." Although appropriate, the greeting sounded ridiculous. But with absolutely no clue regarding Anna's mindset, Flic was wary. Last night had predominantly been her fault, but Anna's totally unfair implication left her insulted and defeated.

Heavy, dark eyes dominated her usual features, and glancing up, Anna sighed heavily and smiled slightly. "Flic, hi. Have you got a minute?"

The inevitable *make up* conversation was unavoidable. Flic sat, determined to say her piece first. "I'm sorry I got carried away last night." Filled with Pernod, she had rehearsed a heartfelt apology as she lay awake until the early hours, but in the harshness of sober daylight, she wondered if she could pull it off and if it was even appropriate. "I'm not going to explain to you how I came to the conclusion that kissing you was the right thing to do. I don't think you'd understand. But I do want you to know my feelings were genuine and in no way disrespectful." She delivered the abridged version.

It was impossible to read Anna's expression until a smile crept through the facade, followed by a serious stare. "I'm sorry I likened you to a pedophile. I know what I said was wrong, and like you, it wasn't my intention to offend or insult."

Flic breathed a visible sigh of relief. "So we're okay?"

Anna nodded. "Can we try again this evening? Dinner? My shout."

Flic was sure she'd blown it. An invitation to start over was the last thing she expected, and she wasn't one to pass up a second chance. It was on the tip of her tongue to say "God, yes please," but instead she grinned and said, "Dee always shouts."

Anna smiled broadly. "I know. Makes it all the more fun, surely? Oh, and we'll need to leave fifteen minutes early for the signing this afternoon."

Flic struggled to keep up with the switch in conversation.

"Sure. No problem. Everything okay?" She was suddenly anxious. "Is there a problem with the venue or route or something?"

"No, all that's in Max's safe hands. We need to leave early because I have to stop at a church on the way and confess my sins from last night."

Flic's anxiety grew into guilt. "I'm terribly sorry." She had no idea there would be repercussions beyond their respective hurt feelings. "Is there anything I can do?"

Anna doubled over. "You're terribly gullible. The look on your face is priceless."

Flic held her chest. "Phew. For a second there, I thought you were serious."

"For a second there, I thought you were going to offer to come with me."

"Do you ever go to confession?"

"Only when I break the law."

"What?"

"I'm kidding."

Flic's heart raced a little. Where had this playful and amusing Anna been for the past month?

Curiosity won over. "I know your faith is important to you, and has been your entire life, but can I ask how that developed?" Flic's tone suggested caution; sometimes tragedy inspired faith.

Anna patted the seat next to her and Flic obliged. "It's no big deal really. Both my parents were in the air force and we moved a hell of a lot. We lived in Ireland when I was very small, and I went to Sunday school with my friends. My childhood was filled with inconsistencies, and I stumbled upon the reality that there's nearly always a church in every town. It became the one thing that was consistent in my life."

"That's why you're Catholic?"

"Yep. When we moved to England, I was older, and was happy to attend the local church, but I always felt more of an affinity with the Catholic faith. It was where I felt the safest as a child."

Anna was one contradiction after another. Artistic, creative, and ambitious in one sense, but ordered and led by faith in another. The more infuriating she became, the more Flic wanted to know her, unravel her, and chip away at her defenses.

"You don't get it at all do you?" Anna was watching Flic mull it all over.

"Nope. But I respect your beliefs and your choices."

"Yes." Anna contemplated. "I think I'm learning to do the same."

❖

For the first time, Flic experienced the authentic buzz of illustriousness. As elaborate and impressive as many of the buildings in Paris were, *Un Monde de Livres*—A World of Books— was a remarkable sight. The store was fitted with tall, foreboding hardwood bookshelves, industrial styled timber, and metal furniture and fixtures, coupled with renaissance tapestries and warm, exposed bulb lighting.

Her appearance had been a success. There was something refreshing about the French's liberal views. They'd been a vocal yet embracing crowd.

Anna had linked a finger through a belt loop at the back of Flic's jeans. At the top of the stairs, she drew her close. "You look every bit the celebrity."

Flic glanced at Anna and then at the crowd below her. For the first time, she *felt* like a celebrity.

Max rested an arm on her lower back. "A few autographs, but don't linger."

She nodded her understanding, and together they descended the stairs as she signed autographs. Max and Anna flanked her, and she easily relaxed into publicity mode.

Outside, the largest crowd to date greeted her. The police presence was enormous, and Max had enlisted the services of a driver so he could accompany Flic personally. Police efficiently cordoned off the massive black Hummer, and her walk from the store's front doors to the car was about thirty meters.

The scene altered with proportionately more protestors than had entered the building. There was little use heckling her during the reading; the police efficiently removed anyone who caused a nuisance, but outside was a different story. She remained unnerved by the insults. She was riding high. After all, everyone had the right to protest, right?

The passion and enthusiasm the French conveyed was unlike anything she'd ever experienced. She was British, after all, and their reputation for a stiff upper lip was hardly unfounded.

With the crowds securely behind barriers on either side of her exit, she truly felt like a celebrity. Like a sponge, she soaked in the atmosphere and adoration. She looked perfect in a French cuffed white shirt, black pinstripe blazer, and figure hugging designer denim jeans. The newspapers and magazines had begun comparing her style to that of the television star Ellen, and today, sporting glamorous sunglasses, she looked every bit the part.

"This is amazing."

Anna was only a step behind her, head down to avoid photographers. "I couldn't have written a better script."

One sign read: *The voice of global gay rights: Felicity Bastone.* Of course the book had gone global from day one, but Felicity had no idea she was being looked upon to lead a global movement. The thought both excited and terrified her.

A reporter yelled from behind the barricade. "One quote, Miss Bastone. Please give us one quote."

So as to avoid any moments of unpredictability, Dee had prohibited all media interaction unless it could be controlled. The last thing they needed was Flic becoming embroiled in a debate on the street, in front of cameras and in front of the world. It was imperative she remained positive and in no way incited violence or provoked the public in such an open forum.

The one quote the reporter requested seemed obvious to her. Filled with adrenaline and emotion, she held her arms out, spun around soaking in the crowd, and simply said, "Love is love."

The crowd clapped and cheered as if she'd just promised to buy them all dinner. Momentum grew and a "Love is love" chant erupted from her followers. Her opposers remained silent.

Flic hoped to God someone was recording this scene because she knew that while she would hardly forget it, she wanted to be able to relive the moment later. Nearing the car, the chant increased in volume. This was no longer about book sales. She already knew she would live a comfortable life from the proceeds. This was about a far greater beast, and she was ready and willing to lead a revolution that could potentially change the world.

As she approached the sparkling black Hummer, she turned to wave one last time. Anna had already entered the vehicle and was waiting for Flic to join her with a beaming smile. Desperate to see and be seen by the majority of people, she stepped onto the doorframe and turned to wave to her adoring fans. Max attempted to persuade her into the vehicle, but she ignored his suggestions, preferring to prolong her moment of fame.

In bright contrast to the crisp whiteness of the shirt beneath her blazer, the perfectly circular red dot of a laser sight—no bigger than a five-pence piece—that danced back and forth in the center of her chest took only milliseconds to register.

Max was the first to respond, but the loud cracking of a gunshot drowned out his words. "Get down," he yelled. Flic could barely hear him and only understood when he lunged toward her.

In painful slow motion, Max launched himself, his arms extending to circle her waist while his shoulder connected with her stomach. Initially, his force was solid, but reasonable under the circumstances, until his forward motion became fierce and violent.

Frightened, Flic largely resisted the backward motion as her body turned rigid with tension and terror. Unable to oppose Max's momentum, she scraped her back and belted her head on the roof of the car before her body buckled under the movement.

The back of her head crashed down hard on Anna's leg, but there was little time to register that pain as Max landed heavily on top of her. The vehicle lurched into action, and although she wanted to scream at the driver to stop because the door wasn't shut, it felt like there was no air in her lungs to push the words out.

Frantically, Max crawled on top of her, reaching for the headrest and holding on as the vehicle sped away, cornering hard in the process. It occurred to Flic that the reason Max collided with her so hard was because the bullet hit him, propelling him forward. She freed her arms and began feeling the length of his back, wanting desperately to provide something to assist in stemming the blood flow while he heroically protected her. Instead of feeling his body under his jacket, she felt something hard and smooth. A wave of nauseous relief rippled through her as she realized he was wearing a Kevlar vest. The feeling was so intense tears streamed down her face.

The sense of respite was short-lived, however, when the back window was shattered. This time Anna screamed and bent forward, covering, with her upper body, the exposed parts of Flic Max couldn't reach.

Lurching back and forth in the back of the car, the rear door flailing open, continually bouncing off Max's legs, the three of them endured the chaos until the Hummer finally came to a halt.

Anna sat back first, taking stock, and began screaming, "She's been shot. Please, someone help."

Flic's heart sank. She hadn't realized. *I've been shot?*

Flic honestly thought she'd survived unscathed. It must have been the shock overtaking her senses because she couldn't feel any pain other than the bump on her head, which was thoroughly throbbing.

Anna held aloft a hand soaked in blood. "Oh, God, please no. Don't die, Flic, please."

I'm going to die? Flic wasn't prepared to hear that information, and panic gripped her. Unsure if her mind had begun playing tricks on her and the end was looming sooner than she anticipated, she began thrashing and screaming for Max to get off her. She hadn't realized she'd been shot, let alone was dying, so she wasn't even sure in reality if she was moving a muscle.

"Call an ambulance," screamed Anna, her voice reaching an unnerving high pitch. "She's bleeding. Someone help."

"Already en route," the driver announced.

It all happened so quickly that while Anna was screaming, Max was moving to sit above Flic to assess any damage. Help arrived in a rush of sirens and yelling.

Flic wished she knew where the hell the bullet had struck. It couldn't have been her heart because she'd probably be dead already, and if it were a lung, she hoped the other one had enough capacity to continue to pump oxygen through her until they could repair any damage. She really wished she hadn't been shot.

"Where am I shot, Max?" Her voice was surprisingly strong.

Without warning, the other rear door opened and Anna was dragged from beneath Flic by the police who quickly handed her over to paramedics. Anna disappeared from earshot almost immediately.

Another wave of panic filled Flic when she realized that Anna had been taken away. Shot and possibly dying, Flic yearned for Anna to stay with her.

"Max," she screamed. "Tell me how bad it is, damn it."

A paramedic entered the vehicle. Without introduction or formality, her gloved hands touched Flic all over. Max was doing the same, and Flic was terrified about what they might find.

"Please, just tell me how bad it is."

The paramedic scruffed Flic's collar and pulled the shirt apart, sending buttons flying. Her eyes scanned Flic's torso before she exhaled deeply and sat back on her haunches. Cradling the base of Flic's skull, she fingered the back of her head before announcing, "Got it."

Got what? Flic wasn't coping with the lack of communication. "Am I shot in the head?"

Suddenly, Max was off her and another paramedic took his place. With excellent English, he spoke calmly to her. "We don't think you've been shot, madam."

The news was such a relief, Flic began crying.

"You have a deep laceration to your head."

Flic could have kissed the man delivering the good news, but if she wasn't shot, then Max was. "Max," she screamed.

Max's head filled the remainder of the gap through the door. "I'm here, love."

"Are you shot?"

He tapped the jacket across his chest. "Hit with a bullet, yes, but not shot."

"What?"

"I've got a bulletproof vest on. Bullet hit me right in the middle of the back. Better me than you today, sweetheart."

Flic remembered feeling the vest. She felt relief beyond words.

Max moved away and it was Anna's face who filled the space. "Oh, thank God you're not shot."

Flic smiled. It was all she could do to reassure Anna she was okay. "I smacked my head hard though, I think. Bloody hurts."

Anna briefly glanced down at Flic's exposed torso. "I saw blood and thought you'd been shot."

"I think when Max tackled me into the car, my head clouted the roof, but it all happened so fast. What went wrong?"

Anna shook her head. "No idea. The police aren't saying much. Although, I'm not convinced they have much to say at this early stage."

All the bravado in the world wouldn't have stopped Flic's tears now. "Someone tried to kill me, Anna. Jesus Christ, I could be dead."

"I know, honey, but you're fine, and the police are going to protect you for the time being."

"Don't leave me?"

"I won't. I'm right here." Anna reached for her hand and squeezed it. "I'm just so glad you're okay."

Much discussion surrounded the police's ability to secure their current location. It was too early for conclusive answers. In fact, they had little idea so soon after the event about what actually happened, so the decision was made to transport them all to a hospital. Hospitals had security cameras, and beyond having Flic stitched up and Max checked out, it would be a logical place to coordinate the next move. History suggested that the shooter, or shooters, would need to regroup in the aftermath of the failed assassination, so the threat, for the time being, had diminished.

Now sitting in the rear of the vehicle, Flic was being prepared to dash with the police, paramedics, and Anna to an ambulance. The bandage wrapped around her head felt too tight, her eyes struggled to focus, and noises seemed muffled. In a sudden movement, she was hauled from the vehicle and rushed the ten steps to the waiting rear of the ambulance.

For the second time in three days, Flic found herself en route to hospital, only this time in a crowded ambulance with the stakes substantially higher.

While the paramedics took her vitals, the word *assassination* echoed in her ears, and again, for the second time this week, she vomited, only this time no one had noticed she was about to.

CHAPTER FIFTEEN

During the early hours of the following morning, Anna tucked Flic into bed, placed a large glass of water on the bedside table, and promised to check on her frequently. Under advice from French police, they had retreated to a secluded chateau where a doctor administered a sedative and Flic was finally able to relax.

"My head's all over the place," Flic said.

"That's only natural, but the sedative will help."

Dee had left England as soon as she received word of the attempted murder. Anna eyed the pill bottle and wished she could take one of the magic sedatives and curl up for the next day or so, but she had work to do. She wasn't sure when, but she'd deal with what she'd witnessed later.

Flic's eyes looked heavy. "Make sure you get some rest, too."

"Never mind me." Anna winked. "Dee turns into a banshee without enough sleep."

Flic smiled faintly. "Where's your room?"

Anna's priority had been Flic and coordinating Dee's arrival. She'd not given her own sleeping arrangements a single thought. "I'll find a room close by. Don't worry."

Flic began to cry. "I know this is too much to ask, but can you come back here?"

Anna hesitated.

"Please? Don't make me beg you. I don't want to be alone. My head won't stop thinking, and if I wake I won't know where you are, where anyone is."

"Of course." Anna couldn't say no. The desperation in Flic's voice frightened her. "Now try and get some sleep."

"Wait with me until I drop off?"

Anna glanced around the room. From the tote bag she knew Flic carried all her personal belongings in, like her laptop and journal, she took the latest novel Flic was reading, opened it at the marked page, and began reading.

Barely a minute passed before Flic twitched a little and her breathing became heavy and sleep finally took hold.

Anna was shattered, but returned to the living room. For the first time in their ten-year history of working together, Dee Macintosh pulled Anna into a tight hug and allowed her to cry on her shoulder. Witnessing the failed assassination of anyone, let alone someone you know and especially when you were also in the firing line, was enough to break anyone. It broke Anna.

"I'm here, honey. I'm so sorry you had to go through that yesterday." Dee spoke gently in Anna's ear.

After many minutes, Anna gathered herself and poured them both a brandy. "This certainly makes the fracas in Dublin look like a tea party."

"She'll be all right, you know."

"Will she?" Dee hadn't been there when the shots were fired, when Flic's blood had covered her. She'd barely seen Flic before the doctor whisked her away to look her over and give her the pills. Anna briefly wondered who'd be looking out for Flic's best interests. She knew who'd be looking out for Griffin's and the book, but would all this only serve to demonstrate to Flic that her life wasn't her own anymore? The life someone had just attempted so efficiently to take from her. Anna felt a weighty responsibility fall upon her. "Dublin turned her into a nervous wreck. What will this do to her?"

"We'll get her some help if she needs it. She'll get through it. I promise. We all will."

Anna wasn't so sure. "She needs to be given the choice to go on or not."

Dee eyed her warily. "I'm sure she'll say if she can't go on."

"That's not fair, Dee."

"If she pulled out now, that would serve you well, Anna. Be careful what you're saying."

"And that's not fair either." It was just as much of a shock to her as anyone else to be thinking about Flic's well-being and not about saving her church. "Dee, someone tried to kill her today. She feels alone and frightened. She's like a child. This is cruel and it's hurting her." Anna paced the room. "She fell asleep crying just now." Her voice began to fail her. "All she wanted was not to wake up alone."

Dee nodded and sighed. "You'll stay with her tonight, then?"

The thought of sharing a bed with Flic both frightened and comforted Anna. In truth, she didn't want to be alone either, but the idea of sharing a bed with Flic, even under these extreme circumstances, was messing with her head. But then, someone hadn't tried to kill her today. It was Flic the bullet was aimed at. She needed to put Flic's needs above her own. "Yes, of course."

"She's grown to rely on you a lot, hasn't she?"

"Her life has changed so much since writing this book. I think today was the first time she really enjoyed the attention and what does she get for it? An attempted murder."

"I think she should go on, Anna. And before you growl at me, it's not for Griffin's or for the money, but for her own good. This is no longer about the pope. It's about love and equality and acceptance. If she fades into the distance now, her message will fade and the cause will be set back years. She needs to go on."

Before the conversation could continue, Max and a police officer arrived. The police had agreed to conduct a regular drive-by, and thus far, no one had claimed responsibility for the assassination attempt. The four of them had things to discuss, and with practiced style, Dee transitioned from friend to unrelenting leader. She set her brandy glass aside and calmly said, "Right. Let's work out how to move forward."

Flic roused and heard voices so she knew Anna wouldn't be there. She rolled over and checked the bed just to make sure. She was alone.

Her head ached, but without the painkillers the doctors had given her, she imagined the dull throb would be an unbearable cracking pain. Her wound was sutured and now sported a six-centimeter-long bald patch where a sliver of hair had been shaved to facilitate the procedure.

Since the world was under increasing attack from terrorists or those with a catastrophic agenda, to question if someone would "claim responsibility" for breaking the law was less absurd than it sounded. She had wondered if some religious, homophobic freak with a bee in his bonnet would bother to claim responsibility for fucking up her murder. She'd refused to contemplate the alternative—that an organized group had somehow paid for a professional job, but even then she didn't understand why they'd admit failure. Perhaps they wouldn't. Perhaps they'd keep going until the job was completed. Her entire body covered with goose bumps before she had a chance to push the thought from her mind.

In any event, she had welcomed the tiny little pill that ensured a sound sleep, not that it had lasted nearly long enough, but she felt drowsy enough to slip back into slumber. She had to believe Anna wouldn't disappoint her, and she allowed her eyes to close again in the hope Anna wouldn't be too far away.

Anna looked at her watch. It was close to three in the morning before the police officer left and she, Dee, and Max could finally go to bed. Dee held her back after they bid good night to each other. "Just be there for her. She needs you now," she said.

Anna quietly entered the bedroom, and Flic was thankfully still sleeping. She looked so peaceful, it hurt to know she'd be waking up to a horrible day. They'd discussed the best way to handle Flic, but Anna knew what she should do and that was to focus on the positive; they were all okay, just a few scrapes and stitches. Obviously, that didn't detract from the fact that someone had attempted to kill her, but every time Flic would be frightened by that thought, Anna would remind her that she was relatively unharmed. She hoped her reassurance would be enough.

Previously, when Flic had asked her to stay, it had felt odd knowing she would undress and sleep next to another woman, but now that it was actually happening, she couldn't imagine being anywhere else. There was no way Anna could sleep away knowing Flic could wake frightened and alone. She quickly changed into her pajamas and slipped beneath the covers. She'd also contemplated just sleeping under a blanket on top of the bed, but that now seemed a redundant thought. There was nothing sexual about the situation. It didn't require dilution.

As she settled into a comfortable position, both she and Flic facing the same direction, she felt a hand reach back in search of her. Without hesitation, Anna took the hand and gently squeezed. Flic's fingers slowly slipped through hers, and as the hand withdrew, Anna watched Flic curl into a tight ball. They both slept.

Although the heavy curtains gave the impression it was still nighttime, the thin crack of light where they met told a different story. Feeling drowsy from the sedative but no longer drowsy enough to doze, Flic reluctantly edged her eyes open. Gaining consciousness by the second, she took stock of where she lay. She was on her side and could feel comforting warmth against her back. Becoming increasingly aware, she realized Anna's arm was draped over her and tucked firmly on her shoulder. The embrace was strong and not half-hearted as one might expect when holding, in bed, someone you'd barely touched. Flic reminded herself that Anna had been there too. This was not an ordinary situation. On a normal day, Flic would have loved to have woken in this position. The rhythmic, soft breath blowing on her neck was soothing. It was impossible to know if Anna was there out of a sense of duty or friendship. Flic decided she didn't care.

Then the flashbacks came. Thick and fast.

Tears fell onto the pillow. Did she really have to face the day and face reality? She wanted to pretend for as long as she could that Anna was holding her under different circumstances and that this scene would be replicated tomorrow and every other day after that, but most of all, she wanted to pretend that no one had tried to murder her yesterday.

"Shhh, it's okay." Anna sounded sleepy.

Flic tensed. "How did you know it wasn't?"

"I don't know. I just knew you were sad."

It surprised Flic that Anna didn't attempt to break their connection. "Are *you* okay? You know, after yesterday."

Anna squeezed. "Besides thinking you had been shot, yes, I think I'm doing okay."

"Who tried to kill me, Anna?" As the words spilled from her mouth, fear constricted her chest and the tears progressed to sobs.

"Come here." Anna turned Flic to face her, pulling her tight. "I don't know. Hopefully, the police will have some answers today."

"Thanks for…" The words were there, but saying them out loud would break the illusion that Anna was in bed with Flic because she wanted to be, not because she felt sorry for her.

"You don't have to thank me. Someone attempting to shoot you has had a profound effect on all of us."

"But this, this isn't you, is it?"

"I disagree. Being here for someone I care about is very much me."

"But me?"

"You challenge nearly all of my beliefs. I can't deny that, but the one thing that has become glaringly obvious to me in the last twenty-four hours, is that you and I are friends. I care for you. I care very much for you as it turns out."

"But I told you I like you. Hasn't that ruined everything?"

"I don't think so. I think we've set clear boundaries."

"I'm sorry I like you."

"Gee, thanks."

"You know what I mean. It complicates things."

Anna shrugged. "It only complicates them if we allow that to happen. I think we can keep on top of it."

Flic left it at that. She'd given Anna ample opportunity to escape, but to her relief, she'd stayed. What she really needed now was coffee.

Anna extracted herself from the embrace. "How about I see if I can source a coffee?"

"Are you a mind reader?"

"Funny. But don't sound so surprised. I just happen to know you."

Chapter Sixteen

It wasn't a shock to see everyone dressed so normally, except for Dee. Flic never contemplated the day she would see Dee Macintosh in anything other than designer suits and dresses. In the space of a day, everything had changed.

Dee advanced toward her with outstretched arms. "Oh, Flic, how are you today, my love?"

She allowed the hug from Dee to last an appropriate time before she squared her shoulders and asked, "Do we have some answers on yesterday?"

Dee nodded. "Not exactly, but let me introduce you."

The man standing to the rear of the room was a French police officer. She didn't catch his name, but she thought it sounded roughly like the designer Pierre Cardin. The person who sparked her interest the most was Agent Bethan Stark from MI5.

"MI5?" Flic couldn't help but sound surprised. "Someone taking a pop at me is hardly a matter of national security."

Agent Stark smiled, barely committing an emotion either way. "We hope not, but your book has stirred a rather large pot. We're currently monitoring the toes upon which you might have trodden."

Flic raised her eyebrows. Were Agent Stark's qualifications in international relations or Shakespeare?

"We need to show you something," said Dee. She ushered Flic to a laptop set up in the adjacent room. "Your sales figures, last updated at midnight GMT."

The figures were nearly double the previous figures Flic had seen two days ago.

Dee pointed to another. "Hits on your website." The figure was in the millions.

"And the social media supplier has had to suspend your account due to the sheer volume of interest generated globally. Their server can't keep up. In its absence, the public have created their own pages. Some are following you, hating you, loving you, inciting violence, the list is endless. Others are attacking the church, some are defending it, some are homophobic, and some are pro choice. The dominant positive theme that is associated with you all over the world, however, is 'Love is love.'"

Flic wondered if she had begun something she had no idea how to end, or more unnerving, had she started something she had little control over. "I presume the authorities are shutting down the dangerous sites? I mean, surely recruiting extremists to bomb the Vatican or kidnap the pope is inciting violence?"

"Yes," said Anna. "But they're understandably struggling to keep up with them all. As soon as one's shut down, another dozen pop up in its place."

"Fucking hell. What have we done?" Flic couldn't stomach the screens and what they stood for. She turned away. "I can't hide forever though, can I?"

She caught Dee and Anna exchange glances. "What?"

"We weren't sure if you'd want to go on," said Dee.

Neither was Flic. "It's not so much that I want to go on, it's more that I can't accept quitting." She searched Anna's face for answers. "Is continuing the right thing to do?"

Dee went to speak, obviously worried about what Anna might say, but Anna jumped in first. "As long as we can get your protection sorted out so you remain as safe as possible, yes, I think you should finish what you've begun."

Dee breathed an audible sigh of relief.

Pierre Cardin cleared his throat. "The trajectories of the bullets indicate the shooter was not at ground level. In fact they were at least eight floors above the street."

"Out a window?" asked Anna.

"We think not because the second bullet, fired through the rear window of your vehicle, matches that of the first and was therefore fired from the same gun. You were traveling down a different street when the second bullet hit. This leads us to believe that the shooter was on a roof. We've narrowed down that location."

"Please tell me the building has some sort of functioning CCTV?" asked Dee.

Everything hinged on this, and Flic was all ears.

"Yes."

Thank God.

"And no."

"What? What do you mean yes and no?"

"We think we have footage of a possible male suspect, but the CCTV on one of the side fire exits is broken. The shooter could have escaped through that exit, but in the interim, of course we are looking closely at the suspect we have vision of. So far, the timings all add up. We think it's our man."

"The building, is it a hotel?" asked Anna.

"Yes, madam, and while their security is obviously questionable, their CCTV system is adequate. A hotel is a preferred option for a shooter. Seeing a member of the public in hallways and elevators is normal practice, so you can remain undetected for longer. The downside for the shooter is that hotels have many more cameras than say, an office block, for example. A stranger is more likely to stand out negotiating different floors in an office building."

"So the obvious question is why? Why try to kill me?" Simply saying the words aloud gave Flic a chilling shudder.

"That we don't know. Of course there are obvious reasons, but until we can get our hands on the suspect to find out which grudge he's holding against you, we're flying blind."

"So you're saying you don't know if it's the homophobic grudge against gays, the pro-Catholic grudge against my book, the pro-Catholic homophobic grudge against me because they believe I've in some way ousted the pope, or perhaps someone just hates my writing."

"Your writing's not that bad." Anna grinned.

"I don't suppose anyone mentioned on social media that I'd be better off dead?"

"If you search for key words such as kill, murder, stab, shoot, hang? Probably close to half a million," said Agent Stark.

Half a million. Flic sat before her knees buckled beneath her.

"The word rape on its own racks up a good few thousand," added Agent Stark.

"Christ, thousands of people would like to see me raped. What the fuck sick world do we live in?"

"Very few of them would see their comments come to fruition. Many of these people are just letting off steam."

"Right, well, next time your mother pulls in front of me at an intersection, don't mind me when I yell to her that she's a shit driver and she deserves nothing but a good raping!" Flic lost control.

Anna was by her side, her arm around her waist. "Hey. It's okay. We're all frightened and angry that this has happened." Her hand slid under Flic's jumper, her touch providing enough distraction to calm Flic down.

Agent Stark pushed her hands deep in her pockets. "That's not possible anyway." She eyed Flic squarely. "My mother is dead."

"That's enough, ladies." Dee's timing was a little late, but it was a welcomed intervention. "We're all a bit stressed. Anna, why don't you take Flic to the kitchen for some breakfast? She needs to eat and so do you for that matter."

Flic stormed from the room and down the hall.

"Um, the kitchen is this way." Anna cocked her head in the opposite direction.

Flic's storming turned to trudging. "I was out of line. I need to apologize to her."

"Later, yeah? She knows you're under pressure."

"Her mother's dead."

"And you can't change that. See her after breakfast."

"I'm really not hungry. I feel empty, like hollow if you know what I mean."

"You need to eat."

Footsteps approached behind them. "You need to eat, Felicity. You faint if you don't eat, remember?" After entering the kitchen, Dee emptied the contents of the fridge onto the table. It would hardly provide a gourmet spread, but it would do. "We have work to discuss."

Flic picked at a thick slice of baguette. Her spirits lifted marginally when she spotted some orange juice.

"The dates for the US are being finalized as we speak, but as of yesterday, they need revising with security in mind. You're now a high risk, and the cost of protecting you has more than quadrupled."

"No Christmas bonus for me then?"

"Sweetheart, you've earned enough bonuses to last you a lifetime. You've written a book that will sell over one million copies in hardcover alone. You're just a pain in the ass to protect now." She patted Flic's shoulder and winked. "It's okay. I promise we'll work this all out."

Anna pushed her hands through her hair. "There are strong indications the Vatican will be making an announcement soon. So we need to get back on top of our game."

Flic struggled to concentrate, but it was no use. "My brain is all mush. Is that good or bad for us at this stage?"

Dee looked to Anna for the answer. "It's inevitable. Don't worry. I figured that by this stage you might be finding it all a little overwhelming. I believe an announcement on the pope and his sexuality will be any day now. It's simply a matter of time. Our strategy understandably takes into account both a denial and admission by the Vatican, but an admission is almost assured. What happened yesterday, however, was *not* in our strategy."

Flic was no defeatist. "So, the show must go on?"

Dee smothered butter on a croissant and filled it with ham and cheese and handed it to Flic. "Eat."

"You do know croissants are made with a ton of butter, right?"

"Yes. I do know that. Now eat. And yes, the show will go on as soon as we arrange for additional people to keep you safe."

"Is that where Max is?"

"Yes, he's liaising with experts to have your personal security sorted ASAP."

"Not just mine." A flashback of Max and Anna frantic in the car yesterday filled her head. "Everyone's life was in danger."

Dee touched her shoulder. "And everyone will be protected, I promise."

Flic couldn't believe that it had come to this.

❖

The day passed with little input required from Flic. Anna checked on her and looked at the stitches in her head late in the afternoon, but besides that, she was left to her own devices and spent most of her time wandering in and out of what she called the "control" room. The gist of the conversation rarely changed—security.

Max and Dee finally sat her down to discuss their completed plan. She struggled to concentrate on the details, but the upshot of it all was that a Scottish firm, mostly staffed with specialist ex-servicemen, would supply a team to coordinate her security. Max would liaise with her and then the team. She would have to get used to a personal bodyguard and limited social engagements for the foreseeable future. On any other day, such a suggestion would have seemed downright ridiculous, but today she shrugged. Her world was changing, and considering she was lucky to be alive, it could only be for the better.

The tour was scaled up and down simultaneously. Up because the venues changed from bookstores to actual auditoriums or conference centers, and down because all smaller localities were canceled completely. She had hoped they would cancel Italy altogether, but so far no one had mentioned it. In her mind, touring the pope's homeland with a controversial book was, at the very least, unpredictable. But then, that's what she had a team of security specialists for, apparently.

If the moment she realized someone had made a calculated attempt to end her life was frightening enough, every second she spent reliving the nightmare was torturous. Flic was feeling tormented so she called Max and Anna to her room.

"I know I should probably speak to you about this separately, but I'm not sure I have it in me to do this twice." Her emotions ran high. She silently cursed her weakness. "Yesterday, two things happened that I would very much like to avoid happening again." Oxygen seemed sparse in the spacious room and she breathed deeply.

"Are you okay?" Anna moved toward her, but Flic waved her back.

"I'm fine, honestly. Just bear with me while I get this out." Her weak smile did little to reassure her audience. "What you did for me yesterday, please don't do again."

"Flic, what exactly are you talking about?" Anna shrugged, clueless, but Max nodded knowingly.

"I don't want either of you putting yourself between me and a bullet ever again; do you understand me?"

"I was wearing a vest, love. It was a calculated risk on my behalf," said Max.

"And I just reacted on instinct. Ducking for cover was a natural move, shielding you was easy when you were on my lap." Anna took her hands. "Please don't make this bigger than it is. I know you're wondering how you would be coping if one of us had been injured or worse, but we're all fine, all here in one piece, and all grateful no one was hurt."

The guilt Flic had been experiencing had weighed heavily upon her. She felt better for having had the discussion. "Just mind yourselves in the future. Promise me that?"

Max draped a bulky arm around her shoulders. "How about we mind each other? Deal?"

All three nodded.

There was a purposeful knock on the door, and Agent Stark poked her head in. "Thought you might like to know they have the suspect in custody."

Max pumped the air with his fist.

"So soon? Are you serious?" It all seemed so fast. Flic wasn't sure if she wanted to laugh or cry.

"Any preliminary reports?" Max was all business.

Stark leaned against the doorframe "Claims he was working alone." She shook her head. "But it's not adding up."

"And what was his motive?" Flic asked. "I mean which cause is he fighting exactly?"

"He reckons he fancied a bit of notoriety, hates gays, and hates books apparently, too."

"And based on that he thought he'd just kill me?" Flic wasn't buying it either.

Max shook his head. "If it looks like a duck and quacks like a duck, chances are it's a duck, but this sounds too good to be true."

Stark nodded. "We've found evidence that he's a member of a breakaway Opus Dei group."

"Isn't Opus Dei already a breakaway group?" Flic was beginning to wonder if Dan Brown was lurking in the shadows, poised to write a best seller based on her life. "This isn't *The Da Vinci Code*. It all sounds so ridiculously clichéd."

"Cliché or not," said Stark, "we know he's part of an extreme Catholic sect, but he's not saying a damn word."

"I suppose he's an albino wearing a hessian sack and all?"

"I'm pretty sure it wasn't a sack in the movie," said Max.

"Whatever! This is getting beyond a joke."

Anna had remained silent until now. "He tried to kill you, Flic. That's hardly a joke."

"So he's lying about his involvement in Opus Dei—"

"No. He's admitting to limited involvement in Opus Dei, but beyond that, he's not saying a word."

"And what is this breakaway group calling themselves?"

"Ordinem Castitate," said Stark.

"The Order of Purity." Flic had picked up enough Latin during her research on the Catholic faith to know the translation. "Give me strength."

"Quit making a joke of this," said Anna. "Regardless of how bizarre this seems, they were pretty darn serious when they shot at you yesterday, so I don't care what they call themselves, I just want to know that you're safe. That we're all safe."

Flic studied Anna. She was frightened. They were all scared in one way or another, but Anna amazed her. She was the glue holding them all together. Flic felt selfish—no more jokes. It touched her to know Anna cared enough not to find any of it amusing. Flic squeezed Anna's hand. "Has he been charged?" she asked.

"No. Not yet. He's not saying a lot. But don't worry. If he's so much as scratched his ass the wrong way lately, we'll find out. We'll keep digging into this Order of Purity. Something will turn up." She shrugged. "Or we'll waterboard him and he'll tell us everything we need to know."

MI5 were beginning to scare Flic almost more than the crazies of the world. "You'll really waterboard him?"

"You want to find out why he did this, don't you?"

"Yeah, but isn't that illegal?"

Stark gently tapped Flic's shoulder in a playful fashion. "I'm kidding. He'll be questioned with all the courtesy in the world." She grinned and left.

Flic wasn't so sure about that. She turned to see Anna staring at her.

Anna coughed, her focus obviously directed back to the issue at hand. "Um, call me daft, but what's waterboarding?"

"Come on," said Flic. "Let's discuss torture techniques over dinner."

They sat silently opposite each other at the table. It was an easy silence. Anna was lost in her own thoughts and she imagined Flic was, too. There was much to consider. Anna liked neat and resolved loose ends, but finding out about this Order of Purity only served to generate more questions, not answers. She had thought that by catching the person who tried to murder Flic, it would all be behind them, except the opposite was true. Nothing felt resolved, and she wasn't convinced the threat against Flic had abated at all.

"What have I done, Anna?" asked Flic. "I look at you and see how this is hurting you, and if I multiply that hurt by the billions of Catholic believers all over the world, I'm beginning to wonder if it's all gone too far. If I've gone too far."

"None of this is your fault," said Anna. The words were out before she deeply contemplated her response.

Flic laughed. "You can't possibly believe that. You tried to tell me what the implications of this book might be and I ignored you. I think I've underestimated the power of faith. People are willing to kill for this. Kill me. You of all people must surely think that this is *all* my fault."

Anna didn't. The extremist group branching out beyond Opus Dei hadn't formed as a result of Flic's book or her actions or the Love is Love campaign. "It's not lip service. You haven't encouraged or facilitated a group of people loosely operating under the Catholic umbrella to kill for their cause. These people aren't true Catholics. Just because they purport to take their faith to an extreme level, doesn't make them true believers, it makes them a bunch of self-serving idealistic twats."

"Wow, Anna, you should say what you really mean."

Anna smiled and reached for Flic's hand. "It's not your fault."

"It *feels* like my fault."

"Well, that's another issue altogether." Anna withdrew and sat back. "What I assumed your agenda was, and what your agenda has turned out to be, are two different things. I was wrong about you, and as much as I don't want the pope to be gay and as much as I can't stand what is happening to my church, I do understand that you honestly believe his sexuality is neither here nor there in relation to his ability to perform his job." Her words flowed and they were heartfelt. It was the first time she'd experienced any clarity in her feelings and opinion toward Flic. "Nobody deserves to be hunted and murdered for that."

Flic looked taken aback, and Anna felt heat rise up her neck. Had she said too much?

"Thank you for clearing that up," said Flic. "It means a lot that you would think that, let alone say it. I know that must have been difficult."

Anna laughed. "No, not really." Flic's eyes widened. "Oh, don't worry, it's as much of a shock to me as I'm sure it is to you, but it wasn't difficult. Don't get me wrong, I don't want the pope to be gay. I don't want the pope to be in love or be in a relationship—unless it's with God—and I certainly don't want him to fail billions of people, but I do at least now understand how you see this. How others might see this."

"But you don't agree?"

"Give me a break here, one step at a time. I'm only just accepting that there's people on earth who aren't troubled by a gay pope."

"And you're friends with one of those people and all," said Flic.

Yes. Anna was Flic's friend, and it was a good feeling, a comforting feeling. But there was something else playing on her mind, something more immediate, and it concerned the sleeping arrangements for that evening. She'd left her belongings in Flic's room, but she wasn't sure if she was needed again. "Has my friend thought about where she'd like me to sleep tonight?"

Flic's eye twinkled and she appeared to do her best to hide her cheeky grin, but she failed miserably. "Same place as last night, but ideally you should lose the pajamas this time."

"You're not amusing, you know. You need to get that filter looked at. You might offend someone one of these days."

"Have I offended you?"

"No. But I know you're joking. And you have an appalling sense of humor."

Flic's eyes became watery.

Anna cut the attitude. "You're making jokes because you're frightened, and when you close your eyes, you can't stop thinking about what happened. Am I right?"

Flic eyed her in surprise.

"Don't worry. It's happening to me, too." Anna had never had anything quite as traumatic as witnessing an assassination attempt on her friend, but her ability to pray and center herself in the arms of God had, until now, served her well. Now, she found the antidote to her anxiety sitting opposite her. Talking to God calmed her sufficiently, but watching Flic soldier on through the crisis settled her nerves almost completely. For the first time ever, Anna found strength in another human being. "If it's okay with you, I'll ask Max to drag another mattress into your room?"

"I was only joking about the pajama thing." Flic looked sad.

"I know, and honestly, I wasn't offended." She smiled in reassurance. "I just think it's better this way."

"No blurred lines."

"No blurred lines."

CHAPTER SEVENTEEN

The world of fashion had reached Kevlar bulletproof vests, unbeknownst to Flic who imagined they would all be like the bulky ones the police sometimes wore. Her jacket of choice was the lightweight concealable vest in white, manufactured right there in Berlin where they were preparing for their first public appearance since the shooting. It did nothing for her figure.

"What little boobs I have are gone." She examined herself in the mirror. Anna rolled her eyes.

"You look fine."

"What about my head?"

"Well, there's little we can do about your ugly mug," said Anna.

Tobias, their friendly bulletproof jacket expert, laughed as he produced a bulletproof helmet with a face shield. "Would madam like it in black or, let me see, ah yes, black?"

"Okay, point taken, but what if the next nutter is a better shot than the last?"

Not surprisingly, Max found it difficult to suppress his smile. "There won't be another one. The vest is just precautionary."

"It seems too thin. Can it really stop a bullet?" Flic wasn't convinced.

"It's stab proof, too." Tobias knew his stuff. "It is a perfect fit." He jiggled and jostled the vest about. "And you'll be able to wear normal clothes over it. Maybe your fans will just think you've had too many bratwurst sausages."

Flic punched his muscular arm. "You're not helping."

Tobias smiled. "I'm a good cook. Want me to help by cooking you dinner later on?"

Without skipping a beat, Anna stepped forward. "I don't know if you know, but Felicity is a lesbian author who's written a book about a gay pope."

"Whoa, steady on," Flic said with a grin. "It's just dinner."

Anna took her aside. "He's flirting with you."

"I know. Kinda cute, don't you think?"

"No, it's inappropriate and disrespectful to you and your sexuality, so, no, I don't think it's cute."

"Oh, give me a break. He's harmless."

"Really?"

"Are you jealous?"

"What? Hardly. That's ridiculous."

Whistling an annoying little tune, Flic smiled broadly. "I think you're jealous. Who'd have thought?"

Anna shook her head and walked away.

Her team of security specialists were polite, professional, and remarkably skilled at their work. They escorted her to and from events with precision, and if she were honest, she felt like royalty. The team selected expensive hotels for their state-of-the-art facilities and discretion. She was, after all, raking in the big bucks, so her comfort and safety became everyone's number one priority.

Although her bulletproof vest was white and designed to wear under clothing, her entire wardrobe had to be rethought, especially the top half, so a stylist was engaged to select new outfits that would hide the vest, yet keep her looking smart and intellectual.

On the surface, Flic certainly appeared to be enjoying herself, and to some extent, this was true. She certainly felt safer than she had previously. Her accommodation was first class and her book was selling better than ever before, but her life had altered so drastically, she was struggling to keep up. Regular telephone calls to Laura and her family kept her grounded, but they also fueled a sense of homesickness only normality could cure. Unfortunately, she was no longer normal. She was a celebrity in an exclusive club. It was the failed assassination club, and her reluctant membership left her feeling frightened and alone.

With clockwork precision, her scheduled visits to Germany, Austria, and Switzerland proceeded without a glitch. Her exposure to the general public remained limited, and more television appearances were scheduled as a counter measure. To capitalize on British book sales and to provide a break from touring, the United Kingdom was scheduled after Belgium. Flic couldn't wait to return home, if only temporarily.

One evening in bed, Flic reflected on the two weeks that had passed since the shooting. A team of social media and PR experts were running the "Love is Love" campaign that had taken on a life of its own, and already she had agreed to formalize herself as the founder of the movement. Subsequently, dates were tentatively being penciled into her calendar to transition from the *Holy Father, Holy Secret* tour to a "Love is Love" seminar type tour. She couldn't believe the momentum of her message.

To top off everything, her friendship with Anna was no longer strained, but easy and natural. Similar to their first night at dinner, they now avoided excessive talk of work, religion, politics, or sexuality, and surprisingly, they could still fill hours of downtime with interesting conversation. It occurred to Flic that if the criteria for having an intellectual soul mate was everything besides sex and intimacy, she would have found hers, but then, if that person truly was your intellectual soul mate, there would be no exceptions. It was a confusing state of mind and was verging on hypocritical; religion shouldn't get in the way of love or friendship, that was her message, yet here they were avoiding the subject because it got in the way. It was beyond confusing; it was infuriating.

Bruges was the last destination before returning to Britain. That thought alone sent Flic's spirits soaring, and similar to the preparation of all other events for the past two weeks, Flic's routine began with a shower, makeup, and a security briefing before she dressed to leave. The vest, while not initially heavy or cumbersome, could weigh her down after a few hours so she left it until last.

Whilst Flic was applying the finishing touches to her limited makeup, Anna knocked and entered her room. "You look great. Excellent choice."

Black was one of the most effective colors when hiding a bulletproof vest, and she wore a pair of beige chinos, distressed brown leather brogues, a black knitted top, and a tweed jacket. It was one of the outfits her stylist put together. "I feel like I've forgotten my horse or I'm late for the hunt."

Anna looked her up and down. "You look fine."

"Oh, that's a great help."

"You look like a smart author."

"A what?"

"A smart, English author, actually."

"I should change."

"Not at all. Just don't yell 'fox' or you might start a stampede."

"I'm changing."

Anna took Flic by the shoulders. "I'm kidding. You look great. Very wholesome."

Flic pushed her away.

Anna recovered wielding a piece of paper. "Dee's sent this through, and I think you should seriously consider doing it as a publicity piece."

Flic snatched the paper from her hand and read. The document was in two parts, the first being an invitation to attend a gathering for gay Catholic men and women with strong faith, who, by their own volition, established a safe environment to meet, discuss, worship, and practice their religion. Flic smiled. It was a perfect opportunity in so many ways. The second half of the document was Dee's list of reasons why she should attend, the opportunities the invitation provided, and a statement strongly advising her to accept.

She needed little persuasion, but Anna didn't need to know that. "I don't know." Flic shrugged for effect. "Do I really want to get into all of this with a bunch of strangers?"

"We'll invite a journalist along, maybe from *Time* magazine, take some pics. It's a great opportunity, Flic. Dee knows her stuff and so do I. From a PR perspective, it's a gem."

Really? We'll see. "Can I think about it?"

"It's tomorrow. We don't have enough time to get it organized as it is. We really need to make a decision on this now."

"Okay."

Anna sighed in relief.

"Hang on, I said okay because I'll do it on one condition."

"And what's the condition?"

"You come with me."

"Oh, no." Anna shook her head. "Not a chance."

"They're Catholic, for God's sake. Why the hell not?"

"They're gay."

"Whoa there. Back it up and be *very* careful what you say next."

"I mean no disrespect, but they can't be practicing the Catholic faith, not properly. Their chosen lifestyle is not in line with my religious beliefs. I don't want to go."

"Then we're not going. I'll leave it up to you to tell Dee the good news." Flic preoccupied herself with collecting her glasses, tablet, and phone.

"That's out of line, Flic. This should have nothing to do with me."

Flic changed her tack. "I'd very much like you to come with me and see how some people, and I'm not suggesting you have to be one of them, but how some people separate their sexuality and their faith, allowing them to coexist harmoniously."

Anna rolled her eyes, but Flic knew she was wearing her down.

"I'm just asking that you come along. That's all. Be an observer, nothing else." Flic could be persuasive when she had to be. "Please? For me? One little meeting is all I'm asking you to give up your time for. I'd really like for you to come with me."

"If I say no, I suppose you'll tell Dee it was my fault?"

Flic determined it wasn't in her best interest to answer that. "It's only an hour."

"You're blackmailing me?"

Again, Flic avoided the question. "It's an opportunity. Let's take it."

Anna shook her head with resignation. "How do I let you do this to me?"

"Don't act so surprised. You let me do stuff to you all the time."

Anna raised her eyebrows until Flic caught up.

"Well, that just got weird. Obviously, I don't *actually* do things to you. More's the pity, but you know what I mean."

"I let you take advantage of me, that's what I do."

"I really wish you would."

"Pardon? Stop mumbling."

Flic spoke up, suppressing a smile. "How is it that I'm taking advantage of you when you're the boss? I'm the one gallivanting around Europe on *your* schedule. If anyone is being taken advantage of here, it's me. This could be one of your elaborate schemes to get me to agree to something I probably don't want to do. Sometimes you just muddle me up with all your words. See, I'm not even sure if I want to do it or not." She playfully punched Anna on the upper arm. "I'm no match for you, Anna. I bow to your superiority."

"Oh, for God's sake, will you just shut up?" Anna's head lolled back on the headrest of the sofa. She grinned and shook her head. "You're impossible sometimes."

"But you still love me."

"I'll come, but I'm not participating. I won't discuss it with you afterward, and don't think I don't know that the only opportunity this offers is for you, not me."

Flic put her hand over Anna's. "Thank you."

"You must have given your teachers a headache at school."

"Only the sexy ones who would put me over their knee if I was naughty."

"I'll put you over my…" Anna trailed off, embarrassed.

The moment was uncomfortable.

Flic let her off the hook. "So you'll confirm it with Dee and organize the journo?" It took some effort, but she managed to suppress a tone of triumph.

Meeting some of her supporters was certainly a great opportunity. There were a growing number aligning themselves with the Love is Love campaign and also another faction calling themselves the Liberated Catholic Movement—a group openly inclusive and openly Catholic. In one sense, it thrilled her to have such a growing number of supporters willing to place a foot firmly in her camp, but on the other hand, it saddened her that a group of people who'd existed for thousands of years—open-minded, pro choice believers—were finding the need to label themselves. Did the world really need to take a step backward to facilitate a leap forward? Regardless, Flic welcomed the opportunity to meet with this group, and she was delighted Anna would be with her, arm slightly twisted or not.

CHAPTER EIGHTEEN

Flic was amazed when her vehicle pulled up outside a quaint little church surrounded by a leafy and carefully manicured garden. For some reason, she imagined the group being forced to meet in secret at a local football clubroom masquerading as a private yoga group. She was a little less impressed when she found out the building was not now, nor had it ever been, a Catholic Church, but in fact was a converted five-bedroom house purchased by the group with the funds from an anonymous donor who so generously wanted to provide them with a place of worship. Of course there was a catch to such a sizable injection of funds. They weren't to attend normal Mass, and they weren't to actively recruit followers. Although not stated, the anonymous donor was obviously the Catholic Church.

Stealing a glance at Anna, Flic wasn't surprised to detect any emotion other than boredom. Anna had been quieter than usual, and Flic knew she had only come along because she didn't want to explain to Dee that she was the reason it couldn't happen. Flic hoped their friendship would endure the conflict of opinion this visit fueled.

"Thanks again for coming." Flic nudged Anna with her shoulder as they were lead past a country style kitchen and a wonderful space filled with worn leather chairs, heavily cushioned sofas, and a wall with books from floor to ceiling, and finally through to the meeting room.

Helene, the thirtysomething member of the group who'd initiated the meeting, had greeted them warmly, speaking fluent English and brimming with enthusiasm. It was clearly a big deal to have a celebrity in their midst, and a strong waft of home baking floated through the building.

"I'm only doing this for you. I really don't want to be here."

"For me? Don't you mean for Dee?"

Anna rolled her eyes. "No, stupid. For you. I know you want me to see this, so here I am."

Flic eyed her seriously. "I appreciate it. I can't tell you how much, but I do." Anna's admission left Flic a little warm and tingly, and it wasn't until Helene motioned for her to sit with the rest of the congregation that she snapped out of her blissful state.

Helene coughed politely to gain their attention. "If it is okay with you, we will conduct our service as we always do and then afterward, perhaps we can invite discussion over coffee and cake."

Max's stomach rumbled on cue, and they all sat, including the journalist and photographer, as the service began. The photographer had been given a clear brief, along with a list indicating those who wanted their identity, and therefore their face, to remain anonymous—they sat to one side of the meeting room. He had also been directed to avoid long-range shots of the outside of the building, avoiding the possibility that the location could be established.

Flic had attended Mass enough times to know the procedure. They all sat, kneeled, and stood at the appropriate time, even Max who claimed the only God he worshipped produced coffee beans and invented the espresso machine. One day, Flic would research who that person was and have a plaque made in his honor.

Flic wasn't surprised to learn that the responsibility of conducting the service lay with a select few senior members of the congregation. Not senior in authority, but senior in knowledge and training. The atmosphere was inclusive and uplifting; even she could feel the enthusiasm. When she asked Anna if uplifting was a word she would ever use to describe going to church, she replied unless it was a funeral, she always found her experience uplifting.

As expected, coffee was barely served before the questions began. Flic was prepared and was happy to be the center of attention initially, but after her celebrity status was exhausted, she had a few questions of her own. It was her turn to take the floor.

"I suppose my first question, and the question of many homosexuals in the world, is how can you purport to be gay, yet worship and invariably support the Catholic Church?"

In reality, Flic didn't need to know the answer. She believed in freedom of choice, but she had read many documents and Catholic teachings on homosexuality and natural law according to the church. In essence, homosexuality was a sin. The church rejected the idea that people were born gay and suggested that chastity was advisable should you experience strong homosexual tendencies that you might be in danger of acting upon.

A middle-aged man raised his hand first to answer. "I'm not gay." This was not news to Flic; it was in her notes that at least one third of the congregation were not homosexual. "I was raised Catholic, I believe in God, and I've had many an occasion to call on my faith." Flic hoped Anna was listening. "But on the subject of homosexuality, I believe the church is wrong. If you teach the scripture, and only the scripture, texts written thousands of years ago, of course the lesson is what we learn today. But life isn't a text written over two thousand years ago. Life is now. It's my family and friends who are gay. It's their committed love. It's their beautiful personalities. It's their kindness, their generosity, and ultimately, it's their business." He nodded, collecting his thoughts. "That's why the church has it wrong."

The group clapped. Anna remained impassive.

Flic wanted to elaborate. "A friend of mine studied economics. In his lessons, the basic assumption to maintain a steady economy was that manufacturers produced tractors." She shrugged. "Sounds simple doesn't it? But there's more. Consumers, in turn, purchased the tractors and worked the land, and the manufacturers purchased the produce from the farmers. Essentially, they were all producers and consumers. Without fail, the economy existed, neither expanding nor contracting because what was earned was spent." People nodded their understanding. "So, as a demonstration of a basic economy, this model is rather effective."

"Faith isn't a demonstration, though," said Helene.

"No. You're perfectly correct. And in that model, we accept it as a demonstration, or an assumption in economic terms, because it helps us understand the bigger picture. We're not stupid. We all understand that some day, someone might want to do something other than manufacture a tractor. They might fall ill and fail to sow their crop. They might prefer to save their money, or buy a fleet of tractors, all of which throw the basic economy out of kilter."

Flic commanded undivided attention.

"But what if I changed my mind?" she continued. "What if I decided our economy should only be a simple tractor/producer scenario in real life? What if, instead of teaching you this as an assumption or demonstration, I taught it to you as a way of life? What if I taught this to you and promised that when you died you'd move on to the bonus round where you could manufacture airplanes and produce food in factories? And what if these teachings were handed down over hundreds and thousands of years? Based on history, based on what others have been taught, based on what is written, based on what we know, without question, we *should* be manufacturing tractors with the view of dying and going to a place where we can manufacture airplanes, and we *should* be producing crops with the view of dying and being able to produce food in factories. Correct?"

Anna stared at her, eyes wide.

"I know I'm preaching to the converted." Flic's smile was broad. "But unlike the gentleman over there, I don't think the church necessarily has it wrong—I understand they have been driven by years of tradition, years of teachings, years of following—but I do believe they are naive and wrong *not* to change."

Anna coughed. "It's not a sin to have homosexual tendencies controlled by healthy spiritual beliefs."

Flic sat back, no longer the center of attention. She was interested to see how far Anna wanted to explore the subject.

"Of course," said one member, a young man, probably gay if his high-pitched voice and heavy eye makeup was any indication. "It goes back to what Miss Bastone said. We *think* that, because we're *taught* that. Regardless of our teachings, we are smart enough to determine for ourselves that a tendency toward the same sex isn't a sin."

She couldn't help herself; Flic raised her hand, determined to challenge Anna. "If you're all so smart, why do you believe in something you can't prove exists?" Her cheeky grin conveyed her words weren't offensive, but it was a valid question.

The young man answered confidently. "The evidence we are taught relates to changes in the universe, things others call fate or destiny. These are all controlled by God. Life and death is controlled by God. The fact that we are here on earth making decisions, choosing, being guided; something has to control that. That guidance comes from God. Miracles," he said enthusiastically, "are the work of God."

Anna shook her head as if predicting where Flic was going with the conversation.

"Thank you." Flic smiled at the young man whom she'd taken a warm liking to. "What you've just described is faith. A belief. And it has to be, because nothing you just explained to me is proof. If I choose not to board a train that subsequently crashes with no survivors, your response could be that God chose to save me that day. Correct?"

Everyone besides Anna nodded.

"Whereas an equally valid point of view could be that Santa Claus chose to save me that day."

The congregation laughed.

"Prove to me that he didn't," Flic said.

Anna found her voice. "Billions of people around the world don't believe in Santa Claus, but they do believe in God."

"That's completely untrue. Billions of children all over the world believe in Santa Claus."

"Yes, but only because their parents tell them to."

"Exactly!" Flic loved it when a plan came together. "They believe it because we tell them to. Sound familiar?" Flic smiled. "The fact that our parents tell us that a big fat man from the North Pole delivers our presents on Christmas Eve doesn't make it true. The fact that the church continues to condemn homosexuality doesn't make it right. We all have capacity for faith and love. In my world"—she gestured to the room full of amazing people—"love is love."

CHAPTER NINETEEN

"My faith is the most important thing in my life." It was the first time Anna had mentioned anything religious since leaving the meeting the previous day, and she had removed her headphones during the flight back to the UK to address Flic.

"I know. I think that's a wonderful thing to have in your life."

"I enjoyed yesterday."

"You did?"

"I did. I'm an intelligent person, just like you said."

"Without question."

"Then why do I feel so confused?" She replaced the headphones and turned toward the window.

After a moment of contemplation, Flic tapped her on the arm. "Anna?"

Anna removed the earpieces.

"Enlightenment, regardless of which way it goes, is a process. Intelligent people become confused because the process is demanding. Ignorant people rarely have the capacity for enlightenment, or learning and growing as a person." She shrugged. "You're working to find a balance between your head and your heart. It takes time."

"You know, I thought I was brilliant the day I found out Santa wasn't real. I thought I'd cracked the conspiracy. I was dead chuffed with myself. I thought I'd outsmarted everyone."

"It's a great thing to believe in as a child though, isn't it?"

"I feel like I'm the one who's been outsmarted now."

"Why?"

"It doesn't matter." She replaced her earbuds, signifying an end to the conversation.

Pushing Anna was a mistake. Flic let it slide.

❖

Elated to be back on British soil and in one piece after the Paris fiasco, Flic was yet again whisked away to a hotel. Going home wasn't an option, not until she could purchase a gated and fenced property and install a security system. Laura reckoned she could break into Flic's flat with her eyes closed and her hands tied behind her back, so she'd moved her belongings to a storage facility and her flat was up for rent. Apparently, to rent the property of esteemed author Felicity Bastone was a status symbol and the real estate agent was negotiating a figure triple the estimated rental income of a property that size and in that location.

Back at the Safire, Flic was bursting to see Laura.

"God, you look so tired." Laura pulled her into a solid embrace. "And rich, you look so rich."

"I do not look rich," countered Flic.

"Okay, you don't, but you are rich, right?" Laura helped herself to the minibar. "Dee still picking up the tab?"

Flic laughed. "You're such a twat." She cuddled in again. "But I can't believe how much I've missed you." Memories of Paris came rushing back, and annoying tears filled her eyes and choked up her throat.

"Hey, hey, hey. That's enough of that. You're all right. You're in one piece, and from what you've told me about your security detail, you're safe as houses now. Speaking of which, is that your woman at the door?"

"That's Marcelle, my number one girl on security. You didn't give her a hard time, did you?"

"Hardly. I wouldn't dare."

"Good. She's been fabulous. Leave her alone. She's straight."

"No way!"

"Yes way. She's married to Carlos, one of my other minders."

Laura threw her arms in the air. "Say no more. A girl knows when the odds are against her."

"Late lunch?" Flic was famished and was keen to enjoy the London pollution she'd missed for weeks now.

"Oh yeah. Can we do Marcus's? Surely this is a special enough occasion for that?"

Marcus's was their favorite go-to Italian restaurant for special occasions due to the menu prices being double other restaurants.

There was no hesitation. Flic agreed, popped her head out the door, and informed Marcelle who promptly phoned Carlos. Within five minutes, there was a knock at the door; security was ready to escort them.

Laura was in awe of the arrangement and its efficiency. For Flic, it was second nature. "They Google the location, check it out on Google maps, and set up a preliminary schedule which may or may not change depending on the day and the circumstance."

"How many will follow us?"

"One that you see and one that you don't."

"Bet I can spot him." Laura fancied herself as a spy.

"Bet you can't."

"What makes you so sure?"

Flic grabbed her hand and dragged her from the room. "It'll be a woman."

The food, the wine, and the company—it had all been delicious and exactly what Flic needed. She'd missed Britain and she'd definitely missed Laura. At four thirty, her phone rang. It was Anna.

"Hi, Flic. I was wondering if you're busy at half five this evening?"

Flic wasn't. She'd planned to soak in the bath, order room service, and watch a movie on her elaborately large television. And she'd only planned this regime of pampering because Laura was doing a business dinner. "What did you have in mind?"

"I'd like to show you something."

It wasn't like Anna to be so secretive. "Show me what?"

"Just say you'll come along. It will only take an hour or so. It's completely informal so just wear whatever."

An hour wouldn't interrupt her plans for the evening. After all, she'd just eaten her weight in Italian. "Sure. Will I meet you somewhere?"

"No, that's fine. I'll pick you up at five and I'll let Carlos know the arrangements." Her voice seemed lighter now that Flic had agreed. They ended the call.

Laura stared at her.

"What?"

Laura cleared the table and leaned on her elbows ready to pounce. "Spill."

"There's nothing to tell."

"Rubbish."

"I swear."

"Then swear again, sweetheart. I can only presume the crush on Mary Magdalene hasn't extinguished?"

The fact that Laura knew her so well grated on her nerves. "It's not a crush."

"No? Look, I'm not judging you, but you obviously have feelings for her." Laura sat back. "Am I right?"

The truth was Flic needed someone to talk to. "I like her."

"Does she like you?"

"Well, that's the thing. I think so, and sometimes our familiarity is so easy it's like we're a couple, but other times we're poles apart."

"A couple? So you've slept together?"

It was all coming out wrong. "No. Not at all. I'm not even sure she's gay. I just really like her. I mean, what makes us like any one person in particular? I wish I knew, but all I really know is that we get on well, we have fun, she's super supportive when I'm doing appearances, and I feel good around her." Flic explained how she'd taken Anna to the meeting in Bruges.

"Do you think she's struggling with her sexuality? Because what you're describing sounds to me like a perfectly straight girl who's made a good friend."

That was certainly something Flic had considered—about a million times.

"You're investing an awful lot of time in someone who might just like you as a friend."

"But what if she doesn't?"

"I think you should let it go." Laura was serious.

"What?"

"You don't chase straight girls, Flic, you never have—"

"But what if she's not straight?"

"And as I was saying, straight Catholic girls are in a league of their own. Enjoy Anna's friendship, by all means, but don't get swallowed up in something that's unlikely to happen."

Remaining silent at this juncture was the only way Flic knew to make Laura let it go. The conversation turned to more catching up and home gossip topics before they paid the bill and returned to the hotel just before Anna was scheduled to arrive. It was going to be a cool evening and she needed a warmer jacket. Anna, as usual, arrived on time.

"So, where are you taking me?"

Anna grinned. "Don't get too excited. You'll probably find it about as much fun as sewing class."

"I'm quite good at sewing."

"Of course you are."

"Well, don't come crying to me when you need a button sewn on." They stepped into the fresh early evening.

Anna cocked her head to one side and raised her eyebrows. "You think I don't know how to sew?"

Accepting defeat, Flic draped her arm through Anna's. "You win. So where are you taking me?"

"Patience, Felicity."

They strolled through Green Park, past Buckingham Palace, and eventually onto Ambrosden Avenue, where Anna stopped. "The other day you opened my eyes and my mind. I'm still processing everything I saw, heard, and learned, but today I'd like to repay the favor."

An impressive building grandly occupied the right-hand side of the street. Flic recognized the stripped brickwork of Westminster Cathedral.

"I'd like to show you my world."

Flic nodded her assent.

"I'm taking you to Mass."

"Interesting choice of location for a date."

Poised to defend herself, Anna clocked Flic's playful expression. "You nearly got me."

"You're catching on and beginning to make it difficult."

"Good, it's about time I caught up, but I'm sure you're up for the challenge." Anna checked her watch. "Come on. We don't want to be late."

"God's a very good timekeeper I hear."

"You can shut up now."

Flic squeezed Anna's elbow and kissed her cheek. "I'm on my best behavior, I promise."

Stalling on the front steps, Anna inhaled deeply. "I want to explain to you where this experience takes me, where I go when I walk through the doors."

Flic nodded.

As they entered the stunning building, Anna pulled Flic to the side. "The moment I enter, the world outside ceases to exist. The very first time I entered a church, I was awash with the most satisfying sense of calm. I expected that sensation to wear off. In fact, I waited for it, afraid that I would never feel it again, but it never went away. Today, walking through those doors, I can honestly say I experienced the same feeling I did as a small child."

Flic took in the beautiful and peaceful space. She felt only a small sense of calm but attributed that to the delightful quiet that surrounded her. She remained silent and let the mild aroma of incense fill her nostrils in the muted light.

"There's something in here. I feel a presence." Anna was speaking from the heart. "I feel it in every church, not just stunning cathedrals in the center of London, but everywhere. It feels like home here."

"Did you ever consider becoming a nun?" It was a serious question.

"Of course, but it was never going to be enough. I wanted a church to call my own, a place where I could welcome *my* flock, lost children *I* could save, broken hearts *I* could mend all in the name of the Lord and all under my roof."

Flic understood. "But the Catholic Church won't allow women priests?"

"No, and I understand why, but I felt my calling wasn't so much to wed God, more to the service of being the caretaker of a church, the giver of God's word, and the holder to the key of the gateway to enlightenment." Mass was about to begin. "Let's take a seat."

If she'd had to put a positive spin on the service, Flic would have described it as interesting. If she'd had to tell the truth, she'd have described it as sensationalist propaganda.

Void of drama—a quality Flic thought would have enhanced the experience—the priest pointed to his foot and announced that murderers and rapists were the lowest of the low and sinners of the highest order that belonged at the very foot of the Lord. He then indicated a place level with his knees and suggested thieves and abusers belonged at this level. Then, placing his hand level with his eyes, he suggested the remainder of the population belonged at that level, high above the sinners he had previously mentioned. Even Flic felt a sense of pride to be in the highest level, but the best news was yet to come. Pointing to the sky, and in effect to God, the priest suggested that because God was so high above us all and so free from sin, no matter how differentiated man had been initially, we were all sinners. Flic deflated in a matter of seconds.

She would have liked to have challenged Anna on the content of the sermon, but today wasn't about challenges; it was about understanding. She watched Anna take communion and participate in the service enthusiastically. The process was essentially the same the world over, but Flic understood that besides her creative marketing and public relations flair, Anna thrived on routine, and church services were certainly routine, if not downright boring.

It was well known that the Catholic Church was one of the richest organizations in the world, but Flic looked on as Anna tossed fifty pounds in the basket during offertory. She quickly calculated that if Anna gave, on average, only five pounds per week over her lifetime, she would have donated near on eight thousand pounds.

She shrugged internally. Perhaps it was a small price to pay for enlightened contentment.

At the conclusion of the service, Anna remained seated. "I wasn't neglected as a child, my parents provided for me, but they worked hard and played hard. I was left to my own devices for long periods of time."

Flic waited patiently while Anna collected her thoughts.

"I was an only child and I was an accident." Her shoulders sagged as if saying the words relieved her burden. "They didn't know I found that out. One night, my parents had friends over and I overheard them talking candidly about children."

"I'm sorry, Anna." Flic covered her hand with hers.

"I didn't love them any less. They didn't speak the truth with malice. It was a fact. That was that."

Flic wondered what it would be like to know your parents hadn't planned for your arrival, and not just at that moment, but ever. There would have been little celebration at the news her mother was pregnant, limited excitement decorating the nursery, and ultimately, probably not enough nurturing to fulfill a child.

"So, do you see why this is the one constant in my life?" Anna asked.

"I can see that."

"I detect a but?"

"But if you let it, there could be many constants in your life. Your experiences as a child shaped you, that's human nature, but I think you're doing yourself a disservice by not allowing your experiences as an adult to shape you also." Flic had much more to say, but she left it at that.

"I don't know if I can."

"You had the courage to find your happy place as a child. Where's that courage now?"

CHAPTER TWENTY

"Y ou took her *where*?"

Anna knew telling Seb was a stupid idea, and when she said it out loud, it sounded like a stupid idea. "I took her to Mass."

"Why on earth would you do that?"

Anna explained she was returning the favor. She told Seb about the gay Catholic group she'd met—that Flic had wanted her to meet.

"We're all free to think and believe in whatever we like." He nodded.

She hadn't mentioned it at the time, or after for that matter, but she'd found the experience positive. Although the church spoke of inclusion, in her experience they did so in fear. They controlled what they feared by defining it in a manner to suit themselves and then selling the hope of redemption to keep the oppressed in the gutter where the church believed they belonged. Ignorance, for the church, was obviously bliss.

It was a rubbish analogy, but Anna felt like a racehorse whose blinders had been removed. Suddenly, she could see the trees around her and not just the muddy old racetrack straight ahead.

"So do you think Flic respects my need for the church?"

"Of course. She's pro choice."

"Yes, but what does that actually mean?" Anna turned to face Seb on the sofa. "For example, I don't believe in abortion, but she does. So which one of us is pro choice?"

Seb shook his head. "How on earth did you get a degree at university?"

Anna punched him.

"Pro choice isn't about which one of you is right or wrong. It's about believing in the freedom to make a choice. In this example, I assume Flic believes a woman should be free to make the choice, based on her unique circumstances."

Anna nodded, finally understanding. "So she might not choose abortion herself, but might agree with others that in some circumstances, it's a valid decision."

"She might. Yes."

"And the church group I met." Anna stumbled on her words, but eventually managed to get them out. "The gay group. They're exercising their right of free choice, but they also want to worship the Lord."

"In fact, they're exercising free choice in many ways. They have the right to be gay, the right to be Catholic, the right to meet and worship as a group." Seb was in full swing. "And the list goes on."

Anna was beginning to feel the neatly segmented parts of her life merge. It frightened the hell out of her. The lines that so clearly defined her creative side and her orderly, faith-driven side, were blurring. She was slowly recognizing the beauty in gray.

The purposeful tap on the door suggested it was Max, but it felt so ridiculously early. Flic was surprised to see it was already eight o'clock. Regardless, her scheduled appearance at England's last surviving LGBT bookshop, Gay's the Word, wasn't until seven that evening. The next knock echoed through her room. *What on earth is so urgent?*

"Max, come on. What is so damned—?"

Flanking Max were two people in suits. One of them was agent Stark. The other was a young man dressed badly in a shiny gray suit. She briefly wondered if real life police deliberately went out of their way to dress exactly as they did on television.

"Flic, you remember Bethan Stark?" Flic nodded. "And this is her colleague, Agent Roman Ali."

Flic nodded and smiled at Stark, but a million thoughts rushed through her sluggish mind. "What's this about?"

"Can we come in?" asked Stark.

Flic ushered them in, including Max, and pressed the button by the bed that raised the blinds. "Can I offer you coffee?"

Both agents nodded. Max shook his head.

Flic dialed room service and ordered fresh coffee. She wasn't the slightest bit hungry, but she ordered a selection of pastries, too. "So now can you tell me what this is about?"

"Miss Bastone." Stark was all business. "Have you received any unusual e-mails or messages lately?"

Flic raised her eyebrows. "Please don't call me that. Flic or Felicity is just fine."

Flic made a point of not looking at any of her messages unless they came from family or very close friends. She had one private e-mail address and a private phone number. Neither registered to her name. Griffin's handled all her social media. Thoughts of Paris and vulnerability filled her head. Seeing Stark again was enough indication that something serious was happening. She sat in a chair that Max swiftly moved beneath her.

"I'll take that as a no?"

A film of sweat caused her instant stickiness.

"Why are you asking?" Max took over.

"We've been able to identify many members of the Order of Purity. We've been taking their involvement in your failed assassination very seriously, and since you've returned to England, at least three members of the Order have travelled to the UK also."

"It's not just the wonderful English summer they're here for, is it?"

"We think not, but by the time we realized they were en route, they'd cleared customs and we've yet to find them."

"So you don't know where they are?"

Stark shifted uncomfortably from one leg to the other. "No."

Before Flic had a chance to ask any questions, a loud knock pounded the door.

Max opened it and Anna came bursting in.

"Well, that's certainly one way to make an entrance." Flic was relieved room service exited the lift while the door remained opened. She needed caffeine urgently.

"Oh, they're here already!" Anna pulled up a chair and attempted to appear composed. She failed. Directing her next comment to Flic, she said, "I only just got the call from Dee that the police wanted to see you. I came as soon as I could."

Resting a reassuring hand on Anna's arm, Flic caught her up to speed and she hit the ground running. "Here's her schedule for the next four weeks." Anna handed them a folder. "All the contact names and numbers are there. If you need either myself or Max, we're available twenty-four hours a day. The team we have keeping Felicity safe is outstanding. They've been on board since the incident in Paris, they know the drill, and we'll all work with you at every juncture."

"We need to find them first," said Stark. "The list of people that might be helping them could be endless, given the reason for their outrage. But rest assured, this issue is a high priority and we're doing all we can." She turned to Flic. "You need to stay smart. No risk taking, and please follow the orders of your security team."

Flic nodded. She was slowly warming to Agent Stark.

The moment MI5 left, Flic logged on to her computer and commenced work to increase her online security. She changed every password, deleted unnecessary files, and saved important documents to her cloud storage. Hacking her personal files was one way to get to her. Anna already had someone on the task of upgrading Griffin's security.

Anna's phone rang. She answered, acknowledged the caller, and hung up. "Turn on the television."

"What now?" Flic had had enough action for one morning, and all before she'd had a chance to shower. She shoved a pastry in her mouth and stared wide-eyed at the television.

Airing was footage of the pope. Pre-recorded and in English. His eyes were sunken, and he appeared drawn and gray, far older than his sixty-three years. All three of them squashed on the sofa and watched as the leader of the Roman Catholic Church announced he was a homosexual, that he had previously been conducting a relationship with the Camerlengo, and that he had resigned as pope. People were glued to their televisions all over the world. News programs showed people watching in Sydney, New York, and all over Europe and Asia. The emotional outcry from those sharing his faith was unfathomable. It was ironic that so many Catholics mourned his sexuality yet happily lived under the suppressed conditions imposed by the church.

After all was said and done, he had no choice but to resign. That, in Flic's opinion, was the only tragedy worth her mourning.

While Felicity hadn't caused this outcome, she was clearly reaping the benefits now, and a small part of her wished she'd never overheard the conversation in Rome many months ago. She felt genuine sorrow for the man who had been outed by a lover no longer content to hide their relationship, and he'd been shunned by a church that couldn't accept his choices. His ability to lead the church had not once factored into this sorry mess. She didn't try to conceal her tears.

Although this outcome was expected, the words of the pope stung. Anna couldn't watch a moment longer and retreated to the bathroom. It was out there now. The pope was gay, and Anna felt conflicted. What would this mean for her church? Would there be a revolt? Would the flock simply just soldier on as if nothing had happened, elect a new pope, and carry on? And what about the man himself? Previously a strong and determined leader, he now resembled an empty shell of a man going through the motions imposed upon him by his employer. She felt sorry for him. She imagined if someone told Flic she could no longer be a writer because she was a lesbian. It sounded absurd. It was absurd, but it was exactly what had happened to the pope. Why was she feeling this way?

She felt an arm around her shoulder and turned toward Flic standing close beside her.

"Are you okay?" asked Flic.

Comforted by Flic's close proximity, Anna allowed herself to lean into the embrace ever so slightly. "It's funny how some things never seem quite true until you see it for yourself or it's spoken aloud. Regardless of the likelihood."

"Disappointment is difficult even when you know it's on the way."

Anna sighed.

"Change is difficult, too, but these things find a way of working out. It may not be today, or for decades to come, but a change is inevitable. Not just for the Catholic Church, but for everyone."

"He seemed like such a good man."

"He still is a good man, Anna."

Anna nodded. "Yes, I think he is. If he had to have a relationship, there's a huge part of me that just wishes he'd been discreet about it."

"You mean hide it like the others?" asked Flic.

Anna nodded. "This would have been easy for me in the past. I would have had a clear standing on this."

"And now?"

"Not so much." Anna blew her nose. "Now there's a nagging part of me that wonders why he should have had to have been discreet about love in the first place."

"I like that nagging part of you. She gives me hope." Flic nudged Anna.

"She gives me a bloody headache."

"What say we get some fresh air and a deliciously naughty breakfast?" Flic looked over to Max who was on the phone talking quietly in the corner. She mouthed "breakfast?" but he shook his head and gestured to the phone. "It's just you and me, then. Come on. Let's get out of here."

❖

No one was willing to predict the impact of the pope's announcement on the crowd that might gather at Gay's the Word.

As it stood, a section of the road was cordoned off, and Flic was to read on a stage directly opposite the shop front. Although England's only surviving LGBT bookstore, Gay's the Word was relatively small and nowhere near the size of the rooms she'd been filling of late. This appearance differed a little from previous outings. Tonight was a celebration, a homecoming of sorts where food, drink, and an array of promotional products would be available. At eight o'clock, a ticketed charity dinner was taking place at a nearby venue where Flic was the guest of honor. Proceeds were being distributed among some of the struggling LGBT support groups, many of which received little or no government funding.

Tonight was important, but Flic couldn't help but feel disappointed that she was possibly being hunted in her own, largely Church of England faith, country. She thought she would be safer in England than in continental Europe. All the fear and worry that had faded since Paris had come flooding back. She was excited about the evening ahead, and she told herself it was madness for the members of the Order to attempt anything at such a security conscious event. She just needed to make it through the night, enjoy herself, and then sit down with Max, Anna, and Dee and discuss her security for the remainder of the tour. Stark had assured her there'd be agents on the ground in London, and between MI5 and her security team, she knew they'd have it covered.

Anna had done her best to maintain Flic's enthusiasm throughout the day. She and Max had met with Agent Stark privately and learned that MI5 were treating the three missing men as serious and as a direct threat to Flic and possibly to London. It wasn't considered a coincidence that the men flew to London the day before Flic arrived. Forewarned was forearmed, but Anna was seriously wondering if keeping up to date with things was worth the worry.

She and Flic occupied the backseat of a black Mercedes SUV on the way to the evening event. She stole a glance at Flic and smiled. Flic loved London. She watched Flic stare at the hustling crowds filling the busy streets. They passed buildings and landmarks famous the world over—Piccadilly Circus, Trafalgar Square, and Buckingham Palace—and she experienced a sense of pride to have returned home for what would be an amazing evening.

Flic's style had certainly evolved since Paris. Today she was dressed in a slim fit designer black suit with styled hair and flattering makeup. She looked like a million dollars. Her security team regularly hit the gym or ran for fitness, and since they came on board in Paris, she knew Flic had taken a number of gym classes and for her own peace of mind, was learning martial arts. She looked fit and she radiated confidence. It might not have been how she felt inside, but Flic was mastering the art of a seasoned celebrity. Summer in Europe left Flic tanned and healthy looking, and her modern hairstyle set off the celebrity style. If she could have found the top of the world, Felicity Bastone would have stood tall and proud upon it.

"You look fabulous," said Anna.

Flic blushed. It caught Anna off guard to realize she was impressed to be able to make her blush. She briefly savored the power. "For once, you actually look like you're enjoying this."

Flic smiled. "I'm enjoying a drive through London on my way to an event in the backseat of a nice car with my favorite person." This time Flic blushed and turned away. "I said that out loud, didn't I?"

"Yep." Anna inhaled deeply as the comment sunk in.

"I'm not the only one who looks good today. You look stunning. That dress is amazing on you."

"Oh, you mean this old thing?" Anna pretended to iron out the creases of her black dress with her hands. She caught Flic's gaze dart down to her cleavage. "Is it a bit low?"

"No. Oh, God, I can't believe I just did that. I'm sorry, I'm just really nervous."

"Do you always focus on inappropriate things when you're nervous?"

"No. Definitely not. Well, probably, yes, now I come to think of it."

"What can I do to take your mind off it?"

"Oh, give me strength. You can't say that to me. I'm vulnerable."

Anna realized her mistake. "I meant to take your mind off the event for a while and relieve your nerves."

Flic closed her eyes and rested her head back. "Phew, because for a while there I thought you wanted me to take my mind off your amazing dress and your great cleavage. Thank goodness we straightened that out."

"You're impossible, Felicity Bastone."

"Maybe, but I feel a little more relaxed."

Flic pulled new black-rimmed glasses from her pocket and slipped them on. "Do I look like an author?"

"I think you always have. You just look like one who wrote a best seller now."

"I'll take that as a compliment."

They traveled the next few streets in silence before Flic said, "I know we're only just beginning this journey. I mean, we have the US and more of Europe scheduled, but this really has been a great achievement so far, hasn't it?"

Anna grinned. "Are you only just beginning to believe that now?"

"Well, I've had a marketing expert tag along and absolutely hate the premise of my book. It's been a little soul destroying at times."

"I've been watching and paying attention, Flic. You didn't write a destructive lie, and the pope was gay all on his own without your help."

"I'm sorry I appeared flippant in my drive to promote the value of an openly gay pope. I think I was blinded by my own belief that love is love. I truly believe that to be the case, but I should have thought about how others would view my opinion."

Anna couldn't help but reach across and take Flic's hand in hers. "We both seem to have come full circle. I honestly thought you should have minded your own business and let the church deal with their problems. But by the same token, why hasn't the church—me included—minded our own business and let people love who they want to love and believe in what they want to believe in?"

Flic shrugged.

"I've believed what I've been taught. I realize I have the right to question that."

"Just like I have the right to look down your top in times of stress."

Anna withdrew her hand and punched Flic's shoulder. "No, idiot. Nothing like that."

Flic was suddenly serious. "Thank you. And I agree. We have come full circle and it's been a most enlightened journey."

Anna changed the subject before she began to cry. She hadn't been expecting sentiment on the journey. "Dee's looking forward to introducing you tonight. It'll be a special moment for her."

"It'll be special for us all. She took a chance on me. I'll be forever grateful."

Anna laughed. "Oh now, don't go too far. Dee Macintosh doesn't take chances; she takes calculated risks. You just happened to be an extremely sound risk."

"Either way, I can't imagine any of this happening without her. Without you all, for that matter."

❖

After deftly negotiating London traffic, Max reverse parked the vehicle on the road running parallel behind Marchmont Street. It was six p.m. and they arrived in plenty of time and on schedule. Flic and Anna entered the tiny offices above the shop and the atmosphere was lively and thrilling. Dee had already arrived, and as someone thrust a glass of champagne into Flic's hand, Dee toasted, "To my most successful author and dear friend, Felicity Bastone."

Flic shot Anna a cheeky sideways glance at the "dear friend" reference but didn't care. It seemed that with her newfound wealth and status, everyone wanted to be her friend. "Cheers!" she declared, raising her glass and taking a long sip of the bubbles.

There were so many people to meet, she simply couldn't remember everyone's names, but she'd learned from her previous experience and restricted herself to the one glass before her appearance. At dinner, however, she intended to let her hair down and celebrate her success. Laura would be there and finally have the chance to engage with Anna under less stressful circumstances than the initial meeting the day she and Flic rushed to the offices of Griffin's. That day seemed so long ago now.

The crowd was gathering outside, and as she stood at the window staring down over excited fans and those less excited and perhaps angry or annoyed, she watched as the police erected subsequent barriers designed to safely accommodate the ever-increasing numbers. The entire street was cordoned off, and powerful speakers stood above the crowd so even those farthest away could hear. To control any unrest—not that violence was expected—the crowds were effectively being penned into smaller sections for containment purposes.

Flic felt the champagne numb her senses, and she wanted to pinch herself. Was this really happening? It was hardly the Oscars. There was no red carpet, only green, and even then it was just to cover the electrical wiring that was likely to trip someone arse over head at the foot of the stairs. But still, for an author no one had even heard of just months ago, a couple of thousand people crammed into a street outside a bookstore seemed a pretty impressive feat.

"You okay?"

Flic heard the voice first then felt the familiar hand rest comfortably in the middle of her back, only this time, instead of an empty space between them, Anna's entire side touched hers. She tingled all over, and for the first time, she refused to fight the addictive sensation.

She pulled her phone from her breast pocket and navigated to a picture of them both at her debut appearance in Dublin. "We've come a long way, don't you think?"

"You look nice in chinos and a blazer." Anna smiled. "But you do look terribly smart in your suit."

"What about my hair back then?" It was only weeks ago, but Flic cringed at the photo and her hair falling in her eyes.

"It's okay to be complacent when the world isn't watching you."

It was true. Flic had always thought her hair was trendy, but then when the stylist showed her some pictures of how it could be, she'd laughed, suggesting she was an author, not a rock star. The stylist had smiled crookedly and said, "You're not a normal person anymore. Stop looking like one."

Her reaction was similar when her makeup artist arrived at the hotel. Flic barely had five items in her makeup routine, and all of them produced a subtle and natural look. When the artist wheeled in a sizable case and took over half an hour to complete a job she'd mastered in under a minute, she was convinced she'd run to the bathroom and wash it all off. But of course she didn't. She looked amazing, and when the artist explained about lighting and the cameras and the fact that the majority of people would be seeing her from a distance, it all made sense. The reflection staring back at her in the mirror looked so foreign she had to stare long and hard to recognize herself. She liked what she saw. She felt ready to be the new Felicity Bastone.

"You know I couldn't have done any of this without you." Flic faced Anna and immediately missed the warmth of her hand on her back. "I'm sorry you were practically ordered to come with me, but I'm so very grateful you did. I think we make a great team."

Anna blushed, but it suited her. "We do make a great team, don't we? And while I know you would be standing here today regardless of who was your right-hand woman, I'm pleased it was me in the end."

"Really?"

"Yes, really, you clown. Oh, don't get me wrong. It's more stressful than I could have ever imagined, but it's worth it. Sales are soaring, your popularity is soaring, and although I'm not sure how I'm going to do it, I'd like to try to convince Dee to keep me on in this role."

It hadn't occurred to Flic that Anna wouldn't continue in her current capacity, but then, she was the head of marketing and PR; there must have been loads of other projects in the pipeline that Griffin's needed her to manage.

Flic stalled, trying to find the right words to mirror Anna's sentiment, but it all became lost in the rush to have Flic ready to take the stage. As she strode through the bookshop, flanked on both sides by two of her security people, she received nothing but praise and congratulations from onlookers. She heard enthusiastic whispers of, "that's her" and "there she is," and as she swelled with pride, she lifted her chin a little, straightened her back, smiled, and took in every single moment. As she exited the bookshop, the crowd erupted into applause. One man, middle-aged and smiling, grabbed her hand and spoke Italian or Spanish, she wasn't sure, but he was beaming at her. "*Ti amiamo. Brucia all'inferno.*" Her Italian wasn't all that good, but she recognized one part as "we love you." She nodded her thanks before her security team moved her on.

"Ladies and gentlemen, please welcome Felicity Bastone." Dee beamed a triumphant smile, and the Love is Love chant echoed around the entire street and beyond. After a kiss and warm embrace, Flic stood behind the speaker's podium waiting for the applause to die down. She was able to find Laura in the crowd, and as per their usual routine, she spotted Anna directly in her line of vision, this time easily distinguishable as the most attractive person at the sound desk.

When the applause and chant reached a level which she could speak over, Flic addressed the crowd. "Thank you, everyone. It's a great pleasure and honor to be here. You certainly know how to make a girl feel welcome—"

Twenty-two words was all Flic said to the crowd that evening. The twenty-second word was drowned out by a thunderous crack. Stupidly, Flic's first thought was confusion as to why the fireworks had launched prematurely. Her second thought was that there were no fireworks. Before blackness overtook her, she realized a bomb had exploded in Marchmont Street.

Chapter Twenty-one

Everyone was a suspect when chaos reigned. By the sheer fact of her survival, it appeared even Flic was a prime suspect.

If the fact that two attempts had been made on her life in a matter of months wasn't enough to make her crazy, the incessant ringing in her ears certainly would. The smell of antiseptic gave away her location. Her thumping headache cemented the fact that she should be there, and when she attempted to open her eyes or move her head, the pain was so exhausting, she succumbed to a sedative-induced sleep.

It was the gentleness of the touch on her hand that woke her. She'd been stirring for an indeterminate period of time, but the touch, which was most certainly Anna's, warranted an extra effort on her behalf to wake up.

"Good girl, wake up for me." An unfamiliar voice encouraged her.

It wasn't the smooth, velvet voice she was expecting, and she forced her eyes open.

"Welcome back." A middle-aged nurse with a cheerful round face beamed at her. "I'm Val. How are you feeling?"

On the third attempt, Flic managed to form words and make a sound. "Where's Anna?"

"I'm not sure where Anna is, love. You received a pretty hard knock on the head and a few scrapes. The doctor will be here in a minute."

"What about Laura? Is Laura okay?"

"Don't you worry about a thing, my love. The doctor isn't far away now."

Flic didn't possess the confidence to determine if Val hadn't understood the urgency of her questions, or if she deliberately evaded answering. She tried again. "Are my friends okay?"

"I don't know who Anna or Laura are, love." She glanced desperately toward the door and looked relieved when someone entered. "Ah, here's the doctor."

Flic felt ill.

"Hi, Felicity, I'm Dr. Phillips. How are you feeling?" Dr. Phillips was probably in her fifties, friendly, with a broad smile, and she smelled of antibacterial hand wash.

"Where's Anna and Laura?" She could feel the throbbing in her head become fiercer and louder.

Dr. Phillips glanced at the machine attached to the wires attached to Flic. "You need to calm down, Felicity."

Frustration and fear gripped her, a dangerous combination when you were pumped full of drugs. Flic projectile vomited all over the doctor.

"Felicity, this isn't doing you any good at all." She checked the monitors again. "You're working yourself into a right state."

Felicity ripped the machine sensors from her chest. "This isn't right." Her brain and mouth were functioning at different speeds. "Are my friends dead?"

Dr. Phillips and Val stopped in their tracks as Flic wiped bile and spit from her mouth. The acrid taste of vomit was nothing compared to the fear that was constricting her heart like a steel vice.

Dr. Phillips and Val exchanged glances before Val shook her head and took Flic's hand. "Your friends are okay, but other than that, we're not supposed to tell you anything."

Relief inflated Flic's chest again, and the urge to vomit began to subside. "What happened at the bookstore?"

After Val eased her from her soiled hospital gown and began cleaning up, Dr. Phillips replaced the sensors on her chest. "I know this must be difficult for you, but by law, we aren't allowed to say. As it is, we shouldn't have told you about your friends, but your health is my priority. The rest is the priority of the authorities. Do you understand?"

"Something bad happened, didn't it?" Flic was thinking out loud, not expecting an answer. "It was a bomb, wasn't it?"

Dr. Phillips smiled. "The police will be here soon. They have a job to do, but so do I, so if you need anything from me"—she patted Flic's shoulder—"just let me know."

After some skillful maneuvering and with the expertise of someone who'd performed the task a million times, Val changed the mucky sheets and rested Flic comfortably back on the pillows.

A purposeful knock sent Flic's pulse racing.

Dr. Phillips smiled and nodded encouragement. "I'll stop it if it becomes too much for you."

Flic inhaled, filling her lungs.

Agent Stark and a stranger entered the room.

"Hi, Felicity, how are you feeling?" Stark didn't wait for a response. "This is Agent Supervisor Colin Murphy."

Murphy was wrinkly, too wrinkly for a human being, but the strong smell of cigarettes suggested he'd aged prematurely. His face gave nothing away. "We're glad you're awake, Miss Bastone. Do you mind if I call you Felicity?"

Something told Flic to be wary. She simply shrugged.

"Do you know why you're in hospital, Felicity?" Stark asked in a singsong tone that seemed out of context.

Flic frowned. Stark was acting weird. Was this a good cop, bad cop routine? Flic needed answers just as much as they did. It wasn't constructive to offer anything but her full cooperation. "Something happened at the bookshop appearance."

"Do you know what happened?" Murphy asked, deadpan.

She had no idea. She guessed a bomb had gone off, but she felt reluctant to say. "Something bad happened, I think, otherwise my friends and family would be here."

"They are here. After we speak to you, you can see them."

"They're here? At the hospital?"

"Yes, but we need to ask you some questions first. Is that okay?" Murphy was thawing. "Felicity, a bomb went off at the bookstore."

Somehow, through the haze of drugs and nausea, Flic finally understood. "And you think I had something to do with it?"

Stark shook her head without hesitation, but it was Murphy who spoke. "Did you? Your book sales increased dramatically after the attempt on your life in Paris. You've managed to survive two assassination attempts. You're like a cat with nine lives."

"And you're just plain fucking daft if you think I could have orchestrated any of this." She looked at Stark. "I know you don't have a shred of evidence to suggest I'm involved. What the hell's going on here?"

"Agent Murphy had a hunch." Stark eyed him and scowled. "But I think we've cleared it up now."

Flic stared at them both. "Jesus, you're actually serious."

Stark turned to stare out the window.

"What the hell happened to the three wise men from the Order?"

"They've completely disappeared," said Stark.

"So now you think I did it?"

"No. We still believe it's the men from the Order, we just needed to eliminate you."

Flic closed her eyes momentarily, longing for the incoherent drug haze to take her over again. Clarity was a bitch.

Stark moved forward to speak, probably to assure Flic they were doing everything they could but they needed to cover all angles, when Dr. Phillips stepped in. "I think you have the answers you came for today. My patient needs rest now. You can see her again tomorrow if need be."

Before the officers reached the door, Flic asked, "Was anyone killed?"

Stark shook her head. "Five seriously injured, including you. The bomb was disguised as part of the speaker system, and it failed to detonate correctly. Everyone was very lucky."

"We know who we're looking for," said Murphy. "We just haven't found them on the CCTV yet. When you look for something suspicious, you see it in every movement. We're in the process of eliminating footage minute by minute."

"Can I see the footage?"

"Why?"

Flic remembered nothing beyond the moment she stood in the window next to Anna. She certainly wasn't a sadist, but she wanted to piece together the final moments before the bomb exploded. She hated not knowing. "I barely remember it; in fact I don't remember being outside at all. Can I see it for myself? I might be able to help."

The agents exchanged glances, and Murphy indicated for Stark to step outside. Flic observed, through the open doorway, the officers deep in conversation, obviously weighing up the pros and cons of her request.

Murphy and Stark returned. "Be our guest." Stark handed Flic her tablet.

Dr. Phillips coughed. "Are you up for this?"

Flic nodded a little too enthusiastically, and it made her head hurt, but she wanted to see. She knew her family and friends were waiting, but it would only take a minute. She didn't want to be in the dark a moment longer, and she hoped reality was better than her imagination. In her mind, it was bloody and horrific, and she needed the truth to replace that disturbing image.

She pressed play and skipped forward, checking her progress every now and again by watching a snippet of the footage.

The images were surprisingly clear.

Stark checked the time on the footage. "They're only just beginning to set up now. You probably haven't even begun to get ready at this stage."

Flic looked at the CCTV time in the bottom left hand corner of the screen. It was early afternoon.

The footage was from a building opposite, and she calculated about two doors down. She starred at the window where she and Anna would look out from later that day. Her stomach lurched at the thought of Anna being hurt, but calmed again when she reminded herself she was safe and nearby. It was Anna she was desperate to see, and she let the feeling of need rest in her chest.

Stark was about to skip forward again when Flic saw it. "Stop!"
Stark jumped.

"Go back!"

Murphy moved in.

"Please, just a few seconds. Go back."

"What is it?" Murphy asked. "What did you see?"

Stark played it again, and this time Flic was sure.

"That man spoke to me. That man there." She pointed to a bald man with olive skin. She was sure it was him.

"What did he say?"

Flic's initial excitement began to fade. She closed her eyes to help remember. "I don't know."

"Please take a moment to think," said Stark.

Flic shook her head. "It couldn't have been anything much or else I would have mentioned it at the time, wouldn't I?" She felt deflated.

"Just give it a few moments. If it is the same man you saw, then it's worth taking a look at simply because he was there so early in the day. We'll also have the facial recognition team check it out against the three missing men from the Order. It's something, Flic." Stark reassured her with a pat of her shoulder. "Get some rest."

Stark and Murphy were just about to close the door when it came to her. "He said something about loving me, my Italian isn't great at the best of times, but I recall thinking how nice it was that he loved me. Can you look that up on your tablet?"

Stark didn't need her tablet. "I love you in Italian is *io ti amo*."

"Of course. I know that. It was like that, but something else. He said two things."

Stark typed on her tablet. "How about *ti amiamo*?"

"Yes. That's it. What is that?"

"He said we love you."

Flic felt relief that she hadn't misinterpreted the man's sentiment. "And he also said something about light or fire, and something about food, like bruschetta or something." Her head hurt from thinking. "Maybe he was asking me to lunch?"

Stark tapped away on her tablet. She frowned. "Did he say *brucia all'inferno?*"

Flic repeated the words silently with her best Italian accent. She felt her blood pressure drop. "That's burn in hell, isn't it?"

Stark nodded.

Murphy was already making a call before he rushed from the room.

"Holy shit. I'm so fucking stupid."

"Not at all." Stark closed her tablet cover and squeezed Flic's shoulder. "It's a start. I have to go." She paused at the door. "You know we'll need to keep you safe, don't you?"

Flic understood.

"I'll be back in an hour."

Flic nodded.

"We can take two of you. As long as the other person has clearance, they can come along." Stark smiled awkwardly before disappearing down the corridor.

Flic knew what she had to do.

Dr. Phillips ensured Flic was comfortable before sending in her family and friends. Her poor mother sat hunched and had possibly aged twenty years in the last twenty-four hours, but her father suggested that with a good feed of Indian that night, she would perk up and look better tomorrow.

Laura held her long and close. "Are you wishing you'd never written that damn book?"

There was no way she'd wish that. If it weren't for the book, Flic would never have met Anna, and soon she had something important to ask her, but in the meantime, she needed Laura to do some things for her.

"Laura, will you make sure my mum's okay?"

"Sure. But you'll be out of here in a day or two, and now that she knows you won't be in a coma for a decade, I think she's pretty chilled out." Laura paused. "Well, as chilled out as I suppose you can be when you know someone tried to blow your daughter up." She finally engaged her brain before her mouth. "Okay, I'll keep a close eye on them both."

"And because I'll be so busy in the next little while, I'll give the property manager of the flat your number to call to make any decisions regarding rentals, et cetera."

Laura nodded, making notes on her phone.

"Oh, and I don't need the rental income, so when she calls, give her your bank details. She's expecting that information."

"Whoa there. Isn't your flat fetching something like three thousand pounds a month these days?"

With a wave of her hand, Flic brushed her off. "I don't need the money and you'll be helping me out, so please, keep it. The only stipulation is that it's to be rented to a female, or females."

"Why?"

"Because that's what I'd prefer, that's all."

Laura eyed her suspiciously, but evidently thought better of pushing the issue because she moved on. "Okay. I can do all that. You sure about the money though?"

Flic squeezed her hand as reassurance. "I'm sure. I want you to have it, and it's my thanks for looking after the place."

"You look so tired you're actually gray." Laura never shied away from the truth. "Anna's waiting to see you. You need to rest. I'll show her in and come back tomorrow, okay?"

"Come here." Flic held open her arms and Laura wrapped her arms around her.

"You okay?"

Flic breathed in Laura's familiar expensive perfume. "You look after yourself, okay? Thanks for being here." Flic choked back tears. "I love you. Promise you won't forget that?"

Laura held her at arm's length. "That must have been some knock you got on the noggin last night." She kissed Flic's forehead. "See you tomorrow."

Good-byes were always difficult, but today, Flic felt like her heart was being crushed. She battled to compose herself before Anna came in, but to no avail. The moment she entered, Flic fell apart. "I'm sorry. I didn't want to cry."

Anna was immediately by her side. "There's no need to apologize."

There was a knock at the door. Stark poked her head in.

"I'm not ready yet," snapped Flic. She'd run out of time.

"Two minutes?" Stark framed it as a question, but Flic knew she didn't really have a choice.

"What's going on?"

Flic took her hand and held it tightly. "I'm being taken to a safe house. I think I've identified the bomber, but regardless, they want to keep me safe until they catch them."

"You saw one of the men there, didn't you?"

"I think so. Look, we don't have much time. The longer I'm here, the longer I'm in danger, and the longer I put you all at risk."

Anna nodded.

"I'm allowed to ask you to come with me."

"Me?"

Flic realized digesting the scenario was difficult at any time, let alone under these circumstances, but there simply wasn't time to explain. "My life is in danger until these people are caught. If you come with me, you won't be able to contact anyone, or be seen in public without a disguise, and I know it sounds horrendous to even contemplate, but the police said they don't imagine it will be for long, but I have to go off the radar, and I want you to come with me." She rambled on, unable to stop until she had it all out.

The movement was slight, but the few centimeters Anna backed away were like unfettering a raft and pushing it from the jetty, left to drift aimlessly. Flic's nausea returned as her stomach constricted and her body worked to pump blood and oxygen to her brain and vital organs. She had never felt so alone.

"I don't think I can do that, Flic." Anna cleared her throat. "I have a life, a job. I can't just give that up. Are we even that close?"

The question stung. "A simple no would have been sufficient." Flic edged from her bed and pressed the buzzer. She was supposed to call Val when she was ready to go. She began to strip off her hospital gown, knowing Anna would make a run for it before she would allow herself to see Flic naked.

"That came out wrong. I'm sorry." Tears reddened Anna's eyes. "It's just that it's been a hell of a time this last twenty-four hours. Can you understand how hard this is for me?"

Flic tried to understand, she pushed herself to see this awful situation from Anna's point of view, but in truth, she was wrestling with her own fears, her own emotions, and the realization that three men were trying their utmost to kill her. The thought was sickening. She felt toxic. "It wasn't fair of me to ask, but I had to. I'm sorry."

Anna could barely speak. "Are you asking me to come with you as a friend, or…something more?"

Flic had finished dressing by this time, although Val was nowhere to be seen, and Anna hadn't budged. It was heartbreaking to think this could be the last time she might see Anna for an indefinite period. "Could you ever love me?" She was raw now and had nothing left to lose.

"We've managed to arrive at this junction well before I thought we might," said Anna.

Val came charging through the door. "Right, my girl, are you—"

"One minute please, Val?" Flic's voice oozed desperation.

Val nodded and swung about-face, leaving them in silence again.

"They really want you out of here, don't they?"

Flic pushed on, embarrassed to be baring her soul, but not willing to miss the chance. "Is there more than just your religion stopping you from feeling anything for me? I mean, it's okay if there is. It probably means you're not gay, but I really need to know. I refuse to say that I don't want to feel this way about you, because I do. I like the way I feel about you. I like the way you make me feel. I just thought, perhaps…" The cold hard truth was excruciating. Flic swallowed hard. "I just thought that perhaps given that I've cheated death twice now and that I have to go away, you might choose to come."

"This is all too much. I'm sorry. I just simply don't know how I feel, Flic."

"Please, Anna? Please come with me?"

Anna shied away from the hand Flic offered. "I can't. I'm sorry." She ran front-first into Val as she rushed from the room.

Flic bundled up all her pain and rejection and stowed it away to unravel and deal with later. Right now, she had to leave.

Behind Val entered Dr. Phillips and Agent Stark. They talked about her pain medication, they told her how she would be taken to the basement, how she would be driven to a safe house far from London, and how a car would follow them to ensure they in turn, weren't being followed. Had it not been for her thumping headache and broken heart, Flic might have been impressed. Instead, she was a shattered version of herself, held together by aching bones and toxic blood that pumped through her overused veins.

They had been driving over an hour when Stark took a brief phone call. She turned to talk to Flic who was resting her head on the seat with her eyes closed. She coughed to gain her attention. "We have some news."

Flic snapped open her eyes.

"The man who spoke to you, and who we saw on CCTV, is Alesso Redi. He's one of the men we're looking for from the Order."

"And the others?"

"Tommaso Rosa and Joseph Stefan."

"Can they leave the country? I mean surely they'll get arrested if they try to leave," said Flic.

"Yes. They would be arrested."

Flic sensed a catch. "But?"

"But the job still hasn't been done. We're not expecting them to try to leave."

"Because I'm still alive?"

"Something like that. We have people talking to experts, religious scholars and the like, and the majority believe they won't stop until they complete their mission."

"Are they martyrs?"

"The general consensus is that they're willing to make the supreme sacrifice, so yes. I suppose they are."

It was unnerving to realize that the people hunting you were willing to die in the process.

"Does this change the goal posts? I mean in terms of my safety and that of my family?" Thinking of Anna, she added, "And my friends."

Stark shook her head. "Not at all. The plan is for you to stay hidden. They're after you and we're after them. They need to lie low and not get caught before they can get to you."

Flic understood, but she couldn't help thinking Anna was better off with her. She wished she'd had more time to try to convince her to come along.

Her ears began to ring and she closed her eyes again.

CHAPTER TWENTY-TWO

There are some things the police couldn't control, and the media had a field day in the aftermath of the explosion at Gay's the Word. Attempting to dampen the fire, the police issued a statement saying that Flic had been moved to a safe location until the culprit or culprits had been apprehended. Photos of the suspects were all over the media and the fact that the men were from a secretive and cult like branch of the Catholic Church just fueled the fires from every angle. Groups were now forming who claimed to be antireligious. The atheists were having a field day.

It was just past midnight, and Flic sat watching the news. The safe house was comfortable enough—old and creaky and like something you'd find the middle class occupying in *Pride and Prejudice*. It was a modern renovation, and she occupied a bedroom and living area that wasn't communal. Not that it mattered. There was usually only herself, one other officer, and the safe house owner—an ex army and police officer—in the house at any one time.

The demand for *Holy Father, Holy Secret* was at its peak. Print editions couldn't keep up with orders, and e-book sales remained steady. The press speculated about Flic's whereabouts in the aftermath of the bombing, inventing ever more elaborate scenarios surrounding her mysterious disappearance. No one seemed willing to report the probable boring version of events—that she was most likely hiding until the assholes that were taking pot shots at her on an increasingly regular basis, were caught. Every story had to be embellished with a conspiracy theory, a mystery entirely unrelated, and lately, Felicity Bastone was supposedly suffering at the hands of God. The bullet in Paris and now the bomb in London, all brought about because she pissed God off. Plain and simple. She wanted to throw her laptop through the TV.

The only reliable information Flic received was from the police—and that was as frequent as a meteor crashing into earth—and from the news, but considering she knew more than those idiots, she was beginning to wonder why she was bothering.

Isolation was its own form of hell. No phone and no contact with anyone other than her safe house minder and the police officer were slowly sending Flic crazy, and it had only been one week. She missed Anna, Laura, Max, and her own team of minders, but she especially missed Anna. She wondered, when it was all over, if she and Anna would be friends again. She supposed not, but allowed the faint twinge of hope to remain.

As the days passed and the assassins remained elusive, the police continued to search for clues and details of the bombing. Flic, in contrast had taken more walks in the woods than she had for years, and read more chapters of *War and Peace* than she ever imagined she could. In a word, she was bored.

❖

"You'll start to believe that crazy chain of thought if you write much more of it." Seb only half teased her.

Anna was taking some well earned time off work, and because Dee had hired someone to cover her touring with Flic, she'd seen no sense in jumping straight back into things at the office after the bombing.

"Does she even know you're pretending to be her?"

"I'm not pretending to be her behind her back." Anna was insulted. "I know Flic. I know she'd want this continued in her absence. I'm the best person to do it, trust me." As soon as the words left her mouth, she realized how ridiculous they sounded.

He was too quick. "Of course. Catholic homophobic girl should definitely write blogs on behalf of the world's best known advocate for free love and freedom of choice."

She let him have his fun. "It's my job to sell the unsellable. I'm just doing my job. And quit calling me homophobic. It's wearing thin now."

He nodded. "That's a fair call, sorry. But are you doing your job or a favor for a friend?"

"Well, I suppose I'm happily doing a favor for a friend."

"A very good friend?"

"What's your point?"

Clearly taking that as all the invitation he needed, Seb snatched the laptop from Anna's lap and sat next to her on the sofa. "You've changed."

Anna began to protest. It had only been a matter of time before Seb became suspicious of all her work toward the Love is Love campaign. She couldn't describe her motivation for wanting to continue Flic's work; it simply seemed like the right thing to do. In fact, it was the only thing she could do to settle her restless mind. The conversation with Flic in the hospital tormented her, and on an exhaustingly regular basis she swung from mildly annoyed with herself to frantically anxious that she may never see Flic again. Maybe it was guilt, maybe it was a sense of loss, but the only time she felt anything resembling calm, was when she posted on the Love is Love site.

Seb was right. Of course she'd changed. How could she have lived through the past months without changing? Regardless of her feelings for Flic, she couldn't imagine how Felicity Bastone could become a part of anyone's life and not impart a positive change. She protested to Seb because she didn't know what else to do. She didn't know what an alternative reaction would mean, where that would take her. She protested, but it was weak and she knew it.

"No, hear me out." Seb inhaled. "You've changed for the better." He surveyed her closely. "You're wearing chinos for starters, and your hair is lighter." He shook his head, trying to focus. "But you seem so different, so relaxed when you're on that thing." He tilted his head toward the laptop. "And you're actually *willing* to do this for Felicity, for the book, and for Griffin's."

"She's a good person, Seb, and someone's trying to kill her. Continuing her work is the least I can do."

Seb nodded. "But not long ago you didn't want anything to do with her, and now you're writing inspirational words that the world is following. Surely you can see my point here?"

"She helped me see things a little differently. That's all."

Seb slouched into the softness of the sofa. "I don't think that's all, Anna. The only time you seem even remotely happy lately is when you're writing this stuff."

"That's not true."

"Yes, it is. It's completely true. You're sad most of the time, you mope all day, and you talk about Felicity like I imagine you'd talk about Dee, or your priest, or someone you admire and idolize."

Seb was right, and Anna didn't know what to do. She had stupidly thought that knowing Flic survived relatively unharmed from the bombing and knowing she was being kept somewhere safe, would allay her fears. But she wasn't sure it was the fear of Flic's safety that was plaguing her. Was fear creating an emptiness inside her only Flic could fill? Was it fear sending tingles to her core when she relived the wanting in Flic's voice when she had asked her to go into hiding at the hospital? Was it fear that left her lonely and helpless? Anna guessed not.

"Do you miss her?"

His change in tack didn't go unnoticed, but she let it slide. Her need to talk about it was stronger than her need to ignore it. She couldn't lie. "I think I do, yeah."

"She relies on you, doesn't she? At her appearances. She needs you there, right?"

"Sometimes I feel like the glue that holds the show together."

"And you like that feeling? The feeling that she needs you, that you have a purpose on a personal level, not just professional?"

"I reassure her, calm her down when she's anxious, and I make sure I'm in her line of sight at all times. We work as a team—me, her, and Max."

"I saw you after the bombing. You were worried sick about her."

Anna stood on the precipice, unsure if she had the courage to jump. She closed her eyes, took a long, deep breath, and stepped from the crumbling edge. "Ask me about something I might feel that would suggest I feel more for her."

Seb's face twisted in confusion.

"I'm asking for your help. Please? I don't know if I'm coming or going. I don't sleep, I can't eat more than two mouthfuls, and I need to know if what I'm feeling equates to more than just friends. I need you to help me work this out."

Seb squeezed her knee. "Okay. Let's find a baseline and work from there."

Anna rolled her eyes.

"I'm a numbers man."

"I don't think maths is my problem here, Seb." Maybe asking Seb wasn't such a good idea.

"Okay." He became a little more urgent. "Scrap that. I'm going to ask you a series of yes or no questions. You just answer them as honestly as you can, and with my vast wealth of relationship knowledge, I'll summarize for you at the end." He smiled genuinely for reassurance.

Anna nodded. She wasn't convinced it would work, but she needed something, anything at this stage to reach a resolution.

"Do you miss her?"

"Yes."

"On a scale of one to ten, how much?"

"That's not a yes or no question."

"No. Turns out I'm not as good at this as I thought."

"Oh, Seb. Come on."

"You miss her terribly, right?" Anna nodded. "She gives you butterflies when you see her?" She nodded again. "You have a strong sense of loyalty toward her?" Another nod. "You would go to extreme lengths to protect her."

"Yes, I would."

"You regret not going to the safe house with her."

"That didn't sound like a question, Seb."

"No. It wasn't." He stared intently. "But I just realized that's why you're so sad."

"And?" Anna wasn't stupid. She just needed to hear someone else say it.

"Because you love her. It's as simple as that."

A protracted silence fell heavy in the room. Neither of them moved a muscle and both stared into space.

It was out there now. Anna's stomach knotted as both fear and relief collided and fought for dominance over her emotions.

She finally broke the silence. "But it's not that simple, is it?"

"Maybe it is." Seb was in deep thought. "Well, besides the fact that you can't see her, talk to her, touch her, or even know where she is, I think it's perfectly simple."

Anna laughed. It surprised even her. "Other than that, it's all just coming up roses."

Seb eyed her carefully. "You're not arguing with my assessment of the situation?"

She shook her head. She felt relieved.

"You don't need a label you know." He shrugged. "You can just love a person. It doesn't matter what gender they are."

"Is that really true? I mean, I know the world has changed, but you forget I've seen and heard all the comments thrown at Flic in the last few months. There's some horrible people out there."

"And there's some amazing people too. I'd suggest you've fallen in love with one of them, so don't let that worry you. The world is full of rapists, pedophiles, murderers, bigots, and homophobic twats. It always will be, but the rest of us love and accept people based on their good bits, not the box they fit in."

"This is the scariest thing I've ever faced."

"But you're not alone. I'm here for you anytime."

Anna smiled. He had a heart of pure gold. "I know. But I don't know where Flic is, and she's the only one who makes me never feel alone."

Seb left the room and returned with the car keys and threw a coat at Anna. "Come on. Let's go find your girl."

"What?"

"You heard me. Let's go." He dragged Anna to a standing position. "There's no point wallowing here any bloody longer."

"But where are we going?"

He held the door open for her. "We're going to talk to the cops. They know where she is."

"MI5 aren't just the police, Seb. You can't just call in."

He seemed determined not to be deterred. "Did that Stark woman give you a card?"

Anna raced to her room and returned to thrust a bent and tattered card at Seb. "It's been in my purse the whole time."

Seb dialed the number and handed his phone to Anna.

Within a minute, Anna and Stark agreed on a meeting place.

Seb drove his Mini Clubman like a maniac to a pub twenty minutes away. Since surviving the journey, Anna believed anything was possible.

Just when the adrenaline was threatening to wear off, Stark rushed through the squeaky pub door in worn jeans and a woolen jumper. Turns out she was human after all.

Anna introduced Seb and Stark indulged the pleasantries, but she quickly moved on.

"What's so urgent, Miss Lawrence? I gather it's not my good company you're here to enjoy."

Anna stalled. What she was about to ask seemed so utterly ridiculous.

"I, um…"

Seb nodded his encouragement.

Anna coughed. "When Flic, Felicity Bastone, was moved to a safe place, she asked if I would go with her." Anna's courage faded and she scratched at the shabby wooden table in front of her. "Can I?"

"Can you see her? No. I'm afraid not." Stark seemed to refrain from suggesting that if anyone could just "go and see her," it wouldn't be a safe place. Thankfully, she simply elaborated. "Unfortunately, that isn't how this works."

"No. I mean can I go to the place now? She asked if I could go with her. I want to go now, to the safe place to stay, not just visit."

Stark finally caught up. She sighed heavily. "I'm afraid that ship sailed, Anna. It's too late."

"But it can't be." Panic and fear saturated her.

Seb stepped up to the plate. "Anna realizes she made a mistake. She realizes she missed an opportunity that was offered to her, but there must be some way we can get her to the safe house. Surely the house has supplies delivered? Surely your officers change shifts? There must be some way one of them can come and get Anna and take her to Flic."

Stark eyed Anna. "If I can get something sorted, and it's a big if, you must understand that when you enter the house, you stay in the house until this situation is resolved. Do I make myself clear?"

Anna nodded, the sudden glimpse of hope lifting her spirits.

"It could be weeks or months. You know that, right?"

She nodded again. "Yes. I understand."

"Right. Stay here. I'll go and make some calls." Stark left through the squeaky door with her phone in hand.

Anna grabbed Seb by the arms. "Oh my goodness, what have I done? This is the right thing isn't it? She'll want me there, won't she?" She knew she was rambling, but couldn't stop.

Surrendering herself to a self-imposed period of exile was probably the most insane thing Anna had ever done. Falling in love with a girl was the scariest.

"Let's just see what she comes back with." Seb was so calm she almost hated him for it.

Twenty minutes later, and Anna was slumped with her head on the table, no longer avoiding touching it because she had no idea which sticky ale or lager had been spilled all over the spoilt surface. Deflated and defeated, she knew that to take this long it must mean the answer was no. Never in her life had she felt so empty from regret. She wasted an opportunity and she would never have the chance to make a different choice. The excessive bile in her stomach left her feeling empty as it churned in response to her anxiety. She let the scratches on the table make an indentation on her cheek.

It was at least another ten minutes later before Stark returned shaking her head. "I'm sorry."

Seb rested a supportive hand on Anna's shoulder.

"I tried, I really did. But they won't budge. There's protocol, and it's just too risky."

Anna forgot to breathe.

"I'm sorry. It's simply not possible at this stage."

She buckled. She clawed at her hair and began to sob. The sick feeling that knotted her insides was like winning the lottery but accidentally throwing away the ticket. It was like every dream she'd had where she ran to get somewhere but never actually made it. In that moment, she swore never to miss an opportunity again. The emotional torment when reality hit was too much to bear.

"What's risky about one woman being sent to the safe house with another woman?" Seb didn't understand.

"It's not like the movies, Seb. In reality, safe houses are rarely discovered, and that's because they have strict protocols surrounding their use."

Anna took Seb's hand. "It's okay. Let's go." She dragged him into a standing position. "Thank you for trying." She was desperate to flee; she just didn't know where now.

The elation at having made some sense of her feelings had disappeared. She also felt more alone than she had the night she found out her parents hadn't wanted her. The end to her lonely torment remained out of reach.

CHAPTER TWENTY-THREE

Flic was tired. She wished she'd never overheard the conversations in Rome. She wished she'd never heard Anna reject her, and she was just plain tired of hearing things she shouldn't hear.

Now, at three a.m. on a day of the week she couldn't name, tonight was no exception. She wished she wasn't hearing the dogs barking from the property one hundred meters down the dirt road, or the outside metal furniture scraping along the concrete patio as it was disturbed, presumably by someone careless and in a world of trouble if he failed. But then she guessed his failure wouldn't be determined by whether he lived or died, but more accurately by whether she did. Above all, she wished she hadn't heard Barney speak sharply on his radio. "We're compromised. Albatross is flying the nest."

Flic was albatross. A fleeting sense of importance filled her before a man dressed entirely in black entered her room and waited the split second it took her to pull her hoodie over her head. She wasn't frightened of this man because it was Barney. In contrast, of the men trying to kill her, she was shit scared. Without ceremony, Barney swiftly directed her through the house toward the internal garage. To facilitate her swift departure, Flic made her body turn adequately limp to assist him in her easy removal.

As the door slammed and Barney thrust her into the waiting vehicle, she heard three gunshots. She wondered if that was one for each of the men trying to kill her. She guessed not. They'd be sent one at a time to increase their chances of success. The thought of enduring another two attempts on her life was unbearable.

The three shots rang in her ears. Doug, the safe house owner had assured her he never missed. She'd never wished anyone any real harm, but she hoped he had been on target this evening.

Her book had pissed off a lot of people. Her message to the church pissed off hordes more, and there were probably just enough psychos in the world who took a liking to the shiny new prize that she was. The men from the Order hunting her now might fail, but she wondered if there'd be more. Flic feared her life might never be her own again. That was assuming she had a life.

❖

It was the middle of the night, but Anna's phone only had the opportunity to vibrate twice before she snatched it up and answered breathlessly. "Hello."

"Is that Anna Lawrence?"

Anna's heart pounded, but she recognized the voice. "Yes."

"Anna, this is Bethan Stark, Agent Stark."

The correction wasn't required. Anna knew who it was.

Stark continued. "That request you made yesterday?"

"Yes."

"I can facilitate that, but I need an answer now." Anna caught her breath. "The window of opportunity will literally be closed at the conclusion of this call. Do you understand me?"

The meaning was crystal clear. If she went, she went now. "Yes, I understand."

"Would you like to proceed?"

"Yes."

"Hold the line, please."

Anna waited, the silence polluted by MI5's irritating hold music.

When Stark returned, her tone had lightened. "You'll be collected by a car in approximately ten minutes. You are to take all of your personal Internet enabled electronic devices and surrender them to the officer in the vehicle. Pack as much as you can carry. You don't have much time."

"Thank you."

"Good luck." Stark hung up.

Seb knocked on her door but entered without invitation. He was in his boxer shorts and barely had one eye open. "What's going on?"

"That was Stark. They're taking me to Flic."

"*What*?" He was suddenly wide-awake.

"I'm going, Seb. They're taking me to her."

"In the middle of the night? It's a bit cloak and dagger isn't it?"

"I guess that's what time you do these things." Anna ushered him out while she dressed. Her body could hardly maintain pace with her brain, which was already out the front door. She inhaled deeply, slowing her breathing so she could at least think.

"You sure about this?" he called from the hallway.

Thrusting him her toiletries bag, she said, "I've never been surer of anything in my life. Now can you please make yourself useful and fill this with as much of my stuff as you can?"

"It's been three weeks. Are you sure Flic won't have changed her mind?"

Anna paused and stared at her reflection in her mirror. Over her shoulder she saw Seb lean in the doorway. "There's only one way to find out, right?"

"That's my girl." Seb threw the toiletries into her duffel bag and began pulling jumpers and tops from her drawers.

They were waiting by the front door staring out into the darkness of her quiet street in Clapham when Seb spoke. "So, this will be it for a while then?"

She hugged him close. "Hopefully, not too long."

"For what it's worth, I think you're doing the right thing."

Anna nodded. She needed that reassurance. "Whatever happens is in my hands now, and I know God would want me to follow my heart. I have to trust that." If there was one thing Anna had come to believe, it was that God wouldn't want all this fuss about love. *Love is Love*, she imagined God would say. Now get on with it.

As a set of headlights pulled into their street and double-parked in front of the house, Seb whispered, "I think God's got your back. Stay safe and I hope to see you both soon."

Anna opened the door as the officer reached the step.

"Are you Anna Lawrence?" She nodded and he held a photo next to her face, scanning from one to the other. "Can I see some identification?"

She handed him her driver's license and passport. He studied them thoroughly before producing a torch with an ultraviolet light. "Do you have your devices?"

"Yes."

"Excellent. I'm Phillip." He handed her his ID as proof and waited for her to take it in. "Follow me please, Miss Lawrence."

Stepping over the threshold was the second leap of faith she'd successfully completed within days. Her final challenge lay ahead, and both anxiety and anticipation filled her.

❖

Barney was a man of few words. Not that it mattered. He wasn't authorized to tell Flic anything anyway. Ethan, the new driver of the vehicle—they'd picked him up at a telephone box in the middle of nowhere an hour or so before—spoke even less. At least Barney was in telephone contact with someone and performed the task of saying "Yes, sir" with predictable regularity.

Barney typed something on his phone. Flic only caught a glimpse and guessed they were map coordinates. Ethan studied it for a moment, nodded, and took the next exit off the motorway. She imagined their vehicle from above, like when you fly over a country in the dead of night and see headlights weaving a path through an unknown land. They met no other cars on their journey, and the monotonous road left her head lolling from side to side as she dozed in the backseat.

The blue glowing clock on the dashboard read six thirty-seven, and the sky was a dusky gray color when Flic woke. Something told her she was near the sea, and she was correct. To the right of the car she could see the coastline. She thought she recognized the location, but instead of asking, decided to wait until she saw a road sign. It seemed ridiculous to continue to ask questions she knew wouldn't be answered, but sometimes the silence was unbearable.

"Are we nearly there? I need the bathroom." Flic wanted a coffee, too, but thought the toilet sounded less pathetic.

"Not far now."

Flic sensed Barney wanted to say more, but other than a crooked smile, he simply nodded and looked to the front again.

"Has there been any word on the man who found me last night?"

"He's one of the three men from the Order, but so far, he's not talking."

Of course he wasn't. That would be too easy. The entire process exasperated her. "Can't someone persuade him with a phone book or something?"

Barney and Ethan laughed. Barney said, "Oh, we have much more effective means of persuasion these days."

"Like teeth pulling?"

"There's that."

"And fingernail removal?" Flic could see the grin on Barney's face.

"Yes, that's a timeless classic."

"Toe removal and finger breaking." Flic couldn't suppress the feeling of satisfaction it gave her to think that the man responsible for trying to kill her this time could at least have *one* finger broken during their interview.

Barney joined in. "What about persuasion with a power saw or drill?"

The thought of such intense pain made her empty stomach lurch. "Okay, you win."

"Don't worry. We're searching the place he was staying and looking through all his stuff. There'll be a clue there somewhere."

"So the three of them have split up?"

"Looks like it. Not surprising though."

"And in the meantime I have you two blokes, right?" It was supposed to be a joke, but disappointment laced every word.

"Are you hungry?" It was the first she'd heard Ethan speak since they picked him up.

"I'm starving and could do with a coffee."

Ethan caught her eye in the rearview mirror. "Thirty minutes, okay?"

She nodded. She'd watched helplessly as hours and days passed. What was another thirty minutes?

❖

The thrill of surging adrenaline was new to Anna, and speeding along country roads in an unmarked MI5 vehicle was certainly nothing like the adrenaline rushes she was used to. Creating a great marketing campaign, Christmas bonuses, charity dinners with Dee, and being the all-round best at her role at Griffin's was the only real adrenaline fix Anna had ever known. It had never occurred to her to take drugs, jump off bridges with a giant rubber band strapped to her legs, jump out of a plane, or hang glide over the Austrian Alps. Her clever mind, until now, had been the source of her satisfaction. Actually *doing* something crazy was so beyond her comfort zone, she was practically a different woman.

Her first question to the police officer had been how long until they reached the safe house. He had vaguely replied that the journey would take "considerable time." That question had been the first of many. Anna's voice was reaching octaves so high, she wondered had the devil himself possessed her. But she couldn't stop. Where were they taking her? Did Flic know she was coming? Was driving people to safe houses all they did all day? Did they always move during the night? Who had authorized her to see Flic? Would Stark come and visit? In the end, Phillip suggested she try to get some sleep.

Even though sleep was impossible, she did stuff her bag against the door and lean into it, pulling her knees to her chest. Barely a second passed before she thought of Flic. The thoughts both excited and terrified her. Perhaps it was the reason she distracted herself for so long annoying the officers with unreasonable and idiotic questions; alone with her thoughts meant alone with Flic, and alone with Flic meant so many things. At the forefront of her mind was the thought process that began developing since confiding in Seb. Her sexual experience was limited. Her desires, even more limited, but the sudden change was sending her around the bend. Sexual thoughts of Flic filled her mind if she let them. And on every occasion, she was quick to remind herself that they weren't dirty. The thoughts she was experiencing were tender, loving, sensual, and like nothing she had allowed in the past. The growing knot of warmth that consumed her had to be love. There was no other explanation, so why on earth would God deny her of that? It was possible that the church would deny her, but not God. Surely not God.

The journey was almost unbearable it was taking so long. The winding road, of which the driver seemed determined to utilize both sides of, was making her feel nauseous, and she wished they could stop for something to eat. She hadn't seen Flic in weeks, but this morning had felt like living days for hours, hours for minutes, and minutes for seconds. The destination was unknown and so was the end to her torture.

A petrol station with a small cafe and steamy windows was enough to lift Flic's spirits. At this stage, she didn't really care what she ate, but coffee was a non-negotiable.

"Here, put this on." Barney tossed a scarf over the seat. "And pull your hood up. The toilet is inside here, so you'll have to get out, but I'll order food for you so you won't have to go to the counter, okay?"

Flic nodded and tucked the scarf into the neck of her jumper and pulled her hood on. A quick glance in the rearview mirror suggested she looked more tired and cold than a person being driven to their second safe house because the first one was compromised only hours before. She ordered an egg and bacon roll, a bag of crisps, a doughnut, a croissant, and a strong coffee. Barney lifted his eyebrows.

She shrugged. "If I stopped eating every time I was stressed lately, I'd be dead."

"You keep eating that shit and you'll be dead anyway."

"What are you having?"

Barney smiled. "Same as you." He pointed. "Bathroom's over there. Ethan will take you back to the car when you're done."

Ethan lingered outside, far enough away from the petrol station to safely smoke a cigarette and close enough to keep an eye on things.

It had been so long since Flic had eaten a big breakfast like this that she felt ill as she stuffed the last of her crisps into her mouth. The doughnut was for later, and she scrunched the top of the paper bag to keep the sugar from spilling everywhere. The coffee wasn't much, but it was wet and it was caffeinated, the only two requirements it needed to fulfill. Ethan delicately wiped dripping egg yolk from his chin and drained his tea before starting the engine.

When Flic had finished in the bathroom, he was waiting for her scrolling through pictures of pianos on his smartphone. They were expensive, and when she asked if he played, he said he was classically trained and still took a weekly lesson. His features suggested he was a hard man, but that was the beauty of an agent undercover wasn't it? A classically trained pianist, whose favorite piece to play was Chopin's "Ballade Number One," pulled the silver BMW back onto the road for what Barney promised was the final leg.

❖

What were the chances of seeing an identical BMW pulling out from the isolated petrol station and cafe stop? It was a different color, but still. Just like the car Anna was in, the rear windows were tinted. She briefly wondered if there was anyone in the backseat of that car and if there was, did they have a story to tell as complicated as hers.

She felt too nervous to eat, but she was also feeling lightheaded from her empty stomach so she settled on plain croissants and a cup of tea. The bathroom was a welcomed sight, and her two chaperones joked lightheartedly while they waited for her to return.

After serving his customers, the man behind the counter took a cloth and wiped the window nearest the cash register. "Must have been a sale on those ones." He jerked his head toward their BMW.

"Excuse me?" Phillip followed his gaze.

"That's the third one of those Beamers I've seen already this morning."

Anna's ears pricked up.

"Common car, I guess. Great on gas, too." Phillip eyed Anna. "Ready to go?"

The moment they were out of earshot, Anna bombarded him with questions. "Was Flic in that car? Where are we going? Don't you people radio each other or something? I could have traveled with her."

Phillip raised his hand to hush her.

Open-mouthed, she paused. Her own racing mind left her silent. If Flic had been in that car, then why? Flic was supposed to be in a safe house. Flic was supposed to be safe. "Something's happened, hasn't it? You're not just taking me to her; we're *all* going somewhere aren't we? That's why I'm allowed to join her because she's also being moved?"

"She was in that car, yes, and she's perfectly fine," he said. "The car previous to that is taking supplies to the safe house." This time he raised his finger to avoid interruption. "We ride on our own as instructed, we let the other teams follow their protocols, and very soon, we'll all be arriving where we need to be, okay?"

Anna stood her ground, her voice low and serious. *"What* happened?"

"Last night her safe house was compromised. We're moving her to a new one today. It's the most appropriate time to deliver you there also."

"She's okay, though isn't she?" Anna couldn't even begin to think about what the term "compromised" actually meant.

"As I said, she's perfectly fine, just in need of a new home for a while." He smiled crookedly at his lame attempt at wit.

Besides the fact that Flic's whereabouts had been discovered when she was supposed to be under MI5 protection, something else was bothering her. "Why now? I know you just said it was the most appropriate time to deliver me to her, but honestly, I know this isn't Hollywood. I know how safe houses work in the UK. They're usually homes of ex-police or security people and they put you up for a while and keep you off the grid. So what difference would it make if I joined her now or days ago?"

Phillip squared up and gave her his full attention. Perhaps he hadn't imagined she was much more than a desperate lovestruck woman. "You were being checked out, Miss Lawrence."

It all made sense. Then it didn't. "Surely I was checked out after the bombing?"

"I can't comment on that. I just know you were being monitored and you came up all clear to join Miss Bastone."

"Well, thank God for that."

"She was extracted safely. You needn't worry."

Something else occurred to her, and she began to wonder if she was a wasted talent in marketing. Perhaps detective work was more up her alley. "Why *do* you all drive the same cars? Bit obvious isn't it?"

"Did *you* notice?"

"As a matter of fact I did." She paused. "Well, not enough to mention it, I guess, but then I only saw one besides ours. That bloke saw three." She'd stick to marketing after all.

"In all honesty, we don't usually have the same vehicles. It's just that last night was a bit of a rush job. Try not to worry, though. They're not the same color, and they actually are a very common car. It's not like we're driving in a convoy or anything. There's sufficient time between us all to not raise suspicion. It's secure. I promise."

As if on cue, the man behind the counter walked by them restacking shelves. "Five Aston Martins the day before last. Now *that* you wouldn't believe round these parts, would you?"

Phillip said some blokey thing about cars as he ushered Anna from the shop. "See? He works in a garage and notices cars all the time. It's nothing out of the ordinary, and it's all going to plan."

Anna nodded and silently thanked God again. She was so close now; it was enough to shoot the nausea right back into her gut.

Phillip handed her a bottle of water and smiled. "Only about an hour now."

Flic was an hour away. She held on to that fact like her life depended on it, and she supposed it did. Flic was her chance to have everything she wanted. Ironically, it was only in the past few days that she realized she needed Flic as much as the air she breathed.

CHAPTER TWENTY-FOUR

Barmston was a small seaside town in East Yorkshire. Flic knew they were driving north, if not by the signage, by the drop in temperature. Beyond a wooded area and up a narrow road sat a vast farmhouse with numerous sheds and barns. She knew one of those outbuildings wasn't what it appeared to be from the outside, and the car parked out front of a small barn, identical to theirs in model, if not in color, reassured her.

At least here, the scenery was better than the previous safe house in north Kent. She sniffed the air—sea and cows. She couldn't see the sea. The green rolling fields were just undulated enough to block the view, but she knew it was there, and although she couldn't actually see any cows either, she could smell the parcels they left behind on the gravel roads.

From the outside, the barn was old and gray, but on the inside, it was converted and luxurious. It was useless to appear interested in the activity being undertaken in the barn. No one would tell her what was going on regardless. Four officers were there in total, and two of them tinkered with the surveillance system while Barney and Ethan set up laptops and began charging equipment.

"Will my stuff arrive later?" Flic realized she didn't even have a clean pair of knickers.

"Yes, ma'am," said one of the men who was flicking from camera to camera on the oversized screen in front of him.

One of the cameras filmed a view from the wooded intersection they had traveled through toward the farm. An identical car passed right by the camera as clear as day, and Flic was pleased. "That might be my stuff now."

The officers glanced at each other.

She felt disappointment. They obviously knew it wasn't her belongings. Clean knickers or not, she was having a shower. "Are there any towels?"

"There are, but the water's probably not hot yet."

She sighed. The car in front of them hadn't arrived soon enough to make the place comfortable, and the car arriving after her didn't have her things.

"It won't be long though." Barney smiled and offered her a jelly sweet.

She reminded herself why she was here, and she forgave herself for being so stupid. Solitude and one bag of belongings was so important to her she could barely believe it. When had it come to this?

Like any television that was on in a room, eyes are always drawn toward it, and Flic's gaze was absently fixed on the monitor systematically showing the various camera images—outside, inside, the driveway, the adjacent buildings, the hallway, the entrance, and Anna exiting a car.

"Hold on!" She reached over the officer and used the arrow keys to find the correct camera.

As plain as day, Anna hauled a bag from the backseat of the car and looked around.

The first thing that crossed Flic's mind was *how*? How in God's name had Anna arrived at the safe house? The second fleeting thought was *why*, and when it at last dawned on her that Anna was just outside the door, her body began to work in unison with her brain and engaged her legs.

Flic ran from the living room, taking the stairs two at a time, and burst through the front door only meters from where Anna stood. She froze.

She wasn't the only one. Anna dropped the bag, and the two officers that had escorted her made no attempt to hide their interest.

Never in her entire life had Flic been so glad to see someone. But not just *someone*, it was the one person she wanted to see more than anyone else in the world. She ran to Anna with all the intent in the world of taking her in her arms, kissing her as if the act in itself would sustain her and haul her inside to make love while the brave men of MI5 kept them safe.

A meter from Anna and reality caught up with Flic's elaborate fantasy. This was *Anna.* Anna wasn't someone you just rushed up to and kissed. But she was there, standing in the driveway of *her* safe house, so what was she there for, if not to kiss?

"This must be a shock for you." Anna's arms dangled gracelessly beside her.

"You could say that."

"Bet I'm the last person you expected to see."

"You could say that, too."

"And I suppose—"

Oh sod it! Flic advanced to place her finger on Anna's lips. "It *is* a shock, you *are* the last person I expected to see, and you can suppose all you like, but I'm about to kiss you. I've missed you, I think I really like you, and this time, I don't think you'll get mad at me if I do."

Anna smiled. It only lasted a moment before fear seemed to set in.

From the corner of her eye, Flic could see the police officers return to their business, thankfully realizing the moment was delicate and required privacy. Flic's heart took over, and when she moved to hug Anna, it felt like the most natural thing in the world to do. She recognized her smell immediately—the citrus scented perfume mixed gently with the fragrance of washing powder. It was Anna's smell, and Flic had missed it beyond words.

"I'm so glad you're here," said Flic.

Their foreheads rested together. Their eyes never strayed from each other's.

Flic took Anna's face between her hands before tracing her thumb over Anna's lips. It only took a split second to move her lips to Anna's. It had been so long since she'd had any real human interaction that being in such close and intimate proximity to someone was like melting ice.

Anna neither pulled away nor participated, but something told Flic she was doing the right thing.

"I've missed you," said Anna.

"It's okay. You're here now."

"Missing you is partly the reason why. I've never missed anyone like I've missed you. I thought I was going bonkers."

Flic laughed. She'd never heard Anna even say the word "bonkers," let alone admit she thought she was going crazy.

"I mean it, Flic. I'll go mad if I can't sort this stuff out. I can't eat, I can't sleep, and half the time I can't even think straight."

Flic laughed harder.

"What? What's so funny?"

Flic knew exactly what Anna's ailment was, but she didn't say. It was something Anna would need to work out for herself. "Nothing is funny, well, you are a little. You're cute actually, but it doesn't matter. You're here now." Flic smiled reassuringly. The last thing she wanted was for Anna to think she was making fun of her. "We're together, and you don't have to worry anymore." Flic winked. "You'll eat like a horse and sleep like a baby now, I promise."

Anna smiled unconvincingly. "They told me you were compromised last night." She shrugged. "I don't really even know what that means. I'm just so glad you're okay."

Flic told her the sequence of events that led her, and now Anna, to Yorkshire. She concluded with a smile. "But it's all right now. Seeing you makes it all right. I promise."

Anna seemed reassured. "Come on," she said. "Show me around your palace."

"No way." Flic required answers of her own. "First, I'll make us both a cup of tea while you tell me how the hell you managed to swing this."

Walking toward the barn, Flic second-guessed herself. "You are here because of—I mean you're not here for work or anything are you? Did Dee swing this?" She was horrified. "Did I just make a complete arse of myself?"

This time it was Anna who moved to prohibit Flic from talking. "You had it right the first time. I promise."

"You're here for me?"

"Yes."

"To be with me?"

"Something like that."

"You're staying, right? I mean, they can't let you go now can they? Now that you know where I am."

"Flic! Calm down." Anna took Flic's hands in hers. "I'm here because I want to be with you, and although you managed to make it sound so dramatic, it's not part of the deal for me to leave before this is all over. As long as you're here, I'm here."

Flic inhaled deeply. "I think I've spent too much time alone." She gathered herself and pushed away her insecurities, hopefully allowing the previously experienced elation to take over once more. She took Anna in her arms again. "I'm just so glad you're here."

Flic carried Anna's bag up the stairs before putting the kettle on. "Now tell me, please. Who'd you have to sleep with to score this holiday?"

Anna glared at her.

"I'm kidding, but seriously, who pulled the strings to get you here? Was it Dee?"

Anna recounted the story, explaining that Dee wasn't the least bit surprised to learn that Anna was disappearing for an indefinite period of time and that Flic was the reason.

Flic smiled and shook her head.

"What?"

"I don't know how you do it, but you just make shit happen."

The color drained from Anna's cheeks and her brow creased. Flic wondered if she'd said something wrong. "Are you okay?"

Anna took her tea to the privacy of the sitting room. Flic followed.

"What's wrong?"

Anna winced. "There are some things I can't just make happen," she said.

"I don't follow." Anna raised her head exposing moist eyes. Then reality dawned on Flic. "Oh, I get it." She filled with disappointment—heavy, soul destroying disappointment. "So it's just friends then?"

"*What*? No. Don't be completely daft. I didn't mean that. I just meant…" Anna turned bright red.

Flic shook her head. She was lost.

"I mean that *you'll* have to make it happen."

Flic shrugged, clueless.

"Really? Do I have to spell it out for you? The burden rests with you."

"The burden? What burden?"

Luckily, Anna had put her tea down because she threw her arms in the air. "I could throttle you sometimes." She took a deep breath. "You'll have to make *us* happen. I've not had any experience in this before. I'm sorry."

"Oh my God. I'm sorry. Of course." A sense of relief washed over Flic like an incoming wave, but when it receded, all that remained was Anna's distorted face of anguish. She went to her. "Please don't worry about that—"

"But I am worried."

"I understand, but I want to reassure you there really is nothing to worry about." She kissed Anna on the cheek.

"You sound so sure."

"I am sure."

"How?" Anna attempted to rub the tension from her forehead.

Flic went to light the small log burner. "Because by the time we get round to any of that naughty stuff, you'll be gagging for it." She promptly threw up her arms in defense of the barrage of pillows Anna hurled her way.

"Felicity Bastone, you're uncouth."

"I'm kidding." Flic tackled Anna onto the sofa. "Well, maybe only just a little." Anna punched her. "But please don't worry. I have a hunch we have a long time to get to know each other."

Anna glanced around at the safe house.

"Not just in here. I think you and I have a long time in general."

"It scares me though, to be honest."

"Which bit?" Flic maneuvered them to cuddle comfortably. She crossed her fingers and hoped she wasn't overstepping the mark. She held her breath until Anna relaxed.

"Falling in love," said Anna.

Flic swallowed hard and loud, suppressing the urge not to choke on her own saliva. "Are you falling in love with me?"

"Maybe."

"Maybe is good."

"Are you falling in love with *me*?"

"Maybe. Actually, it's a maybe with a possibly definitely undertone."

"For an author and journalist, you have an appalling command of the English language."

Flic returned to the fire to tend its dwindling flame.

"I should kick your arse for coming here and putting yourself in danger."

Anna laughed. "I'm sure we're safe now."

Flic stared out the window over the green fields with cows and beyond to the sea. "That's what I thought last time. But they found me." She turned to Anna, tears in her eyes. "They always keep finding me."

"Oh, hey. I'm sorry. I can't imagine how you must feel being hunted. But this time, I'm sure it'll be okay. The police are thorough, and they'll catch them soon."

"They caught one last night."

"Exactly. And they'll catch the others, too. Please try not to worry. You *are* in the safest place. You have to believe that."

"I'm beginning to wonder if I'd have been better off just disappearing myself."

"Yes, that's a good plan. No police protection, and how on earth was I going to find you?"

"The plan has flaws, I admit." Flic smiled to reassure Anna it was okay.

She changed the subject. "How's the book doing?"

They both settled on the sofa while Anna shared everything she knew regarding book sales, future tour plans, and of course the Love is Love campaign. The success of the book was certainly phenomenal, and although she had been thankful for the break, she really wanted to be back out there talking to people and spreading a positive message.

Fine drizzle began to obscure the view from the window, and they opted for the comfort of the sitting room for most of the day. It was true that if you didn't go out in the rain in England, you might not go out for days, but it wasn't the drizzle that kept them glued to each other in front of the fire.

CHAPTER TWENTY-FIVE

They spoke of a future where they each featured in the other's, but neither made reference on how they might get there. Flic continually reminded herself that they had all the time in the world, and although the ball had been firmly placed in her court, she was determined not to rush anything. It was a delicate situation.

So, it was with great surprise to find, after two bottles of red, that Anna's hand slid down her thigh as they lay side by side on the sofa.

Flic flinched. Anna's hand gently stroking her inner thigh was the last thing she was expecting.

"I feel butterflies in my tummy," said Anna. She smiled, but her breathing had changed.

Flic cupped her face and drew it toward her. Their lips met, but this time it was a tender, elongated touch. Had Anna's hand not been gently massaging her leg, Flic might not have taken things further, but it had been a long time since someone stirred such deep feelings. And Anna had started it. Hell, Flic had intended to wait weeks before she touched Anna in any of her sexy spots. She hadn't been entirely sure how she was going to achieve such abstinence, but it had certainly been her intention. Intentions be damned. She reached down to unbutton her jeans.

She paused to gauge Anna's reaction. Besides her cheeks flushing an even brighter red, she didn't shy away.

Flic made a dash for second base and guided Anna's hand inside her jeans, on top of her underwear. Because it had been so long since she'd felt this aroused, the moisture in her pants shocked her.

They kissed again, and this time Flic pushed her tongue inside Anna's mouth. She noticed the hand between her legs press harder against her. *Oh, sweet Jesus!*

"A first time together doesn't count, right?" said Anna. It was more of a statement than a question. "I mean, they get better, so forgive me if it's a bit rubbish."

"Nonsense. You'll be fine." Flic couldn't see how anything Anna was about to do could be judged as rubbish. "Plus give yourself a break. This might not be our first time; it might just be fooling around. There's no pressure."

Anna had already made her wet, made her heart beat as fast as a galloping racehorse, and her head was giddy with passion.

Anna's fingers found her clit. Through her pants, it was probably just a lucky stroke, but there it was. Flic gathered herself long enough to say, "Stop anytime if you don't want to go on, okay?" It took all her willpower to pull away and look Anna in the eye. "I mean it." She meant it, but she didn't want it to stop.

Flic was torn. She wanted to undress Anna, but at the same time, didn't want Anna to remove her hand from beneath her jeans. And this scenario certainly wasn't how she imagined this to play out. Not once did it occur to her that she would be at the mercy of Anna so early on.

"I dreamt about this you know?" said Anna. "An actual dream." She slipped her thumb under the band of Flic's knickers. A long way under the band. "In it, you took me to bed and made me feel the most incredible things."

Flic could barely breathe. "I can do that, if you like."

"I'd like to touch you first, if that's okay." Flic managed a nod. She fleetingly remembered her first time and how, oddly, it was easier to touch than be touched.

Anna's entire hand disappeared down Flic's pants.

"Oh, Jes..." Flic's voice trailed off, firstly because she remembered it probably wasn't a good thing to mention Jesus at this point, and secondly because Anna was succeeding in taking her breath away.

The scene was exquisite. Flic lay on her back, her jeans pushed down to her thighs, her knickers bunching there too. She was squirming. Anna lay propped beside her, her fingers playing dangerously with Flic's opening.

Although Flic's desire was powerful, she wanted to show Anna she was doing it right. She placed her hand over Anna's and guided a finger inside her.

Thankfully, Anna was a quick learner.

"Put in a second," whispered Flic.

Whether it was a fluke or by design, as Anna slowly pumped her fingers rhythmically in and out, the palm of her hand applied just the right amount of pressure on Flic's clit. All the stresses of the last twenty-four hours faded into oblivion. The only thing occupying Flic's mind was the generous and gentle fucking she was receiving at the hands of Anna.

"You sure you've never done this before?" asked Flic.

"In my mind, I've done this to you a thousand times." Anna increased the tempo.

"Well, in *my* mind, this scenario unfolded rather differently indeed."

Anna silenced Flic with her lips in a deep and sensual kiss.

All Flic could do was close her eyes and enjoy the ride. She never once imagined her first time with Anna would be like this, nor would it be so soon. It had never occurred to her that Anna was ready *now*, and had she been honest, she'd been worried that being intimate with her might feel a little creepy because she might be persuading her to do new things. Things she might have perceived as unnatural in the past.

Flic doubted Anna was feeling unnatural now.

Anna was reacting to every change in Flic's body—her breathing, the increased pulse of thrusting, and as Flic drew near to orgasm, Anna moved faster and pumped her fingers deeper inside. With the final thrusts hitting directly on Flic's G-spot, she cried out loudly, but briefly, allowing the breathtaking wave of completeness to engulf her.

Flic finally caught her breath. "Surely that can't be a sin?"

Anna went to remove her finger.

"Please, not yet?"

"I know it's taken me a while to see it, but I'm quite sure that the Lord would never have wanted to deny anyone the ability to connect with another human being in an act of love." Anna remained inside Flic and nestled into her neck.

Flic knew Anna would never be capable of sex if love weren't involved. The all-consuming emotions of true love were impossible to suppress. Of course you could ignore them or wait years until you'd turned bitter and the love had finally faded, but there was no off switch. There was nothing on earth that could compare to it, and once true love had a hold on you, to share it was the most beautiful feeling.

"Can I ask you a personal question?"

Anna nodded. "Of course."

"Did that…Just now, did…Did what we just did, you know, did that turn you on?"

Anna whispered something, but Flic couldn't make out the words.

"Pardon?"

"Why don't you find out?" Anna was barely audible.

Flic reached between her legs and slowly removed Anna's fingers from inside her. Severing their connection, even if only for a moment, left her feeling empty—physically and in her heart. She quickly stood and removed her clothing, standing naked in front of Anna.

"You're beautiful," said Anna.

Flic smiled but remained silent. She realized she could tell Anna how she felt a thousand times over, but showing her and letting her feel her love was how it should be, especially this first time.

There were so many ways she wanted to take Anna, and in the fullness of time, she would explore those and many more. But tonight she wanted Anna to feel her tenderness, to look her in the eye as she made her come and witness Flic making love to her.

Flic maneuvered Anna into a sitting position. She gently pulled her jumper from her and then her T-shirt. Anna sat staring up at her in a pink lace bra. Flic pushed her knees apart just enough to kneel between them. She kissed both sides of Anna's neck and unclasped the bra from behind. A fantasy flashed in her mind of coming home from work one day and taking Anna over the back of the sofa without saying a word. Moisture coated the inside of her thigh. She would worship Anna, in body and mind.

She traced a line from Anna's belly, up between her breasts and then around the back of her neck before she took a nipple in her mouth. Anna's response was nothing short of outstanding.

"Oh, shit."

A flash of reality hit Flic. Anna's nipple was in her mouth. She was about to make love to her. The thought was blissful.

With her tongue encircling Anna's firm nipple, she negotiated the button on Anna's jeans before she unzipped them. Loathe to break the connection, she took the jeans by the ankles and pulled them off.

"Can we turn off the lamp?" Anna sounded timid, but determined.

Flic switched off the light and was pleased the fire radiated a steady glow. She didn't want to frighten Anna, but she wanted to see her.

Flic stood between Anna's legs and tipped her chin to face her. She smiled reassuringly before she pulled Anna into a standing position. She slipped her hands down the back of her knickers and they kissed. Now Anna portrayed a sense of urgency, and Flic knew the time was right. She lowered herself to the ground to kneel before her. She wanted the first thing Anna felt between her legs to be her tongue.

Anna was trim and inviting. Flic encouraged her to lift one foot onto the sofa, opening herself. As she took Anna's bottom in both hands, Flic licked her from deep inside her opening slowly to her clit where she applied pressure and felt Anna go weak at the knees.

The only encouragement Flic needed was Anna's lightning fast hand gripping the back of her hair and pushing her face deeper between her legs.

"Will you....touch me?"

It was the last thing Flic expected to hear so soon. Her seduction was intended to be slow, but it was too soon in their exploration of each other to make Anna wait. Ready to share with Anna what she knew she needed, Flic dipped her tongue deep inside her then pulled away to sit on the sofa. She encouraged Anna toward her and guided her into a kneeling position over her lap. Spreading her own legs a little wider, she in turn spread Anna's.

Flic rested a hand on Anna's hip and rested two fingers just beyond her opening. With a nod of encouragement and with downward pressure on her hip, Flic lowered Anna onto her fingers and she pushed them inside her fully.

Anna let out a gasp of satisfaction. Flic loved that moment when she was finally entered; it was encouraging that Anna did too.

With her arm firmly around Anna's waist, and a nipple between her lips and teeth, Flic pushed her fingers in and out of Anna encouraging her to ride her hand, which Anna instinctively did.

With a cry that she was sure would summon the police officer that had remained in the house, Anna came hard and fast.

"That was indescribable." She twisted off Flic and collapsed on the sofa. "You're amazing."

Flic smiled. What Anna had just allowed her to do was monumental, and she expected tears but none came. In fact, she released a sigh of relief as Anna grinned from ear to ear, and in the flickering fire light, she simply glowed.

"I never imagined I'd feel like this."

"With a woman or at all?" Flic wanted to tread carefully.

"At all." Anna shrugged. "It's always women in my fantasies. It never occurred to me that I might one day experience that fantasy for real."

Flic felt bold. "Can I admit something to you without scaring you?"

"Go on."

"When I was stripping you naked, I imagined coming home from work and taking you over the back of the sofa the moment I walked in."

Anna shuddered. "There's so many things I want to explore with you."

"Like what?"

"First you have to understand that until I met you I had suppressed my fantasies and kept them very private. They're real and certainly vivid, and they're the only outlet I've had to express myself, and I was in constant angst about letting them surface or pushing them deep inside." Anna was suddenly shy.

"Please keep going. I won't judge you."

"In bed at night I let scenarios play out in my mind. I don't make a sound and I don't move. I just lie there thinking of different ways you might..." Anna paused, lowered her eyes, and whispered. "Fuck me."

It sounded odd hearing Anna speak like that, but Flic dared not interrupt.

"It's been part of my confession when I go, of course. And other than confessing to inappropriate thoughts, I don't elaborate, but I do admit it. When you're alone and lonely you crave something, someone. Those fantasies are the only thing I have."

"Had."

Anna laughed. "Yes, it seems they're coming true."

"And are you sure you're okay about this? I mean, this is a huge leap for you."

"I never knew what it meant to be madly in love. But for the first time in my life, I felt out of control and I loved it. Fancy liking the feeling of lack of control. Fancy *me* liking that feeling. I talked to Seb about it. I really was going bonkers, and he helped me see that it was you who sent my world spinning. It's always been girls and not boys that interested me, but until you came along, I honestly thought it didn't matter because I felt I would never fall in love, never act on my feelings, and never have to worry about it." Sadness drained her face. "Then it occurred to me that the pope might have felt that way about the Camerlengo. Then I imagined a life without love. I imagined my life without you, and it made me so sad."

"You've done a lot of thinking and soul searching since I've been away." Flic stroked Anna's belly. "I'm glad you did."

"I thought I understood love just by reading and hearing about it. But no one understands love until you experience it."

Flic kissed her on the cheek. "I'm glad you've let me love you."

"You really love me?"

"Of course." Flic laughed. "Who the hell am I kidding playing it cool? I've loved you for a long time."

"I couldn't have done this if I didn't love you, you know that?"

"I know." Flic raised her eyebrows. "So?"

Anna hid her face behind her hands. She peaked through a crack between her fingers before finally allowing her hands to fall. "So I love you more than anything."

More than anything. The words rung in Flic's ears, and she believed it wholeheartedly. For Anna to love anything more than the church was something monumental indeed. She silently vowed to protect Anna's heart always.

"You wouldn't make us a cup of tea, would you?" Anna winked.

"Oh, here we go, domesticated bliss at its very best."

CHAPTER TWENTY-SIX

It was odd lying in bed next to Flic. Naked.

Although Anna had her conscience to battle, she also had the endorphins, or whatever she thought they were called, of love to deal with. One moment she would remember, with alarming clarity, the moment she orgasmed, and she could swear her heart would double in size, but another moment, that same thought would scare her and send shocking waves of guilt and shame to her core. The rollercoaster ride continued.

"You okay?" asked Flic.

It was three in the morning, and although Anna had slept soundly until then—pure exhaustion ensured that every time Anna was on the verge of drifting back to sleep, a jolt of guilt would awaken her.

"I feel like a cheating wife."

"No, you don't."

"Pardon?"

"Oh, I'm sure you feel guilty, but you've not hurt anyone. You've not even cheated on God really. A nun would have a strong argument, I'll grant you that, but you're not married to God. You haven't cheated. You'll never have to look at the person you cheated on and admit you've behaved like the lowest of the low. Hopefully, you'll never wear that label, because no matter how hard you try, you can't take cheating back."

"This sounds like the voice of experience."

"It's the voice of someone who wears the label with shame. We all burden guilt in some way or another. Some things are harder to forgive yourself for. Trust me, you're not a cheater."

"Will you tell me about it some time?"

"One day I will, but for now, all you need to know is that the person you made love to is right beside you, and she'll help you through absolutely anything."

Anna snuggled into Flic's open arms. "It's fleeting when it comes over me, but it's real."

"It won't last forever. I promise. Plus, surely the world is a better place if we're all filled with love? I honestly can't see the real God, if there is one, begrudging you that. In fact, I'd say she's pretty pissed off with organized religion right now. She'd be delighted for you though, I bet."

"She? Since when did God become a woman?"

"Since in my mind she can. Prove to me she's not?"

"Oh no, we're not going through this again. If I hear one peep out of you about Santa or the bloody Easter Bunny—"

"What about the tooth fairy?"

"Or her too—"

"Him."

"What?"

"In my mind, the tooth fairy is a man. A big raving—"

"Yes, thank you. I get the drift." Anna nuzzled closer. "You challenge just about every belief I have."

"That's good, right? I mean imagine if I just agreed with everything you said and did."

"Can't see any problem with that."

Flic continued unperturbed. "And regardless, it's not so much that I want to challenge you; it's just that I hope you learn to see that we can all make choices about who we are and what we believe."

Anna pinched Flic's backside. "I think your mantra is sinking in."

"Yeah, well, it doesn't make us any less a good person."

"Is that correct English?" Anna was finally feeling drowsy. She looked at her phone. It was four thirty. "I feel better now."

"You do?"

She was keen to relieve Flic of her sermon duty for the night. "I do. I've found love. I'm not hurting anyone. I have nothing to feel guilty for."

"And?"

Flic knew her so well. Anna loved that about her. It astounded her how someone, just one person in the world, could know her more intimately than absolutely everyone else. And the best thing about it was its effortlessness. They understood each other without effort. In fact, she realized, she loved Flic without effort. The only obstruction was her beliefs—the ones she had previously thought expanded her mind. She was beginning to wonder if the *knowledge* of religion would continue to expand her mind, not necessarily her faith. By forging her own path and choosing her destiny, in partnership with that knowledge, she determined that only then would she truly be open-minded.

Flic nudged her, waiting for an answer. "Well, with all the wars and suppression in the world caused by religion, I'm beginning to see your point that God would just want people to be in love and at peace. Why do so many people have to hate so many other people?"

Flic yawned. "I think that's a discussion for another middle of the night chat."

Anna turned her back to Flic and pushed her backside into her middle, encouraging Flic's arm to encircle her. "I've imagined you holding me like this."

Flic squeezed. "I'm your big spoon."

"Night night, big spoon." Anna could barely whisper the words.

"Night, little spoon."

❖

Anna made it to seven o'clock sleeping soundly, but her need for the toilet and a strong cup of tea saw her slip out from beneath Flic's arm. She scrounged around the floor for her pajama bottoms and a hoodie and padded into the kitchen. The smell of coffee greeted her only moments before an MI5 agent.

"Good morning," he said.

"Morning." Anna eyed the coffee and decided to forgo the tea. "Do you mind?"

"No, of course not. Help yourself." He seemed to fidget for a moment. "Um, is Miss Bastone up yet?"

Anna eyed him warily. "No. She's still asleep. Why? Is everything okay?"

The officer appeared undecided. "Yeah, I guess. Well, maybe no." He sighed. "Look, perhaps I'll wait until she's up."

"Is she compromised again?" Anna didn't want to even contemplate what another attempt on her life would do to Flic.

"No, nothing like that." He reassuringly touched her shoulder.

Of course they weren't. If they were, organized chaos would reign. She tried to relax.

She spotted a newspaper on the table. "Do you mind if I take a look at that?"

"What? That newspaper? It's yesterday's tabloid shite. You don't want to read that."

With the days all merging into one, it made little difference what paper it was, tabloid rubbish or not. "Sure, it's better than none."

"Oh, no, no, no." The officer stood firm. Firm and weird. "Sorry, miss. It's Anna, right?" Anna nodded, eyebrows raised, wondering if he'd overdosed on caffeine. He sighed again, clearly uncomfortable. "I'll show you. I'm Leo, by the way." He went to the table and turned the paper over to reveal the front page.

Anna's hand covered her mouth in shock and sadness.

The ex pope was in hospital. He'd suffered a stroke.

But the officer didn't linger on the front page. He continued two or three pages in. Anna gasped.

"It's not good is it?" Leo said. "I mean as hard as it is, I'd want to know that that was in the paper." He shook his head for a long moment. "It's probably better coming from you anyway."

The headline read—*Bastone Body Parts Arriving by Mail.*

Similar to charts seen in doctors' surgeries, an anatomically correct picture of a woman with a superimposed image of Flic's head filled the front page. Blackened out were body parts that the newspaper claimed to have been sent to them by those holding Flic captive. Body parts that the sender was claiming to be Flic's. "It would take the paper five minutes of actual journalism to find out that this is all rubbish." Anna was disgusted.

Leo shrugged and looked embarrassed. Usually people with alarmingly low IQs bought this particular newspaper. "I like the crossword," he said.

"Do they really expect people to believe that someone has sent Flic's finger, hair, little toe, and eyeball to a newspaper with the threat of more body parts if her book isn't removed from shelves?" Anna thought for a moment. "Could this really have come from the people after her?"

Leo shook his head. "I've no doubt *someone* has sent body parts to the paper. But the Order aren't claiming it's them. And it's hardly their style."

Anna agreed. Plus it didn't make sense. The Order don't have Flic. MI5 do.

"I reckon it's some other wacko with access to dead people and a grudge against Flic's, sorry, I mean, Miss Bastone's, book," said Leo.

Poor Flic.

Anna closed the paper and poured a coffee. The ex pope was in hospital—probably caused by stress—and Flic's body was being chopped up and delivered to the crappiest newspaper in Britain. She had to tell Flic about it.

"I'm sorry," said Leo. "Of course I can throw out the paper and ask the officers who come here not to mention it, but I just know if it were me I'd want to know."

"She'll want to know, too. She'd be disappointed if she found out I knew and didn't tell her."

"She's famous. I suppose as shit, sorry, I mean as rubbish as it is, it'll only be news for a day or two."

Anna had her doubts, and even if it did blow over that quickly, she doubted Flic would bounce back with the same speed. Isolation was wearing her down, and this wouldn't help. Anna tipped the remainder of her coffee down the sink. She closed the paper and folded it neatly before disappearing with it into the bedroom.

Flic didn't stir as Anna slipped out of her clothes and slid under the covers. The newspaper on the bedside table was the only reason she couldn't relax.

Flic rolled over and wrapped an arm around her. "Where'd you go?"

"Coffee. I needed a coffee."

"Where's mine?"

That was a good question. She'd forgotten. "I'll get you one in a minute."

"Is everything okay?"

"Of course." Anna knew she was rubbish at lying, and it was certainly a ridiculous lie. Everything was not okay, and pretending that it was and then waiting until Flic woke fully to tell her was just stupid. "Actually, no. There's something I wanted to talk to you about."

Flic shot into a sitting position. "I'm glad you feel comfortable enough to talk about it. If there's anything about last night you didn't like or you want me to change—"

"It's not about last night, Flic." There was nothing Anna could do to prepare Flic for what she was about to see. "I need to show you something and it's going to upset you." Anna retrieved the paper.

"The pope, a stroke? How sad." Flic obviously copped a glimpse at the cover page.

"No, unfortunately, that's not it." Anna turned the pages and rested the paper on Flic's lap.

"Oh, my fucking hell. I've been shot and blown up and now some clown is sending body parts to a newspaper and claiming they're mine."

"I know. It's ridiculous."

"No, what's ridiculous is that the paper is printing this shit. How on earth, even if they were dumb enough to think the odd limb arriving at their office was actually mine, do they think printing this would help me?"

Anna wanted to say something helpful, something positive, but nothing sprang to mind. She knew Flic was upset because her life had now been reduced to newspaper sales. Anna looked on helplessly as Flic's eyes darkened.

"I've risked everything for this fucking book. Half the world wants me burnt at the stake and the other half probably couldn't give a fuck because I'm making shed loads of money out of a gay pope." She threw the paper at the wall. "Well, everyone's making money out of my fucking misery now."

"Please try not to let this get to you."

"Get to me? It's already got to me" Flic's face was red and her eyes were moist. "I can't take much more of this."

Anna pulled her into a strong embrace. She'd wondered how long it would be before Flic finally broke. Everyone has a threshold and it looked like Flic had finally reached hers. Anna wasn't surprised that this had toppled Flic over the edge. Having Anna there as support was probably what gave her permission to fall apart. Sometimes all it took was knowing that there was someone there to pick up the pieces before you broke. Anna rocked her back and forth. Flic was well and truly broken.

"You're still here?" Flic said after many minutes.

Anna held her at arm's length. "And where on earth did you think I would go?"

"I'm famous for this book. Soon I'll be famous for having a relationship with my Catholic PR expert. All of this will stay with me forever."

"And if you play your cards right, so will I."

"Forever is a long time."

"I don't want to put pressure on you, but what does forever look like to you?" asked Anna.

"It means commitment. It means a romantic marriage proposal followed by a simple but elegant wedding, and it means a lifetime of happiness."

Anna smiled, relieved. "Then maybe forever isn't long enough at all, but for the time being I think it sounds reasonable."

"I feel empty."

Anna guessed Flic's dally into a whimsical life together would be short-lived.

"I wish I could make the hurt stop." Anna squeezed her tightly.

"I just feel so hopeless, so disconnected."

"I'm not sure this'll help, but we have to try to move forward. If we think of a problem, we try to think of the solution at the same time. Sound like a plan?"

"I can think of a problem."

"What's that then?"

"There's fucking mad men out there trying to kill me, and our country is full of idiot bloody newspapers that publish utter shite."

"And your solution?"

"Blow them all up."

"Great plan, Einstein." Anna squeezed Flic. "You're a wasted talent as an author."

Flic stared at Anna. "How on earth did I manage to win your heart? And all in direct competition with the church."

"Perhaps I found something to love more than I love the church."

"I just want this to end."

"And it will. I promise. In the meantime, we have to learn to live with it."

"I'm the source of scandal after scandal. I think my author days are over."

"Nonsense. What a ridiculous notion. Although you can't see it now, and I'll forgive you if you can't see it for some time, but all of this is an opportunity."

Flic rolled her eyes.

"Write a book about it. About the attempts on your life and about the safe houses. That will shut them up."

"A book?"

"Yes, silly. A book."

"I really can't see how that's a good idea. I'm finished as an author."

"Think about it. It'll make a great story."

Flic seemed to process the thought. "Maybe it's not a bad idea."

Anna watched her mull it over.

Flic developed a grin. "I think it could work."

"Trust me, it *will* work. It's my job to spin lines for stuff like this. I harness quality opportunities out of rubbish situations, do I not?"

"Will you help me?" Flic was excited.

"Of course I will. But get Cameron to help you with the actual plotting and writing. He's the best of the best."

Flic agreed.

Griffin's editor was the best person to help her, but she appeared keen to begin immediately. "I'll make a start on it today and then speak to Cameron when we're out of here." The prospect of writing again was exciting her. "I mean, when will I have time on my hands like this after we're safe and allowed to go home?"

Flic smiled warmly causing Anna's head to go all mushy. "It's a great plan, and when better to begin than now?"

Flic eyed her thoughtfully. "Where will home be for us when this is over?"

"London, I presume."

"No, I mean for *us*. Will we have the same home?"

This time it was Anna's turn to laugh. "Can I make a confession?"

"There's a million jokes in there somewhere, but go ahead, my child, I'm all ears." Flic pretended to cross herself.

"I had no intention of sleeping with you when I came here."

Flic raised her eyebrows.

"Well, I told myself I had no such intention."

"Then what exactly was your intention?"

"I wanted to explore what it would be like with you. I came because I realized I couldn't function without you in my life. I ridiculously told myself that we'd be married before we had sex for the first time and then we could live together."

"And now?"

"And now we should move in together."

"Oh, that's so lesbian!"

"What? It is not."

"You know the lesbian joke, right? One date and then move in together."

"Well, in that case, it's smooth sailing for us and not stereotypical at all."

"How do you figure that?"

"Because we haven't been on a date yet."

CHAPTER TWENTY-SEVEN

Flic knew she'd fallen in love, but by the end of their first full day and night together, it was clear she was done for. Anna let her explore her body, allowing her to do things to her that she'd never before experienced, and Flic found herself experiencing things for the first time, too. She'd never felt more responsible for someone else's body or heart. She'd never felt so protective, so adoring, and so gently nurturing of the love that was developing between them.

The countryside was spectacular—when the rain stopped—and they spent their days anonymously exploring the coast discussing the contents of her new book, often taking notes as they sat and watched the dull gray water of the North Sea. On rare occasions they encountered other walkers. No one recognized her or bothered with much more than a friendly hello. If they intended on going too far, an officer would accompany them, but on shorter walks, they relished time alone.

❖

Flic lay on top of Anna, both facedown, and pushed her fingers deep inside. Anna drew a sharp intake of breath. Flic loved being the cause of that joy.

It was late one evening, and because the days had rolled into one, Flic had no idea what day or date it was, just that it was, at a guess, about a week since Anna arrived. Not one night had passed without them making love, and tonight was no different.

"Can you move up to your knees?" Flic removed her fingers and slid off Anna.

It surprised her, but nothing she asked of Anna seemed to shock or intimidate her, and it wasn't as if Anna was shy about pushing the boundaries of her own comfort zone. They shared a giggle when things didn't run smoothly, when a position just wouldn't work, and on more than one occasion, Anna asked for more or something different, knowing what it would take to reach orgasm. Flic realized that Anna's most alluring characteristic was her genuine openness. Of course, she remained nervous at times, a little apprehensive, and occasionally unsure of her own prowess, but the new Anna—the Anna that loved Flic—was a tower of strength and absolutely everything Flic needed.

Anna moved to her knees and rested her head on her arms. "I feel a bit exposed like this."

Flic was quick to respond. "We can change if you like."

"No. I've fantasized about it this way. I just never thought what it would feel like with someone kneeling behind me staring at my arse."

They both laughed.

"Well, if it makes you feel any better, you have a great arse." Flic encircled both bottom cheeks with her tongue and reached beneath Anna to fondle her breasts. She bit her backside.

"Ouch!"

Without another word, Flic straightened and slid the palm of her left hand along Anna's spine. At the same time, she entered her again, intent on finishing what she had begun.

"I wish we had something to use," muttered Anna.

"How do you mean?" Flic slowed her thrusting hand to a gentle pulse.

"I just feel like—Oh, it doesn't matter."

"No, what? Tell me, please."

"I don't even know if you like toys or things or whatever they're called, but I'd love you to somehow be inside me, to you know…"

Flic smiled as Anna struggled to say the word. "You mean fuck you?" Anna never ceased to surprise her.

Anna sighed. "Yes. But at the same time have your hands free and maybe on my hips."

"When we get out of here we can go shopping."

"In an actual store?"

Flic laughed at the dread in Anna's voice. "Or online." She reached around and caressed Anna's clit as the tips of her fingers concentrated on her G-spot.

Anna let out a deep moan.

"That's better. Now no more talk, okay?"

Although Flic and Anna had explored eastward toward the sea many times, today was such a horrible day they wanted to avoid the coastal wind and venture inland. There were so few people around, especially in the unpredictable weather, that Flic had assured Ethan they would only be gone for an hour and his escort wasn't required. He'd taken one look at the blustery conditions and agreed, telling them not to walk more than an hour's distance from the house and to walk due west, no deviations.

The initial stage of the walk required them to negotiate the hill behind the farmhouse. After only fifteen minutes, with the wind propelling them upward, Flic stopped.

"It'll be hell on the way back into this bloody wind." She turned to face the sea, and the cold air whipped about her face, cutting through her scarf and hat.

She spotted a black car weave along the dirt road toward the house.

"At least we have some respite heading west first." Anna panted and tucked her trousers into her socks.

It looked like a BMW.

"It might blow like this for days," said Anna.

Flic couldn't be sure at this distance, but it could also have been a Mercedes.

"We should just soldier on."

The occupants of the car could be lost.

Anna raised her voice against the wind. "You know how it is in England. If we didn't go out in rubbish weather, we'd never get out."

That was true. There was no such thing as bad weather, just bad clothing.

Flic took in the surrounding area. The black car was on the road to their safe house. It was either lost, or the driver knew exactly where they were going.

"No wonder I gain weight in the winter. Months of this and too much hibernation," said Anna.

The black car slowed to a crawl.

"I should have packed some thermal trousers. I wonder should we suggest the south of Spain might be a great location for a safe house."

Flic stared at the car.

"Hello? Earth to Felicity."

It was true that Flic had been preoccupied since Anna had arrived, but she knew the agents' routines inside and out. The team guarding her, and now Anna, operated like a precision timepiece. Not one change of shift had occurred late, and although she'd only bothered to study the roster magnetized to the refrigerator once, she knew Leo was on his days off and Ethan was currently in the house, three hours into his shift. Relief wasn't scheduled until later that evening.

"Sorry. I'm just catching my breath."

The black car stopped.

From behind, Anna slid her arms around Flic's waist and seductively kissed her neck. "I can think of a few little indoor activities that might raise our heart rate if you'd prefer?"

Flic watched as a figure emerged from the vehicle below.

The wind howled. The top of the hill loomed above them, and as soon as they commenced descending the other side, the wind would be tolerable.

"I think we should continue on." Flic watched as the figure pulled something from the vehicle. She couldn't be sure what it was because the person was on the far side of the car, the driver's side.

"Well, that's a knock back if ever I heard one."

From this distance, Flic wasn't sure what the person behind the black car was doing until she saw something being lifted onto the roof of the car.

"Run!"

Flic grabbed Anna by the hand and hauled her up the hill. The thick damp grass—the reason why Anna had tucked her socks into her trousers—made it difficult to gain any speed.

Before Anna could object, or Flic could offer any explanation, she heard a cracking sound, and although the wind was blowing and in reality she knew it was such a low probability, she could have sworn a tuft of grass beside her exploded. From the horrified expression on Anna's face, she just realized they had been shot at.

At a push, they were no more than four hundred meters from the farmhouse. Flic knew that on a calm day, she would probably be dead now. Her security team had talked a lot about what could influence a good shot, and unpredictable winds were at the top of their list for a missed target. Just minutes ago, she cursed the wind. Now it was their saving grace. She prayed a wayward bullet wouldn't hit Anna.

A split second after the second cracking noise, Flic hit the ground. She thought back to the incident in Paris, and it momentarily amused her how stupid she was to have even considered she'd been shot back then. With the most agonizing, burning pain ripping through her shoulder, she now knew firsthand what it felt like to have a bullet penetrate your body.

Anna shrieked.

Facedown on the sodden grass, Flic's body flinched again as a second bullet tore through her side. Had the breath not have already been taken from her, she would have screamed.

It was the second bullet that seemed to jolt Anna into action. Nothing like a repeat performance to silence your doubts. At first, she screamed—short, piercing, and terrified, but then instinct seemed to take over. "Fucking hell!" She hauled Flic to her feet. "Get up, please, just get up!"

Flic felt like her entire left side was crippled and knotting in agony, but she was overwhelmed with relief to know her legs were willing to cooperate.

The apex of the hill loomed tantalizingly close, and as Anna gripped Flic around the waist, her fingers pressed tightly below the bullet wound. The pain was so intense she was afraid she might pass out.

The shooter was relentless. Another shot cracked through the wind, and when neither Flic nor Anna dropped to the ground, she assumed he had missed.

Crack!

The sound of a rifle was the most terrifying noise Flic had ever heard. To be shot at, to know someone was trying to end your life, was horrifying in the least. Although not consciously forming the thought, Flic was aware her life could end at any moment. She began to ignore the pain.

Anna began to weave back and forth—difficult when you're trudging uphill through thick grass. The movement made Flic feel disorientated, but she gripped Anna with her good arm and simply held on.

Crack, crack. Crack.

Three more shots, fired in desperate succession, pierced the wind, and as they reached the top of the hill, Anna pushed Flic headfirst over the brow before following her. The pain was excruciating, but Flic knew it was the most efficient way to get her head and torso out of the firing line.

Although filled with adrenaline, Flic wasn't convinced she couldn't prevent herself from passing out. Anna was by her side in moments.

"There's two isn't there?" Anna was frantic. "Flic! Answer me, just two, right?"

Flic nodded and looked down. The bullet had passed through her shoulder, and it was bleeding a lot, but it was nothing compared to the shot on her side. There was no exit wound. The bullet remained inside her and it hurt like hell.

Before she could even speak, Anna was hauling her into a sitting position to tightly wrap her scarf around her waist. The pressure on the wound caused her to scream in absolute anguish. At least she'd found her voice. "Is he coming after us?"

The sound of two more bullets pierced the air. She wasn't sure, but Flic thought they might have been coming from a different direction. They certainly sounded sharper, as if from a handgun, not a rifle.

Anna was unzipping her jacket.

"Do we need to keep going, Anna?"

Anna wrapped her jacket firmly around Flic's shoulder.

The thought of the shooter discarding the rifle to pursue them on foot with a handgun sent the most nauseating stab of panic through her. A fit man, or woman—the gender was irrelevant—chasing them would catch them in no time. The killer could probably reach the top of the hill before Flic could even run barely half the distance with her wound.

She made the most agonizing decision, but it was the only decision.

"You have to leave me."

Anna stared at her in horrified disbelief.

"I'm his target, not you. He won't chase you after his job is done." It wasn't in her nature to beg, but she had to make Anna see sense. "Please, Anna, don't make me watch you die. Please, just run and keep running and don't look back."

Valuable time was ticking.

"I'm not leaving you."

"Damn it, Anna, just go!"

Anna hauled Flic to her feet. "If *I* go, we both go."

"Anna, no. I'll slow you down."

"If you don't want to watch me die, Flic, I suggest you shut up and move your bloody legs. Now run!"

She'd lost a lot of blood, but somehow Flic managed to persuade her legs to move. It was barely a jog, let alone a run, but even this slight chance of survival was better than lying in wait for a cold-blooded killer to shoot her in the back of the head.

Her legs burned with the effort. Her body was attempting to do too many things at once, all of which required precious blood and oxygen. She knew they only had until the killer reached the peak of the hill to put any real distance between them. After that, they were sitting ducks, and with the wind blowing considerably less on the west side of the hill, she imagined the shooter would be more accurate the next time he fired his gun.

Before too long, Flic calculated they had probably been struggling down the hill and through the fields for longer than it would have taken a fit man to reach the top of the hill. Had he simply given up?

"Where is he? Can you see him?" Loathed to halt their momentum, she turned back toward the hill. "He should be there by now, surely."

Anna only gave the hill a cursory glance before gripping the waistband of Flic's jeans and hauling her back into action. "I don't care where the bastard is. We have to keep going."

Flic didn't want to care either, but she did, and Anna was right; either way, they should keep going. The sooner they found shelter, the sooner they could try to get help. She felt naked without her phone. Somehow, the Order of Purity had found her, and it obviously wasn't through sheer good luck on their behalf. It begged the question, however, how *did* they find her?

They traipsed no more than fifty meters before they heard yelling.

Flic heard her name.

They both turned to see Ethan running down the hill toward them.

Flic collapsed into Anna and began to cry.

CHAPTER TWENTY-EIGHT

There was something deliriously satisfying about being bounced toward the farmhouse on a trailer, behind a tractor, and over fields with a rescue helicopter approaching. The police obviously hadn't identified a four-wheel drive as an imperative addition to their equipment, preferring the speed and agility of the sedan vehicles instead, so a tractor from a nearby farmer it was. Although every movement sent stabbing pain through Flic's entire left side, the fact that Ethan had confirmed the shooter, Tommaso Rosa, was dead and his mate, Joseph Stephan, was in custody, traced through Tommaso's mobile phone, was enough to lift Flic's spirits—even in her current, less than adequate condition.

Ethan assured her her injuries weren't life threatening as long as she was delivered to hospital safely and with haste. It was his gun that she had heard shooting two quick bullets, both apparently hitting Rosa, killing him instantly. She thanked God Ethan was a better shot than he was. She had been wrong, however. She had thought it was a handgun, but it was actually a high-powered MI5 issue rifle. Ethan was impressed she'd noticed a difference in the shots at all.

Although not yet confirmed, Ethan suspected there was a mole working within MI5. It was the only solution to the Order discovering, on two occasions, where she was hiding. He confirmed with a bit of digging it wouldn't be hard to find the culprit, but until then, he refused to leave Flic's side.

"Who says you aren't the mole?" Flic was beyond grateful to Ethan for saving her life, but she was also beyond political correctness, too.

"That's a good question. I can see why you're a writer." He winked at Anna. "But I've had plenty of opportunity to knock you off. If you've survived this far, I'm a lousy assassin."

Flic knew it was true. Ethan was one of the good guys. "Thank you for being such a good shot."

"It's just good fortune it's a windy day. Under more favorable conditions, the outcome may have been disastrous."

"Well, you got him in the end."

Ethan's eyes lowered.

"What is it?" asked Anna.

"I should have had him earlier, but the wind caused the sound of the shots to ricochet back and forth between the buildings. For the first three shots, I was concentrating on looking for him on the wrong side of the house. I was looking out the northwest windows when I should have been on the southwest side." He shook his head at his mistake.

Anna shrugged as the tractor came to a standstill in an open area behind the farmhouse. It was becoming difficult to hear from the sound of the helicopter approaching. "I didn't see him at all." She yelled. "I'm just glad you two had it covered."

The paramedics on the helicopter were clinically professional and quick to assess Flic's damage, radioing ahead to St. James's University Hospital in Leeds with an ETA in under an hour. Flic knew she would inevitably require surgery after scans. There was a bullet floating around inside her somewhere, but at least she wasn't critical. The pain medication worked within minutes, and pretty soon she could barely feel a thing.

Only the slightest hint of color had returned to Anna's cheeks by the time the helicopter landed, but it soon faded. Although comfortable for Flic—all drugged up and flat on her back—the bumpy ride and probably a hard dose of reality proved too much for Anna. She vomited the entire contents of her stomach before the paramedic jabbed her with a needle to make it stop.

❖

After the rocky ride in the helicopter, Anna was taking the situation in her stride. Flic loved her more every day.

Agent Stark, in contrast, had just entered Flic's hospital room sporting an awkward smile.

"If you tell me one bit of bad news, I'll throw you out of here," said Flic.

Stark raised her eyebrows and flashed a charming smile before she said, "There's no delicate way to say this, but the leak concerning your whereabouts in the safe houses came from us."

"What?"

Stark shifted her weight. "It was one of us. MI5."

"Bloody hell." Flic was pleased to learn the truth, it just wasn't what she'd expected to hear. "How and why?"

"The short version; your book pissed him off."

"Him and millions of others." Flic wondered if she'd ever be safe again. "Was he a member of the Order?"

"No. Well, we don't think so. He denies a connection to them and we can't make one stick. It looks like he sold the information for a hefty sum."

"But it was my book that pissed him off. It just happened to piss him off with a price tag." Flic shook her head. "His moral high ground just sunk into the shit. How dare he make this about religion? The moment he accepted money it became something else altogether."

Anna glanced at the machines Flic was connected to. Flic knew her heart rate was increasing.

Stark intervened. "He's been caught now. They all have. The best thing you can do is concentrate on getting better."

"My sentiments exactly," said Anna.

Stark said her good-byes and left Flic and Anna alone again.

"Things have been running surprisingly smoothly in our absence." Anna changed the subject and read a memo from Dee.

"I see you've at least waited until one day post surgery to bring this up."

It sounded dramatic, but being shot—twice—wasn't as painful as Flic had anticipated. She was taking some super strength painkillers, and she couldn't be sure if the warm fuzzy feeling was because of the opiates or because of Anna. Either way, she was ready for whatever Dee and Anna had in store for her.

"You have a new agent and PA."

"I do?"

"Laura's on board, has been since I left to be with you in the house, and as far as I can tell, she's got the Love is Love campaign completely under control."

"Laura?"

"Apparently, we offered her a rather attractive package. How could she say no?"

Flic shook her head and shrugged. She couldn't believe it.

"Cameron's ready to discuss your new book whenever you are. Dee will clear his calendar the moment you give the word." Anna smiled. "She's predicting book number two will be a best seller."

The luxury of experiencing some notoriety was all coming back. She'd forgotten how high people would jump when she asked them to.

"And Dee's already scheduled and finalized the US tour." Anna shrugged. "Well, obviously not Dee on her own, I mean. That would be a complete balls up from the onset."

Flic was struggling to keep up. Did another promotional tour mean leaving Anna behind? "Will you be coming?"

"I don't think that's part of Dee's plan, sorry, honey."

It was the first time Anna had used a term of endearment. It hadn't sounded half as good as she'd imagined—she hated that it was on the end of bad news. If Anna wasn't going with her, she wasn't sure she wanted to go at all.

"I'm kidding." Anna delicately hugged her close. "Dee knows we're a great team. She wouldn't dare put that in jeopardy. I'm all yours for as long as you want me."

Flic looked Anna squarely in the eye. "I want you forever."

Anna smiled. "Then that's exactly how long you'll have me for."

"No. I'm not talking about work."

Perched on the edge of the bed holding Flic's hands in hers, Anna was like an innocent child. She was beautiful and Flic knew what she was asking was serious indeed.

"Can you imagine being with someone else? Because I can't."

Anna shook her head.

"So if you can't imagine that, and I can't imagine that, I think we should just give it up as a bad joke and when we're ready, I think we should get married."

Anna began to cry, and although she attempted to speak, nothing came out.

"Anna Lawrence, will you be my wife?"

"You're proposing to me full of painkillers from a hospital bed?"

"I sure am, but I promise to make up for the lame proposal with a smashing wedding."

"You'd better."

"I will. So what do you say?"

Just at that moment, Laura and Dee burst into the room full of cheer and full of gusto.

Laura glanced from Anna to Flic and back again. "Did we just interrupt something?"

Flic never took her eyes off Anna. "I'm waiting to see if Anna will say yes to marrying me."

Dee gasped. "You mean we just burst in on your proposal?"

Flic nodded.

"Just this very minute?"

She nodded again.

"Well, Lawrence? What in God's name are you waiting for?" Dee asked.

About the Author

Michelle is Tasmanian born and now resides in the UK, just north of London, with her wife. She's a fair weather golfer, a happy snapper, and a lover of cafes, vinyl records, and bookshops.

Michelle harbors an unnatural love for stray pieces of timber (she promises her wife she'll build her something one day), secondhand furniture shops, and the perfect coffee.

She can play six chords on her guitar, stumble through a song on her drum kit, and if you see her wearing headphones, she's probably listening to Mumford and Sons while dreaming up stories and plot twists.

It goes without saying that writing is Michelle's favorite thing to do.

Michelle can be contacted at: michellegrubb@me.com

Website: www.michellegrubb.com/

Books Available from Bold Strokes Books

Dyre: By Moon's Light by Rachel E. Bailey. A young werewolf, Des, guards the aging leader of all the Packs: the Dyre. Stable employment—nice work, if you can get it...at least until silver bullets start to fly. (978-1-62639-6-623)

Fragile Wings by Rebecca S. Buck. In Roaring Twenties London, can Evelyn Hopkins find love with Jos Singleton or will the scars of the Great War crush her dreams? (978-1-62639-5-466)

Live and Love Again by Jan Gayle. Jessica Whitney could be Sarah Jarret's second chance at love, but their differences and Sarah's grief continue to come between their budding relationship. (978-1-62639-5-176)

Starstruck by Lesley Davis. Actress Cassidy Hayes and writer Aiden Darrow find out the hard way not all life-threatening drama is confined to the TV screen or the pages of a manuscript. (978-1-62639-5-237)

Stealing Sunshine by Tina Michele. Under the Central Florida sun, two women struggle between fear and love as a dangerous plot of deception and revenge threatens to steal priceless art and lives. (978-1-62639-4-452)

The Fifth Gospel by Michelle Grubb. Hiding a Vatican secret is dangerous—sharing the secret suicidal—can Felicity survive a perilous book tour, and will her PR specialist, Anna, be there when it's all over? (978-1-62639-4-476)

Cold to the Touch by Cari Hunter. A drug addict's murder is the start of a dangerous investigation for Detective Sanne Jensen and Dr. Meg Fielding, as they try to stop a killer with no conscience. (978-1-62639-526-8)

Forsaken by Laydin Michaels. The hunt for a killer teaches one woman that she must overcome her fear in order to love, and another that success is meaningless without happiness. (978-1-62639-481-0)

Infiltration by Jackie D. When a CIA breach is imminent, a Marine instructor must stop the attack while protecting her heart from being disarmed by a recruit. (978-1-62639-521-3)

Midnight at the Orpheus by Alyssa Linn Palmer. Two women desperate to make their way in the world, a man hell-bent on revenge, and a cop risking his career: all in a day's work in Capone's Chicago. (978-1-62639-607-4)

Spirit of the Dance by Mardi Alexander. Major Sorla Reardon's return to her family farm to heal threatens Riley Johnson's safe life when small-town secrets are revealed, and love may not conquer all. (978-1-62639-583-1)

Sweet Hearts by Melissa Brayden, Rachel Spangler, and Karis Walsh. Do you ever wonder *Whatever happened to ...*? Find out when you reconnect with your favorite characters from Melissa Brayden's *Heart Block*, Rachel Spangler's *LoveLife*, and Karis Walsh's *Worth the Risk*. (978-1-62639-475-9)

Totally Worth It by Maggie Cummings. Who knew there's an all-lesbian condo community in the NYC suburbs? Join twentysomething BFFs Meg and Lexi at Bay West as they navigate friendships, love, and everything in between. (978-1-62639-512-1)

Illicit Artifacts by Stevie Mikayne. Her foster mother's death cracked open a secret world Jil never wanted to see...and now she has to pick up the stolen pieces. (978-1-62639-472-8)

Pathfinder by Gun Brooke. Heading for their new homeworld, Exodus's chief engineer Adina Vantressa and nurse Briar Lindemay carry game-changing secrets that may well cause them to lose everything when disaster strikes. (978-1-62639-444-5)

Prescription for Love by Radclyffe. Dr. Flannery Rivers finds herself attracted to the new ER chief, city girl Abigail Remy, and the incendiary mix of city and country, fire and ice, tradition and change is combustible. (978-1-62639-570-1)

Ready or Not by Melissa Brayden. Uptight Mallory Spencer finds relinquishing control to bartender Hope Sanders too tall an order in fast-paced New York City. (978-1-62639-443-8)

Summer Passion by MJ Williamz. Women loving women is forbidden in 1946 Hollywood, yet Jean and Maggie strive to keep their love alive and away from prying eyes. (978-1-62639-540-4)

The Princess and the Prix by Nell Stark. "Ugly duckling" Princess Alix of Monaco was resigned to loneliness until she met racecar driver Thalia d'Angelis. (978-1-62639-474-2)

Winter's Harbor by Aurora Rey. Lia Brooks isn't looking for love in Provincetown, but when she discovers chocolate croissants and pastry chef Alex McKinnon, her winter retreat quickly starts heating up. (978-1-62639-498-8)

The Time Before Now by Missouri Vaun. Vivian flees a disastrous affair, embarking on an epic, transformative journey to escape her past, until destiny introduces her to Ida, who helps her rediscover trust, love, and hope. (978-1-62639-446-9)

Twisted Whispers by Sheri Lewis Wohl. Betrayal, lies, and secrets—whispers of a friend lost to darkness. Can a reluctant psychic set things right or will an evil soul destroy those she loves? (978-1-62639-439-1)

The Courage to Try by C.A. Popovich. Finding love is worth getting past the fear of trying. (978-1-62639-528-2)

Break Point by Yolanda Wallace. In a world readying for war, can love find a way? (978-1-62639-568-8)

Countdown by Julie Cannon. Can two strong-willed, powerful women overcome their differences to save the lives of seven others and begin a life they never imagined together? (978-1-62639-471-1)

Keep Hold by Michelle Grubb. Claire knew some things should be left alone and some rules should never be broken, but the most forbidden, well, they are the most tempting. (978-1-62639-502-2)

Deadly Medicine by Jaime Maddox. Dr. Ward Thrasher's life is in turmoil. Her partner Jess left her, and her job puts her in the path of a murderous physician who has Jess in his sights. (978-1-62639-424-7)

New Beginnings by KC Richardson. Can the connection and attraction between Jordan Roberts and Kirsten Murphy be enough for Jordan to trust Kirsten with her heart? (978-1-62639-450-6)

Officer Down by Erin Dutton. Can two women who've made careers out of being there for others in crisis find the strength to need each other? (978-1-62639-423-0)

Reasonable Doubt by Carsen Taite. Just when Sarah and Ellery think they've left dangerous careers behind, a new case sets them— and their hearts—on a collision course. (978-1-62639-442-1)

Tarnished Gold by Ann Aptaker. Cantor Gold must outsmart the Law, outrun New York's dockside gangsters, outplay a shady art dealer, his lover, and a beautiful curator, and stay out of a killer's gun sights. (978-1-62639-426-1)

White Horse in Winter by Franci McMahon. Love between two women collides with the inner poison of a closeted horse trainer in the green hills of Vermont. (978-1-62639-429-2)

Autumn Spring by Shelley Thrasher. Can Bree and Linda, two women in the autumn of their lives, put their hearts first and find the love they've never dared seize? (978-1-62639-365-3)

The Renegade by Amy Dunne. Post-apocalyptic survivors Alex and Evelyn secretly find love while held captive by a deranged cult, but when their relationship is discovered, they must fight for their freedom—or die trying. (978-1-62639-427-8)

Thrall by Barbara Ann Wright. Four women in a warrior society must work together to lift an insidious curse while caught between their own desires, the will of their peoples, and an ancient evil. (978-1-62639-437-7)

The Chameleon's Tale by Andrea Bramhall. Two old friends must work through a web of lies and deceit to find themselves again, but in the search they discover far more than they ever went looking for. (978-1-62639-363-9)

Side Effects by VK Powell. Detective Jordan Bishop and Dr. Neela Sahjani must decide if it's easier to trust someone with your heart or your life as they face threatening protestors, corrupt politicians, and their increasing attraction. (978-1-62639-364-6)

Warm November by Kathleen Knowles. What do you do if the one woman you want is the only one you can't have? (978-1-62639-366-0)

In Every Cloud by Tina Michele. When Bree finally leaves her shattered life behind, is she strong enough to salvage the remaining pieces of her heart and find the place where it truly fits? (978-1-62639-413-1)

Lightning Source UK Ltd.
Milton Keynes UK
UKOW05f1249160617
303518UK00001B/25/P